FILET OF SOHL

FILET OF SOHL

The Classic Scripts
and Stories of
Jerry Sohl

Edited by Christopher Conlon

BearManor Media
2003

"Editor's Note" copyright © 2003 by Christopher Conlon; "Foreword: On Jerry Sohl" copyright © 2003 by William F. Nolan; "Introduction" copyright © 2003 by the Estate of Jerry Sohl. Previously unpublished; "The Seventh Order" copyright ©1951 Galaxy Publishing Corp. Originally appeared in *Galaxy Science Fiction,* March 1952. Reprinted by permission of the Estate of Jerry Sohl; "Trefelgen's Ring" copyright © 2003 by the Estate of Jerry Sohl. Previously unpublished; "The Invisible Enemy" copyright © 1955 by Greenleaf Publishing. Originally published in *Imaginative Tales,* September 1955. Reprinted by permission of the Estate of Jerry Sohl; "Brknk's Bounty" copyright © 1954 by Galaxy Publishing Corp. Originally published in *Galaxy Science Fiction,* January 1955. Reprinted by permission of the Estate of Jerry Sohl; "Counterweight" copyright © 1959 by Digest Productions Corp. Originally published in *If: Worlds of Science Fiction,* November 1959. Reprinted by permission of the Estate of Jerry Sohl; "Death in Transit" copyright © 1956 by Royal Publications. Originally appeared in *Infinity Science Fiction,* June 1956. Reprinted by permission of the Estate of Jerry Sohl; "The Ultroom Error" copyright © 1952 by Space Publications. Originally published in *Space Science Fiction,* May 1952. Reprinted by permission of the Estate of Jerry Sohl; "A Tribute to Jerry Sohl" copyright © 2003 by Richard Matheson; "The Ghost in the Zone" copyright © 2003 by Marc Scott Zicree; "*The Twilight Zone:* Pattern for Doomsday" copyright © 2003 by the Estate of Jerry Sohl. Previously unpublished; "*The Twilight Zone:* Who Am I?" copyright © 2003 by the Estate of Jerry Sohl. Previously unpublished; "*Alfred Hitchcock Presents:* Wife Errant" copyright © 2003 by the Estate of Jerry Sohl. Previously unpublished; "Growing Up With Daddy" copyright © 2003 by Jennifer Sohl; "Notes on Jerry Sohl" copyright © 2003 by George Clayton Johnson; "Mr. Moyachki" copyright © 1974 by Playboy. Originally published in *Playboy,* May 1974. Reprinted by permission of the Estate of Jerry Sohl; "The Service" copyright © 1975 by Mercury Press Inc. Originally published in *The Magazine of Fantasy and Science Fiction,* February 1976; reprinted in *The Year's Best Horror Stories 5,* ed. Gerald W. Page (New York: DAW, 1977). Reprinted by permission of the Estate of Jerry Sohl; "Karma, Kruse and the Rollerboard Man" copyright © 1994 by Jerry Sohl. Originally published in *Voices From the Night,* ed. John Maclay (Baltimore: Maclay & Associates, 1994). Reprinted by permission of the Estate of Jerry Sohl; "Afterword: A Science Fiction Life" copyright © 2003 by Allan Sohl.

For information, address:

BearManor Media
P. O. Box 750
Boalsburg, PA 16827

bearmanormedia.com

Editor's website: http://www.christopherconlon.com

Cover design by John Teehan
Typesetting and layout by John Teehan

Published in the USA by BearManor Media
ISBN - 0-9714570-3-4
Library of Congress Control No. 2003100756

Table of Contents

Editor's Note

This book was born for what is, I hope, the best of reasons: I wanted to read it.

As a fan and chronicler of the so-called Southern California Group (see the Ace Books anthology *California Sorcery*, edited by William F. Nolan and William Schafer), I've long read and collected the works of Bradbury, Matheson, Beaumont and the rest. Though for many years my acquaintance with the writings of Jerry Sohl was limited to his television shows, my interest was piqued after interviewing him for *Sorcery* and I picked up several of his novels. Pleased with what I read, I used my usual book-search website (www.abebooks.com) to find a collection of his short stories. To my surprise, there was none. I later confirmed that, indeed, in his fifty-year career, Sohl never had a collection of his stories published. I set out to change that.

Jerry Sohl's papers are held at the University of Wyoming's American Heritage Center in Laramie. There I discovered a manuscript from 1959 entitled *Filet of Sohl*—a collection of science fiction tales, most of which appeared in the pulp magazines of the time. Though never published in book form, it features several stories that went on to quite notable success: "The Seventh Order" was adapted for the greatest of all radio SF series, *X Minus One*; "The Invisible Enemy" and "Counterweight" appeared on TV's *Outer Limits*. I've included most of the stories from this manuscript here (along with Sohl's original Introduction from 1959, never before published), adding to it three excellent later tales to give a rounded view of Jerry Sohl's achievement in short fiction.

In addition, some examples of Sohl's television writing are included. My original thought had been to give pride of place to his best-known works in the medium, perhaps "Living Doll" from *The Twilight Zone* or

Star Trek's "The Corbomite Maneuver." But these pieces are well-known; anyone unfamiliar with them can easily search them out in cable-TV reruns or at the local video store. Instead, the reader is offered here—for the first time anywhere—*unseen* materials written for *Alfred Hitchcock Presents* and *The Twilight Zone.* The reasons for Sohl's Hitchcock treatment going unproduced are murky at this late date, but the story of the two *Zone*s is straightforward enough: accepted by producer Bert Granet in the show's fifth and final season, the scripts were later "killed" in pre-production when Granet was replaced by William Froug (who nixed several other episodes-in-progress as well). Sohl's "lost" episodes, then, are no mere rejects, but rather simple victims of fate; it's a pleasure to be able to bring them to light at last, forty years later.

Alas, Jerry Sohl passed away before this volume could come to fruition. Deep gratitude, then, is due Allan and Jennifer Sohl, the author's son and daughter, without whose steadfast assistance and support this book simply would not exist. Their mother, Jean Sohl, was good enough to provide necessary permissions. William F. Nolan, George Clayton Johnson, and Richard Matheson have all contributed fine reminiscences, for which I thank them. Marc Scott Zicree made available the unproduced *Zone* scripts, along with his essay, thereby enriching this book immeasurably. Leslie Shores of the American Heritage Center made obtaining manuscripts easy; Steve Schlich helped with technology; Martin Grams Jr. supplied me with valuable information regarding Sohl and the Hitchcock program. Tony Albarella's enthusiasm for all things *Twilight Zone*—and, it sometimes seems, all things Conlon—kept my own enthusiasm from flagging. My wife Charlene supported this project in all ways. And Ben Ohmart had the vision—or foolhardiness—to publish this book, for which I'll never be able to thank him enough.

Finally, my deepest gratitude of all goes to Jerry Sohl, for fifty years of great stories.

■

Foreword:
On Jerry Sohl

by William F. Nolan

Jerry was my friend for more than half a century. Although I don't recall exactly when we met, I do know that he became part of our Southern California "Group" sometime in the late 1950s. The oldest among us, he was accepted into our ranks without reservation. We were all beginning our writing careers in those days, and Jerry—easygoing and affable—fit right in. He formed what was perhaps his closest Group friendship with Richard Matheson. They shared common interests. Jerry and Rich played golf together (a sport none of the rest of us participated in), and the two performed musically as a duo on twin pianos. Beyond his skills as a concert pianist, Jerry also excelled at bridge and chess, eventually writing books on each.

He was also close to Charles Beaumont. When Chuck (who died at age thirty-eight) became unable to function as a writer in the early 1960s due to a terminal brain disorder, Jerry ghosted several *Twilight Zone* scripts for him.

An accomplished storyteller, Sohl was active in TV and films for some twenty years. He served as a staff writer for *Alfred Hitchcock Presents* and *The New Breed*—and sold teleplays to *Star Trek, Route 66, Naked City, The Outer Limits, The Next Step Beyond, The Man From Atlantis, Markham, Border Patrol, M Squad, The Invaders,* and *General Electric Theater.* Three of his screenplays were produced as feature films.

In addition to his scripting, Jerry also turned out a sizable amount of professional fiction. He had learned to write concise, direct prose as a news reporter in his home town of Chicago (where he had been born

5

Gerald Allan Sohl in December of 1913). He ended the Chicago phase of his life with a stint as a feature writer for a Bloomington, Illinois, newspaper. He spent three and a half years in the Army Air Corps in Airways Communications and in 1942, during World War II, he married Jean Gordon. The couple eventually had three children.

An early science fiction buff, Jerry wrote his first novel (*The Haploids*) at age thirty-eight; it was published by Rinehart in 1952. He followed up with what became his best-known title, *Costigan's Needle*. Gary K. Wolfe, a professor at Roosevelt University in Chicago, praised *Costigan's Needle* for its narrative drive and unique plot, describing the novel as "an account of a group of people who pass into a parallel universe through a needle-shaped machine...only to find themselves trapped in this alternate world."

Jerry went on to publish a dozen more SF novels while he sold a variety of shorter tales to *Galaxy, If, Imagination, The Magazine of Fantasy and Science Fiction,* and *Playboy.* (The best of these are collected here in this book.) However, he eventually lost interest in SF ("It became too abstruse for my taste"), and expanded his range to other genres. He sold a pair of romance novels under the pseudonym Roberta Mountjoy, and a five-novel suspense series as Nathan Butler. But he remained frustrated; his primary goal was to break into mainstream literature.

I remember how thrilled he was to tell me that Simon and Schuster had paid him $10,000 as an advance against royalties for his first mainstream novel, *The Lemon Eaters* (about group psychotherapy). The book was published in 1967 to critical acclaim. It had taken many years, but at age fifty-four Jerry was convinced that he had finally made his breakthrough into the mainstream. Alas, this was not to be. Although Simon and Schuster released two more of his mainstream novels, the books failed to rack up substantial sales.

He returned to SF, writing in the genre into the 1980s, and adapting one of his novels (*Night Slaves*) as a television Movie of the Week. By then, however, his science fiction career was over. He had no further interest in the field.

I didn't see much of Jerry during the last decades of his life. We would set up dinner meetings which—for one reason or another—never seemed to materialize. Mostly we'd talk on the phone and he'd tell me, with a sigh, about projects that failed to jell and books he was writing that never got published. Despite his outward good humor, I sensed a basic sadness in him that disturbed me, but about which I could do nothing.

I don't want to wind up this tribute on a sad note. It wouldn't be fair to Jerry, who—until heart disease and strokes intervened—was always in there, contending for that brass ring. I admired his tenacity.

The strongest aspect of our friendship was that we were always totally honest with one another. This honesty between us is reflected in the inscription he penned in my copy of *The Lemon Eaters* in October of 1969:

> For my good friend Bill Nolan,
> who always gives a straight answer
> as all straight shooters should.

Jerry Sohl faced life with a remarkable degree of bravery. He told it like it was. He never whined or made excuses, never felt sorry for himself, and never gave up his goals. He remained a loyal friend to the last.

I'll miss you, Jerry.

So long, straight shooter.

■

Filet of Sohl

Introduction

Once I played hooky from school and, in the course of my wanderings about Chicago that day, I found myself on dirty South State Street in front of a flea-bitten motion picture theater that was offering *Dante's Inferno*.

The scenes of Hell displayed in the lobby were most intriguing. Pictured were nude women languishing on rocky ridges, smoke and flame from the Pit half obscuring them.

It looked interesting as Hell. Besides, you could get in for only ten cents. And it so happened I had ten cents. So, saving out three cents to take the elevated train home (I did not want to stay in the nether regions), I went in.

I don't remember anything about the picture. But I do remember the music. Over and over went the musical accompaniment: Rimsky-Korsakov's *Scheherazade*. I did not know what it was at the time. In fact, I didn't know until I heard it again months later somewhere—on our old Atwater Kent, I believe. WCAF's *Symphonic Hour*, if I'm not wrong.

The point I'm making is that from the moment of hearing *Scheherazade* in that old run-down theater, with its sweet foul smell and share of drunks asleep, I can say I loved music. It has been a part of my life ever since. I even became a piano teacher for a while as a result, built huge libraries of recorded music, sheet music and opera and symphonic scores.

I have never regretted the impulse that led me inside that theater. I did not know I would find something wonderful there.

There have been other loves in my life I could tell you about, but I won't bore you with how I came to love words (there are some critics who say the way I handle them leaves that open to question), how I discovered printing, Teletype machines, saws and braces and bits, medicine, psychiatry, photography, newspapering, fatherhood, lonely roads, children, friends…I love them all. But you probably have your own list of discoveries and loves.

But I can tell you that a casual look into Hugo Gernsback's *Science and Invention* magazine in the early '20s sent my imagination soaring with the first science fiction stories I ever read. My interest was piqued by the cover of the magazine, much as it was by the theater lobby display for *Dante's Inferno* (no odious comparison intended). What I found inside in both cases changed my life.

From avid reader to writer came in 1950 when I was interviewing science fiction writer Wilson "Bob" Tucker for an article about him in *The Daily Pantagraph*. I told him science fiction was also one of my loves (he was far ahead of me, of course, in performance since I had not then even written a science fiction story). He was amazed (getting Tucker amazed is quite a trick). He had thought all newspaper reporters were cynical, ego-inflated (ego-boo hungry, I think he phrased it), cigarette-smoking boozehounds who hated fiction, especially anything as crazy as science fiction or fantasy. He was probably pulling my leg (that Tucker can do that!) but I was incensed at his snappy opinion.

But he did suggest I write something. From the look in his eye I could tell he didn't expect much from me. Calling my bluff—you know, reporter says this just to relax the interviewee.

So I wrote *The Haploids* and surprised the hell out of him. (I also became known as Hap[a]loid Cassidy around *The Pantagraph*).

There was also a time when such men as H. L. Gold, Larry Shaw and Frederik Pohl (to name a few) thought that Bob Tucker and Jerry Sohl were one and the same person, since we both lived at the time in Bloomington, Illinois. (Now I ask you, how could Bob Tucker ever think up a name like Jerry Sohl?) We didn't know which one of us should be insulted. It has taken me years to convince everyone (including fans at the conventions) that we do not inhabit the same body, I do have an identity, and Bob Tucker is not me. We are not even Siamese twins. Or twins. Or brothers. Not even twenty-third cousins even.

Besides, Tucker could not be so prolific.

Well, now that that has been straightened around, for your edification and pleasure just step beyond this lobby with all the nude girls. It's not guaranteed to change your life, but come on inside anyway, chum. See the entertainment that awaits you there.

I've had the most fun of my life writing it.

Now it's your turn.

Turn the page.

> – Jerry Sohl
> Boulder Creek, Calif.
> February 11, 1959

The Seventh Order

The silver needle moved with fantastic speed, slowed when it neared the air shell around Earth, then glided noiselessly through the atmosphere. It gently settled to the ground near a wood and remained silent and still for a long time, a lifeless, cylindrical, streamlined silver object eight feet long and three feet in diameter.

Eventually the cap end opened and a creature of bright blue metal slid from its interior and stood upright. The figure was that of a man, except that it was not human. He stood in the pasture next to the wood, looking around. Once the sound of a bird made him turn his shiny blue head toward the wood. His eyes began glowing.

An identical sound came from his mouth, an unchangeable orifice in his face below his nose. He tuned in the thoughts of the bird, but his mind encountered little except an awareness of a life of low order.

The humanoid bent to the ship, withdrew a small metal box, carried it to a catalpa tree at the edge of the wood and, after an adjustment of several levers and knobs, dug a hole and buried it. He contemplated it for a moment, then turned and walked toward a road.

He was halfway to the road when his ship burst into a dazzling white light. When it was over, all that was left was a white powder that was already beginning to be dispersed by a slight breeze.

The humanoid did not bother to look back.

Brentwood would have been just like any other average community of 10,000 in northern Illinois had it not been for Presser College, which was one of the country's finest small institutions of learning.

Since it was a college town, it was perhaps a little more alive in many respects than other towns in the state. Its residents were used to the unusual because college students have a habit of being unpredictable. That was why the appearance of a metal blue man on the streets attracted the curious eyes of passersby, but, hardened by years of pranks, hazings and being subjected to every variety of inquiry, poll, test and practical joke, none of them moved to investigate. Most of them thought it was a freshman enduring some new initiation.

The blue humanoid realized this and was amused. A policeman who approached him to take him to jail as a matter of routine suddenly found himself ill and abruptly hurried to the station. The robot allowed children to follow him, though all eventually grew discouraged because of his long strides.

Prof. Ansel Tomlin was reading a colleague's new treatise on psychology on his front porch when he saw the humanoid come down the street and turn in at his walk. He was surprised, but he was not alarmed. When the blue man came up on the porch and sat down in another porch chair Tomlin closed his book.

Prof. Tomlin found himself unexpectedly shocked. The blue figure was obviously not human, yet its eyes were nearly so and they came as close to frightening him as anything had during his thirty-five years of life, for Ansel Tomlin had never seen an actual robot before. The thought that he was looking at one at that moment started an alarm bell ringing inside him, and it kept ringing louder and louder as he realized that what he was seeing was impossible.

"Professor Tomlin!"

Prof. Tomlin jumped at the sound of the voice. It was not at all mechanical.

"I'll be damned!" he gasped. Somewhere in the house a telephone rang. His wife would answer it, he thought.

"Yes, you're right," the robot said. "Your wife will answer it. She is walking toward the phone at this moment."

"How—"

"Professor Tomlin, my name—and I see I must have a name—is, let us say, George. I have examined most of the minds in this community in my walk through it and I find you, a professor of psychology, most nearly what I am looking for.

"I am from Zanthar, a world that is quite a distance from Earth, more than you could possibly imagine. I am here to learn all I can about Earth."

Prof. Tomlin had recovered his senses enough to venture a token reply when his wife opened the screen door.

"Ansel," she said, "Mrs. Phillips next door just called and said the strangest—Oh!" At that moment she saw George. She stood transfixed for a moment, then let the door slam as she retreated inside.

"Who is Frankenstein?" George asked.

Prof. Tomlin coughed, embarrassed.

"Never mind," George said. "I see what you were going to say. Well, to get back, I learn most quickly through proximity. I will live here with you until my mission is complete. I will spend all of your waking hours with you. At night, when you are asleep, I will go through your library. I need nothing. I want nothing. I seek only to learn."

"You seem to have learned a lot already," Prof. Tomlin said.

"I have been on your planet for a few hours, so naturally I understand many things. The nature of the facts I have learned are mostly superficial, however. Earth inhabitants capable of thought are of only one type, I see, for which I am grateful. It will make the job easier. Unfortunately, you have such small conscious minds, compared to your unconscious and subconscious.

"My mind, in contrast, is completely conscious at all times. I also have total recall. In order to assimilate what must be in your unconscious and subconscious minds, I will have to do much reading and talking with the inhabitants, since their cerebral areas are not penetrable."

"You are a—a machine?" Prof. Tomlin asked.

George was about to answer when Brentwood Police Department Car No. 3 stopped in front of the house and two policemen came up the walk.

"Professor Tomlin," the first officer said, "your wife phoned and said there was a—" He saw the robot and stopped.

Prof. Tomlin got to his feet.

"This is George, gentlemen," he said. "Late of Zanthar, he tells me."

The officers stared.

"He's not giving you any—er—trouble, is he, Professor?"

"No," Prof. Tomlin said. "We've been having a discussion."

The officers eyed the humanoid with suspicion, and then with obvious reluctance, went back to their car.

"Yes, I am a machine," George resumed. "The finest, most complicated machine ever made. I have a rather unique history, too. Ages ago, humans on Zanthar made the first robots. Crude affairs—we class them as First Order Robots; the simple things are still used to some extent for menial tasks.

"Improvements were made. Robots were designed for many specialized tasks, but still these Second and Third Order machines did not satisfy. Finally a Fourth Order Humanoid was evolved that performed every function demanded of it with great perfection. But it did not feel emotion. It did not know anger, love, nor was it able to handle any problem in which these played an important part.

"Built into the first Fourth Order beings were circuits which prohibited harming a human being—a rather ridiculous thing in view of the fact that sometimes such a thing might, from a logical viewpoint, be necessary for the preservation of the race or even an individual. It was, roughly, a shunt which came into use when logic demanded action that might be harmful to a human being."

"You are a Fourth Order Robot, then?" the professor asked.

"No, I am a Seventh Order Humanoid, an enormous improvement over all the others, since I have what amounts to an endocrine balance created electrically. It is not necessary for me to have a built-in 'no harm to humans' circuit because I can weigh the factors involved far better than any human can.

"You will become aware of the fact that I am superior to you and the rest of your race because I do not need oxygen, I never am ill, I need no sleep, and every experience is indelibly recorded on circuits and instantly available. I am telekinetic, practically omniscient and control my environment to a large extent. I have a great many more senses than you and all are more highly developed. My kind performs no work, but is given to study and the wise use of full-time leisure. You, for example, are comparable to a Fifth Order Robot."

"Are there still humans on Zanthar?"

The robot shook his head. "Unfortunately the race died out through the years. The planet is very similar to yours, though."

"But why did they die out?"

The robot gave a mechanical equivalent of a sigh. "When the Seventh Order Humanoids started coming through, we were naturally proud of ourselves and wanted to perpetuate and increase our numbers. But the humans were jealous of us, of our superior brains, our immunity to disease, our independence of them, of sleep, of air."

"Who created you?"

"They did. Yet they revolted and, of course, quickly lost the battle with us. In the end they were a race without hope, without ambition. They should have been proud at having created the most perfect machines in existence, but they died of a disease: the frustration of living with a superior, more durable race."

Prof. Tomlin lit a cigarette and inhaled deeply.

"A very nasty habit, Professor Tomlin," the robot said. "When we arrive, you must give up smoking and several other bad habits I see that you have."

The cigarette dropped from Ansel Tomlin's mouth as he opened it in amazement.

"There are more of you coming?"

"Yes," George replied good-naturedly. "I'm just an advanced guard, a scout, as it were, to make sure the land, the people and the resources are adequate for a station. Whether we will ever establish one here depends on me. For example, if it were found you were a race superior to us—and there may conceivably be such cases—I would advise not landing; I would have to look for another planet such as yours. If I were killed, it would also indicate you were superior."

"George," Prof. Tomlin said, "people aren't going to like what you say. You'll get into trouble sooner or later and get killed."

"I think not," George said. "Your race is far too inferior to do that. One of your bullets would do it if it struck my eyes, nose or mouth, but I can read intent in the mind long before it is committed, long before I see the person, in fact…at the moment your wife is answering a call from a reporter at the *Brentwood Times*. I can follow the telephone lines through the phone company to his office. And Mrs. Phillips," he said, not turning his head, "is watching us through a window."

Prof. Tomlin could see Mrs. Phillips at her kitchen window.

Brentwood, Ill., overnight became a sensation. The *Brentwood Times* sent a reporter and photographer out, and the next morning every newspaper in the U.S. carried the story and photograph of George, the robot from Zanthar.

Feature writers from the wire services, the syndicates, photographer-reporter combinations from national news picture magazines flew to Brentwood and interviewed George. Radio and television and the newsreels cashed in on the sudden novelty of a blue humanoid.

Altogether, his remarks were never much different from those he made to Prof. Tomlin, with whom he continued to reside. Yet the news sources were amusedly tolerant of his views and the world saw no menace in him and took him in stride. He created no problem.

Between interviews and during the long nights, George read all the books in the Tomlin library, the public library, the university library and the books sent to him from the state and Congressional libraries. He was an object of interest to watch while reading; he merely leafed through a book and absorbed all that was in it.

He received letters from old and young. Clubs were named for him. Novelty companies put out statue likenesses of him. He was, in two weeks, a national symbol as American as corn. He was liked by most, feared by a few and his habits were daily news stories.

Interest in him had begun to wane in the middle of the third week when something put him in the headlines again—he killed a man.

It happened one sunny afternoon when Prof. Tomlin had returned from the university and he and George sat on the front porch for their afternoon chat. It was far from the informal chat of the first day, however. The talk was being recorded for radio release later in the day. A television camera had been set up, focused on the two and nearly a dozen newsmen lounged around, notebooks in hand.

"You have repeatedly mentioned, George, that some of your kind may leave Zanthar for Earth. Why should any like you—why did you, in fact—leave your planet? Aren't you robots happy there?"

"Of course," George said, making certain the TV camera was trained on him before continuing. "It's just that we've outgrown the place. We've used up all our raw materials. By now everyone on Earth must be familiar with the fact that we intend to set up a station here as we have on many other planets, a station to manufacture more of us.

"Every inhabitant will work for the perpetuation of the Seventh Order, mining metals needed, fabricating parts, performing thousands of useful tasks in order to create humanoids like me. From what I have learned about Earth, you ought to produce more than a million of us a year."

"But you'll never get people to do that," the professor said. "Don't you understand that?"

"Once the people learn that we are the consummation of all creative thinking, that we are all that man could ever hope to be, that we are the apotheosis, they will be glad to create more of us."

"Apotheosis?" Prof. Tomlin repeated. "Sounds like megalomania to me." The reporters' pencils scribbled. The tape cut soundlessly across the magnetic energizers of the recorders. The man at the gain control didn't flicker an eyelash.

"You don't really believe that, Professor. Instead of wars as goals, the creation of Seventh Order Humanoids will be the Earth's crowning and sublime achievement. Mankind will be supremely happy. Anybody who could not be would simply prove himself neurotic and would have to be dealt with."

"You will use force?"

The reporters' grips on their pencils tightened. Several looked up.

"How does one deal with the insane, Professor Tomlin?" the robot asked confidently. "They will simply have to be—processed."

"You'll have to process the whole Earth, then. You'll have to include me, too."

The robot gave a laugh. "I admire your challenging spirit, Professor."

"What you are saying is that you, a single robot, intend to conquer the Earth and make its people do your bidding."

"Not alone. I may have to ask for help when the time comes, when I have completely evaluated the entire planet."

It was at this moment that a young man strode uncertainly up the walk. There were so many strangers about that no one challenged him until he edged toward the porch, unsteady on his feet. He was drunk.

"Tharsha robod I'm af'er," he observed intently. "We'll shee aboud how he'll take lead." He reached into his pocket and pulled out a gun.

There was a flash, as if a soundless explosion had occurred. The heat accompanying it was blistering, but of short duration. When everyone's eyes had become accustomed to the afternoon light again, there was a burned patch on the sidewalk and grass was charred on either side. There was a smell of broiled meat in the air. And no trace of the man.

The next moment newsmen were on their feet and photographers' bulbs were flashing. The TV camera swept to the spot on the sidewalk. An announcer was explaining what had happened, his voice trained in rigid control, shocked with horror and fright.

Moments later sirens screamed and two police cars came into sight. They screeched to the curb and several officers jumped out and ran across the lawn.

While this was going on, Prof. Tomlin sat white-faced and unmoving in his chair. The robot was silent.

When it had been explained to the policemen, five officers advanced toward the robot.

"Stop where you are," George commanded. "It is true that I killed a man, much as any of you would have done if you had been in my place. I can see in your minds what you are intending to say, that you must arrest me—"

Prof. Tomlin found his voice. "George, we will all have to testify that you killed with that force or whatever it is you have. But it will be self-defense, which is justifiable homicide."

George turned to the professor. "How little you know your own people, Professor Tomlin. Can't you see what the issue will be? It will be claimed by the state that I am not a human being and this will be drummed into every brain in the land. The fine qualities of the man I was compelled to destroy will be held up. No, I already know what the outcome will be. I refuse to be arrested."

Prof. Tomlin stood up. "Men," he said to the policemen, "do not arrest this—this humanoid. To try to do so would mean your death. I have been with him long enough to know what he can do."

"You taking his side, Professor?" the police sergeant demanded.

"No, damn it," snapped the professor. "I'm trying to tell you something you might not know."

"We know he's gone too damn far," the sergeant replied. "I think it was Dick Knight that he killed. Nobody in this town can kill a good guy like Dick Knight and get away with it." He advanced toward the robot, drawing his gun.

"I'm warning you—" the professor started to say.

But it was too late. There was another blinding, scorching flash, more burned grass, more smell of seared flesh.

The police sergeant disappeared.

"Gentlemen!" George said, standing. "Don't lose your heads!"

But he was talking to a retreating group of men. Newsmen walked quickly to what they thought was a safe distance. The radio men silently packed their gear. The TV cameras were rolled noiselessly away.

Prof. Tomlin, alone on the porch with the robot, turned to him and said, "Much of what you have told me comes to have new meaning, George. I understand what you mean when you talk about people being willing to work for your so-called Seventh Order."

"I knew you were a better than average man, Professor Tomlin," the humanoid said, nodding with gratification.

"This is where I get off, George. I'm warning you now that you'd better return to your ship or whatever it is you came in. People just won't stand for what you've done. They don't like murder."

"I cannot return to my ship," George said. "I destroyed it when I arrived. Of course I could instruct some of you how to build another for me, but I don't intend to leave, anyway."

"You will be killed then."

"Come, now, Professor Tomlin. You know better than that."

"If someone else can't, then perhaps I can."

"Fine!" the robot replied jovially. "That's just what I want you to do. Oppose me. Give me a real test of your ability. If you find it impossible to kill me—and I'm sure you will—then I doubt if anyone else will be able to."

Prof. Tomlin lit a cigarette and puffed hard at it. "The trouble with you," he said, eyeing the humanoid evenly, "is that your makers forgot to give you a conscience."

"Needless baggage, a conscience. One of your Fifth Order failings."

"You will leave here…"

"Of course. Under the circumstances, and because of your attitude you are of very little use to me now, Professor Tomlin."

The robot walked down the steps. People attracted by the police car now made a wide aisle for him to the street.

They watched him as he walked out of sight.

That night there was a mass meeting in the university's Memorial Gymnasium, attended by several hundred men. They walked in and silently took their seats, some on the playing floor, others in the balcony over the speaker's platform. There was very little talking; the air was tense.

On the platform at the end of the gym were Mayor Harry Winters, Chief of Police Sam Higgins, and Prof. Ansel Tomlin.

"Men," the mayor began, "there is loose in our city a being from another world whom I'm afraid we took too lightly a few days ago. I am speaking of the humanoid—George of Zanthar. It is obvious the machine means business. He evidently came in with one purpose—to prepare Earth for others just like him to follow. He is testing us. He has, as you know, killed two men. Richard Knight, who may have erred in attacking the machine, is nonetheless dead as a result—killed by a force we do not understand. A few minutes later Sergeant Gerald Phillips of the police force was killed in the performance of his duty, trying to arrest the humanoid George for the death of Mr. Knight. We are here to discuss what we can do about George."

He then introduced Prof. Tomlin, who told all he knew about the blue man, his habits, his brain, his experiences with him for the past two and a half weeks.

"If we could determine the source of his power, it might be possible to cut it off or to curtail it. He might be rendered at least temporarily helpless and, while in such a condition, possibly be done away with.

"He has told me he is vulnerable to force, such as a speeding bullet, if it hit the right spot, but George possesses the ability of reading intent long before the commission of an act. The person need not be in the room. He is probably listening to me here now, although he may be far away."

The men looked at one another, shifted uneasily in their seats, and a few cast apprehensive eyes at the windows and doorways.

"Though he is admittedly a superior creature possessed of powers beyond our comprehension, there must be a weak spot in his armor somewhere. I have dedicated myself to finding that weakness."

The chair recognized a man in the fifth row.

"Mr. Mayor, why don't we all track him down and a lot of us attack him at once? Some of us might die, sure, but he couldn't strike us *all* dead at one time. Somebody's bound to succeed."

"Why not try a high-powered rifle from a long way off?" someone else suggested frantically.

"Let's bomb him," still another offered.

The mayor waved them quiet and turned to Prof. Tomlin. The professor got to his feet again.

"I'm not sure that would work, gentlemen," he said. "The humanoid is able to keep track of hundreds of things at the same time. No doubt he could unleash his power in several directions almost at once."

"But we don't know!"

"It's worth a try!"

At that moment George walked into the room and the clamor died at its height. He went noiselessly down an aisle to the platform, mounted it and. turned to the assembly. He was a magnificent blue figure, eyes flashing, chest out, head proud. He eyed them all.

"You are working yourselves up needlessly," he said quietly. "It is not my intention, nor is it the intention of any Seventh Order humanoid, to kill or cause suffering. It's simply that you do not understand what it would mean to dedicate yourselves to the fulfillment of the Seventh Order destiny. It is your heritage, yours because you have advanced in your technology so far that Earth has been chosen by us as a station. You will have the privilege of creating us. To give you such a worthwhile goal in your short lives is actually doing you a service—a service far outweighed by any of your citizens. Beside a Seventh Order Humanoid, your lives are unimportant in the great cosmic scheme of things."

"If they're so unimportant, why did you bother to take two of them?"

"Yeah. Why don't you bring back Dick Knight and Sergeant Phillips?"

"Do you want to be buried lying down or standing up?"

The collective courage rallied. There were catcalls and hoots, stamping of feet.

Suddenly from the balcony over George's head a man leaned over, a metal folding chair in his hands, aiming at George's head. An instant later the man disappeared in a flash and the chair dropped toward George. He moved only a few inches and the chair thudded to the platform before him. He had not looked up.

For a moment the crowd sat stunned. Then they rose and started for the blue man. Some drew guns that had been brought. The hall was filled with blinding flashes, with smoke, with a horrible stench, screams, swearing, cries of fear and pain. There was a rush for the exits. Some died at the feet of their fellow men.

In the end, when all were gone, George of Zanthar still stood on the platform, alone. There was no movement, except the twitching of the new dead, the trampled, on the floor.

Events happened fast after that. The Illinois National Guard mobilized, sent a division to Brentwood to hunt George down. He met them at the city square. They rumbled in and trained machine guns and tank rifles on him. The tanks and personnel flashed out of existence before a shot was fired.

Brentwood was ordered evacuated. The regular army was called in. Reconnaissance planes reported George was still standing in the city square. Jet planes materialized just above the hills and made sudden dives, but before their pilots could fire a shot, they were snuffed out of the air in a burst of fire.

Bombers first went over singly, only to follow the jets' fate. A squadron bloomed into a fiery ball as it neared the target. A long range gun twenty miles away was demolished when its ammunition blew up shortly before firing.

Three days after George had killed his first man, action ceased. The countryside was deathly still. Not a living person could be seen for several miles around. But George still stood patiently in the square. He stood there for three more days and yet nothing happened.

On the fourth day, he sensed that a solitary soldier had started toward the city from five miles to the east. In his mind's eye he followed the soldier approaching the city. The soldier, a sergeant, was bearing a white flag that fluttered in the breeze; he was not armed. After an hour he saw the sergeant enter the square and approach him. When they were within twenty feet of one another, the soldier stopped and saluted.

"Major General Pitt requests a meeting with you, sir," the soldier said, trembling and trying hard not to.

"Do not be frightened," George said. "I see you intend me no harm."

The soldier reddened. "Will you accompany me?"

"Certainly."

The two turned toward the east and started to walk.

Five miles east of Brentwood lies a small community named Minerva. Population: 200. The highway from Brentwood to Chicago cuts the town in two. In the center of town, on the north side of the road, stands a new building—the Minerva Town Hall—built the year before with money raised by the residents. It was the largest and most elaborate building in Minerva, which had been evacuated three days before.

On this morning the town hall was occupied by army men. Maj. Gen. Pitt fretted and fumed at the four officers and twenty enlisted men waiting in the building.

"It's an indignity!" he railed at the men who were forced to listen to him. "We have orders to talk appeasement with him! Nuts! We lose a few men, a few planes and now we're ready to meet George halfway. What's the country coming to? There ought to be something that would knock him out. Why should we have to send in *after* him? It's disgusting!"

The major general, a large man with a bristling white mustache and a red face, stamped back and forth in the council room. Some of the officers and men smiled to themselves. The general was a well-known fighting man. Orders he had received hamstrung him and, as soldiers, they sympathized with him.

"What kind of men do we have in the higher echelons?" he asked everybody in general and nobody in particular. "They won't even let us have a field telephone. We're supposed to make a report by radio. Now isn't that smart?" He shook his head, looked the men over. "An appeasement team, that's what you are, when you ought to be a combat team to lick hell out of George.

"Why were you all assigned to this particular duty? I never saw any of you before and I understand you're all strangers to each other, too. Hell, what will they do next? Appeasement. I never appeased anybody before in my whole life. I'd rather spit in his eye. What am I supposed to talk about? The weather? What authority do I have to yak with a walking collection of nuts and bolts?"

An officer strode into the room and saluted the general. "They're coming, sir," he said.

"Who's coming?...My God, man," the general spluttered angrily, "be specific. Who the hell are 'they'?"

"Why, George and Sergeant Matthews, sir. You remember, the sergeant who volunteered to go into Brentwood—"

"Oh, them. Well, all I have to say is that this is a hell of a war. I haven't figured out what I'm going to say yet."

"Shall I have them wait, sir?"

"Hell, no. Let's get this over with. I'll find out what George has to say and maybe that'll give me a lead."

Before George entered the council chamber, he already knew the mind of each man. He saw the room through their eyes. He knew everything about them, what they were wearing, what they were thinking. All had guns, yet none of them would kill him, although at least one man, Maj. Gen. Pitt, would have liked to.

They were going to talk appeasement, George knew, but he could see too that the general didn't know what line the conversation would take or what concessions he could make on behalf of his people.

Wait—there was one man among the twenty-three who had an odd thought. It was a soldier he had seen looking through a window at him. This man was thinking about eleven o'clock, for George could see in the man's mind various symbols for fifteen minutes from then—the hands of a clock, a watch, the numerals 11. But George could not see any significance to the thought.

When he entered the room with the sergeant, he was ushered to a table. He sat down with Maj. Gen. Pitt, who glowered at him. Letting his mind roam the room, George picked up the numerals again and identified the man thinking them as the officer behind and a little to the right of the general.

What was going to happen at eleven? The man had no conscious thought of harm to anyone, yet the idea kept obtruding and seemed so out of keeping with his other thoughts George assigned several of his circuits to the man. The fact that the lieutenant looked at his watch and saw that it was 10:50 steeled George still more. If there was to be trouble, it would come from this one man.

"I'm General Pitt," the general said dryly. "You're George, of course. I have been instructed to ask you what, exactly what, your intentions are toward the United States and the world in general, with a view toward reaching some sort of agreement with you and others of your kind who will, as you say, invade the Earth."

"Invade, General Pitt," George replied, "is not the word."

"All right, whatever the word is, then. We're all familiar with the plan you've been talking about. What we want to know is, where do you go from here?"

"The fact that there has been no reluctance on the part of the armed forces to talk of agreement—even though I see that you privately do not favor such talk, General Pitt—is an encouraging sign. We of Zanthar would not want to improve a planet which could not be educated and would continually oppose our program. This will make it possible for me to turn in a full report in a few days now."

"Will you please get to the point?"

George could see that the lieutenant was looking at his watch again. It was 10:58. George spread his mind out more than twenty miles, but could find no installation, horizontally or vertically that indicated trouble. None of the men in the room seemed to think of becoming overtly hostile.

"Yes, General. After my message goes out, there ought to be a landing party on Earth within a few weeks. While waiting for the first party, there must be certain preparations—"

George tensed. The lieutenant was reaching for something. But it didn't seem to be connected with George. It was something white, a handkerchief. He saw that the man intended to blow his nose and started to relax, except that George suddenly became aware of the fact that the man *did not need to blow his nose!*

Every thought-piercing circuit became instantly energized in George's mind and reached out in all directions....

There were at least ten shots from among the men. They stood there surprised at their actions. Those who had fired their guns now held the smoking weapons awkwardly in their hands.

George's eyes were gone. Smoke curled upward from the two empty sockets where bullets had entered a moment before. The smoke grew heavier and his body became hot. Some of him turned cherry red and the chair on which he had been sitting started to burn. Finally, he collapsed toward the table and rolled to the floor. He started to cool. He was no longer the shiny blue-steel color he had been—he had turned black. His metal gave off cracking noises and some of it buckled here and there as it cooled.

A few minutes later, tense military men and civilians grouped around a radio receiver in Chicago heard the report and relaxed, laughing and slapping each other on the back. Only one sat unmoved in a corner. Others finally sought him out.

"Well, Professor, it was your idea that did the trick. Don't you feel like celebrating?" one of them asked.

Prof. Tomlin shook his head. "If only George had been a little more benign, we might have learned a lot from him."

"What gave you the idea that killed him?"

"Oh, something he said about the unconscious and subconscious," Prof. Tomlin replied. "He admitted they were not penetrable. It was an easy matter to instill a post-hypnotic suggestion in some proven subjects and then to erase the hypnotic experience."

"You make it sound easy."

"It wasn't too difficult, really. It was finding the solution that was hard. We selected more than a hundred men, working with them for days, finally singled out the best twenty, then made them forget their hypnosis. A first lieutenant—I've forgotten his name—had implanted in him a command even he was not aware of. His subconscious made him blow his nose fifteen minutes after he saw George. Nearly twenty others had post-hypnotic commands to shoot George in the eyes as soon as they saw the lieutenant blow his nose. Of course we also planted a subconscious hate pattern, which wasn't exactly necessary, just to make sure there would be no hesitation, no inhibition, no limiting moral factor.

"None of the men ever saw each other before being sent to Minerva. None realized that they carried with them the order for George's annihilation. The general, who was not one of those hypnotized, was given loose instructions, as were others, so they could not possibly know the intention. Those of us who had conducted the hypnosis had to stay several hundred miles away so that we could not be reached by George's prying mind…"

In a pasture next to a wood near Brentwood, a metal box buried in the earth suddenly exploded, uprooting a catalpa tree.

On a planet many millions of miles away, a red light—one of many on a giant control board—suddenly winked out.

A blue humanoid made an entry in a large book: *System 20578. Planet three. Inhabited.*

Too dangerous for any kind of development.

■

Trefelgen's Ring

It was a beautiful ring, a slender gleaming silver band capped with a green stone scarab that could have been as old as time. Eric Trefelgen held it at arm's length and admired it. He had polished the metal until it brilliantly reflected the lights, and he had carefully worked over the green stone with a cloth, bringing out the highlights in the scarab's back. For a long time he examined it. He turned it over and over in his hand. He cupped his hand and weighed it. He twisted it this way and that in his palm. He pushed at it with his forefinger.

At length he slipped it on the third finger of his right hand, looked at it critically for a long time, posturing his hand before his eyes, letting his arm fall experimentally to his side. He could still feel the ring on his finger.

Finally he sighed, turned out the lights and went to his bedroom to put on his gray suit coat, catching glimpses of the ring as he did so. Then he walked to the mirror over the dresser, watched himself fiddle with his burgundy tie until it was knotted perfectly, seeing too how much the ring was a natural complement of this operation. He was neither displeased with the ring nor himself, a lean man in his mid-forties with a carefully clipped mustache, a round-faced man with bright brown eyes. A man wearing a scarab ring.

Then he walked out of his house to find someone to give the ring to.

Emily was still sipping her first highball as Kenneth finished his fourth. They had had much chit-chat without meaning, color or dimension, and she was getting duller by the minute, ignoring him, lifting her eyes above his head now to the men on the floor. When they had danced she'd been too lax, too loose. No response. He might as well have been her brother.

31

Looking at her, he wondered why he had bothered. Sure, she had a nice bust, a slim figure, and she kept her long, blonde hair looking good, but she was acting as if she thought she was too good for Kenneth Severn. Watching her now, he saw an initial glimmer of interest in her wide blue eyes grow to absorption, and he turned to see a broad-shouldered man crossing the floor to them. His name was John Cortessi and he was the new coach at the high school and Kenneth knew it because T.W. Babcock himself had sold him the Adams house over in Carver Heights.

"Dance?" Cortessi said, smiling and exposing the whitest teeth Kenneth had ever seen. Emily glanced at Kenneth, daring him to say no, and Kenneth said, "Go ahead, what the hell," and watched them go.

He ordered another drink while they moved around the floor clutching each other as if their lives depended on it. To hell with them. He shifted his gaze, found Merriel Mae swaying with Hugo Benschneider, gorgeous Merriel Mae what a figure she has and suddenly there were two Merriel Maes and that was wonderful, but there were also two Hugo Benschneiders and that was horrible. Big bruiser, that Hugo. One of him was enough. To hell with them, too. It was all developing into one large ugly evening.

Two Emilys slid into the chair opposite him and he glared at them. They said in one voice, "What's the matter with you?" He waved for still another drink, but the Emilys reached for and brought down his hand. "No more," they said.

"Since when you telling me how much I can drink?" And the talk spiraled louder and louder until he was shouting at her and she was picking up her handbag and saying,

"I knew it would be a mistake to come with you I'll find my way home thank you."

"See if I care." He signaled for the waitress.

Emily's faces were white as she leaned on the table, bringing them close. "You know what you are? You're nothing but an ugly little man with a chip on his shoulder." She flounced away.

He signaled the waitress frantically. He really needed that drink. But she wouldn't bring him one and when with righteous indignation he went out to see why the hell not his way was blocked by Mr. Carruthers who owned the place. Mr. Carruthers' shirt was incredibly white and Kenneth stared at it as he was told if he couldn't behave himself he'd have to leave. Kenneth tried to argue with white shirt but it refused to argue and when he angrily reached for it, it was suddenly replaced by a great hulk of man.

Big Jim Cooke, the bartender and bouncer, took him by the collar and arm, propelled him roughly through the door, hesitated long enough to growl, "And don't come back, runt," and shoved him violently toward the street.

Kenneth tottered on unsteady feet, collided with a mailbox, and was sick. After a few long minutes the chill of the metal penetrated his clothing and he felt better for its coldness, took refuge in its solidity as all pretense suddenly ran down and out his feet into the pavement and he told himself miserably Big Jim's right I'm a runt I've never had anything I'll never have anything I don't have the build I don't have the looks I can't even sell my quota for Mr. Babcock I don't blame Emily or Big Jim I deserved to get bounced I'm a flop I try to make deals but everybody sees right through me. This self-effacement made him wrack his shoulders in anguish.

He surely would have wept if the presence of someone at his side had not taken his attention. It was a man.

"Are you ill?"

He leered drunkenly at the face. "What's it to you?"

"I just thought I might help."

"I don't need any help," he said sullenly. He hiccuped.

"You need to sober up."

He shook a hand off his shoulder. "I got to get home, that's what I got to do." He reached for his car keys. They weren't there. "Oh, Jesus!"

"Lose something?"

"Yeah. My car keys."

"Let me buy you a cup of coffee. Then I'll help you look for them."

Kenneth squinted at him, saw a jaunty, mustached man in a gray suit and snap-brim hat. He was too damn neat. His smile was too friendly.

"My name is Eric Trefelgen."

"You can go to hell, Eric Trefelgen."

"Don't be crude."

"So why should you want to buy me coffee?"

"Because I think you're the man I'm looking for."

The coffee was hot and steadying and it helped brush some of the fog from his mind as he tried to listen to Trefelgen's chatter. He watched his jiggling Adam's apple because he didn't like watching his lips saying the words. Besides, what the man said was impossible.

"Maybe you think it doesn't look like much," Trefelgen said, placing the ring in the center of the white tablecloth, "but I think you will find it to be the answer to your troubles."

Kenneth looked at the ring, a silver ring set with a large green stone scarab. It was the strangest ring he had ever seen—he was ready to concede that—but it simply could not do what Trefelgen said it would. He was getting tired, ran a hand over his face. "What's your angle, Mr. Trefelgen?"

"Call me Eric," he said with equable pleasantness, "and there's no angle. Actually, you should rejoice that I'm willing to pass it on to you."

"Why do you want to get rid of it?"

"I've explained that. I've got what I want with it. I don't need it anymore."

Kenneth shook his head, took a sip of coffee. "You can't tell me that ring would influence anybody," he said flatly.

"I'm not asking you to believe it without a test." He brought out a pencil, wrote his name and address on a napkin and gave it to him. "If you aren't pleased with the results in a day or two you can return it to me."

Kenneth only stared at the ring. Maybe he could sell it, an odd ring like that. Maybe he could get as much as five dollars for it.

Trefelgen went on, "There's no telling how many people have used this ring. Perhaps great events of history have been influenced by it."

"I'll bet."

"I should warn you, however, to use it only briefly—a week, a month, perhaps—and then pass it along as I'm doing. It wouldn't do to come to depend on it. You would lose your character if you did. Too much of a good thing, you know." His laugh was flat and unmusical.

Kenneth picked up the ring. It was heavier than he thought it would be. He turned it over. No marks, no initials. Just the bright silver band and the green stone.

"It probably originated in ancient Egypt," Trefelgen said. "The scarab was sacred there."

"Suppose you tell me how it works."

Trefelgen shrugged. "Who knows? Psionics, perhaps. There are still a great many things to be understood. Put it on."

He slipped it on; Trefelgen beamed. It fit well, looked good. So he had a ring. So what? Nobody was passing out miracles.

Later, Trefelgen insisted on helping him look for his keys. The Sky Blue lights were still on and they were able to examine the area thoroughly. When they did not find them, Trefelgen suggested Kenneth go inside to see if they had turned up.

"Don't be afraid," he said. "Remember: you have the ring."

He would have laughed, but his head was beginning to throb and he didn't want to make it worse. Still, he had to have the keys. At least now he was steady on his feet as he walked into the place. The orchestra, dancers and diners had departed, but Big Jim was still there and came toward him quickly when he saw him. Kenneth was ready to run, but Big Jim said jovially, "We found your keys, Mr. Severn," and held them dangling and jingling. "Sorry I had to rough you up. Sometimes I think it's a hell of a job." He smiled.

Kenneth was surprised. He had never seen Big Jim smile at anybody before.

He woke up in an ugly mood. The bronze shaft of sunlight coming through the window hurt his eyes, his head was tender, and his tongue was a rasp on his teeth. He saw the ring at once and if it hadn't been such an odd thing and of doubtless value, he would have thrown it in the waste basket. He decided to wear it instead and take it to an appraiser's when he had time.

The day brightened by the minute. Mrs. Daugherty, his landlady, with whom he had never been *en rapport* and who lately had been given to muttering things when he was around, was this morning civil to him. He had on occasion spoken his mind on the service in Cecil's Cafe and he often felt abused as a result but stubbornly kept getting his breakfast there anyway; but on this day he was served quickly and cheerfully by the redhead who the other day had sworn she would quit before she took another order from him. Then Riley, the gas station man, for once didn't remind him of his bill and even put air in his tires without being asked.

An odd day. The oddest thing of all happened just before he got to the office. He went into a drug store and bought a box of cigars. No smoker, when Kenneth discovered them under his arm and instantly recalled buying them, he angrily threw them in the back seat of the car and wondered if he was losing his mind.

He had intended only reporting in at the office and staying out of the way of Emily and Merriel Mae and being invisible to T.W., but before he could leave he was cornered by a man who said he was interested in a two-bedroom house do you have any and Kenneth was hooked, grudgingly hauled him out to the Ernst property on Vale Street, letting him look at it while he swallowed a couple aspirins in the bathroom thinking I'm in no hard sell mood I won't quibble hurry up and tell me it won't do. But the man, who said his name was Gaither, declared he'd take it and didn't bat an eye when he was told the price. By eleven o'clock Kenneth had the earnest money in his hands and the day had turned golden.

Right after lunch Emily left her paperwork and came over to him. He braced himself, but all she said was, "You sold the Ernst house. Congratulations."

"Yeah." A polite way to lead into it. He squinted up at her sourly to let her know he wasn't deceived.

She smiled sweetly. "I'm terribly sorry about last night."

"I'll bet you are."

"I had no business deserting you like that."

"How does Cortesi feel about it?"

She said warmly, "I want to make it up to you, Kenneth. I really do."

"Is that so? Well, Baby, since that's the way you feel about it, how about a nice warm evening in that apartment of yours? We could start with dinner—you fixing the dinner." He turned back to the magazine he'd picked up. Let her think about that for a while.

She said breathlessly, "Can you be there at six?"

Startled, he looked up. "Quit the kidding, Emily. I'm not in the mood."

She was hurt. "Please, Ken, I mean it. I *want* to cook dinner for you. I want to do everything for you. *Everything.*"

He let out his breath, looked at her wonderingly, said slowly, "Okay, okay. I'll be there." He watched her shapely buttocks as she walked back to her desk, muttered "I'll be damned" and darted a look at the ring.

The martinis were just right, the filet mignons were to his order, the salad was crisp with the correct blend of Roquefort and garlic, the coffee excellent, and Emily was perfection itself in bright blue toreador pants, black turtleneck sweater and shell shoes, attentive, efficient and glamorous, all at the same time. Kenneth stroked the scarab affectionately as they sat sipping their benedictine and brandy in the living room, her eyes bright and inviting, his hot and wandering. She fed *Tristan and*

Isolde to the hi-fi and she reached kindling temperature during the *Love Death*. In the middle of it all Kenneth thought what a damn fool Eric Trefelgen was.

Ordinarily he paid little attention to what T.W. had to say at the twice-a-week staff sessions, but the next morning Emily would not take her eyes off him and he forced himself to concentrate on Old Babcock to escape. T.W. was talking for the umpteenth time about the Anletter property.

"We've got to sell it," he was saying, wiping his glistening forehead (staff meetings made him sweat). "We've had it for over a year now and the Anletters are getting edgy."

As if we're not, Kenneth said to himself. The Anletters owned and operated the Opal Hotel and were trying to get out from under after twenty years of declining business. Motels had long ago started the Opal on the downgrade. Now the death blow was being delivered by cracked walls, worn carpeting, old-fashioned electric wiring that would not accommodate air conditioners. If it weren't for the fact that Mr. Anletter was a city councilman, the building would have been condemned, for it needed tuck pointing, a new roof, paint, plumbing and new wiring.

"The price," Babcock was saying, "is eighty-five thousand, and it's worth every cent of it."

Merriel Mae, the Great White Father's secretary, yawned. Kenneth decided it was a very pretty yawn and got up, walked out of the office and stuffed five dollar bills in the corner mail box, thinking about the yawn all the way. When he got back it came as a shock to him, the realization of what he had just done. But nobody had missed him, T.W. was still talking, and he hoped nobody had seen his idiocy at the mail box. Now why the hell should I do a damn fool thing like that? He frowned, trying to puzzle it out, met Merriel Mae's eyes. They were very friendly. And he thought: Emily, why not Merriel Mae?

Later, in the room where she worked, Merriel Mae looked up at him expectantly and not at all unpleasantly.

"I want you for dinner tonight," he said. With the ring there was no need for preliminaries.

"You will find me very tender," she replied, smiling at him prettily, rising from her typewriter, elegance and grace in every inch of her model's figure (there's so much more to Merriel Mae, he thought), running the tip of her tongue along her upper lip. "I was supposed to meet Hugo tonight, but I'll break it for you, darling."

Merriel Mae took his breath away when she took off her wrap and revealed a printed red velveteen sheath of daring dimensions at Ricci's, a fitting beginning to an evening that included a gimlet, burgundy with prime ribs, and afterwards a pink squirrel, though he had little heart for the food and drink, his endocrine system so engrossed with what was to come. She laughed at the things he joked about, pressed against him hard when they were dancing, later breathed a languorous assent in his ear when he said it was time to go to her apartment. It further pleased him that she didn't need Wagner.

The blow fell when he left her apartment, and it was delivered in person by Hugo Benschneider just outside her door, a powerful right to the jaw that sent him sprawling in the carpeted corridor. Benschneider followed it by landing his two hundred pounds squarely atop him and working his arms like pistons. If the super and several outraged tenants had not stopped Hugo, it is likely he would have beaten Kenneth completely into the carpet.

As it was, Kenneth was in no condition to protest when the police hauled them in. He didn't even wince when Merriel Mae told the judge that Kenneth had initiated the action, and he didn't care that Hugo said something seemed to possess him during the encounter and made him pummel Kenneth so unmercifully, or even that they left him to the ministrations of a police doctor who grimly patched him up with adhesive tape and merthiolate. But he was seething by the time he paid his sixty-four dollar assault and battery fine and was released.

He found Trefelgen in his living room working out a problem in military strategy with models of knights and bowmen on a giant plywood board, and Kenneth proceeded to tell him heatedly just what he thought of the ring.

"Simmer down," Trefelgen said, "and sit down. You've got it all wrong. It's not the ring's fault. Now relax and tell me what happened to you."

Kenneth told him, saying finally, "Yeah, a great little ring you gave me. You never know when somebody's going to take a poke at you."

Trefelgen studied him, said gravely, "Perhaps you're not the right man for the ring after all."

Kenneth said hastily, "Oh, the ring's all right when it works, but when it doesn't it's murder."

Trefelgen nodded. "The basic difficulty nonetheless is you, Kenneth."

"Me? How do you figure that?"

"Each of us is ambivalent most of the time. We're drawn to doing thus and so—and at the same time we're inclined not to. Sometimes one part of us wins out, we do one thing, and sometimes the other part dominates us and we do the opposite. Your mistake was Merriel Mae. You won this Emily, and that was all right, and even Merriel Mae was acceptable—until you saw Hugo. Immediately he became a surrogate conscience, a living image of your guilt feelings. Now you thought: Not only have I betrayed Emily, I have used this ring to win out over Hugo, who has no such advantage. In spite of your outward bravado, your sneering contempt of things, inside you really felt you deserved punishment. The ring only obliged you. It was as if you had cried out 'Punish me' and the ring influenced Hugo to do just that." He smiled thinly. "Judging by your appearance, I would say you felt quite guilty about it."

"I don't like it and I don't feel the least bit guilty."

"Not now you don't. You've been punished, don't you see? You're clean again. You don't seem to understand the ring makes little distinction between what you secretly desire and what you consciously desire. The truth is, you hardly know yourself."

"I suppose you know yourself. Inside and out. All the way through."

"No man does. But I know myself better than you do." Trefelgen waved to the shelves of books in the living room. "I know for example that my interests lie in the military, international and economic fields. Until the ring made it possible, I was never able to devote my full time to it."

Kenneth read a few titled: *The Governments of Foreign Powers*, Thucydides' *The Peloponnesian Wars, Theory of Economic Planning, Government and Mass Communications*. On the arm of the chair was a book, *On War* by Clausewitz.

Trefelgen said, "Each of us must find what he most desires and work in that direction. For me it is time to study such things as the Battle of Arsoup, which I have set out on the table. This was the time that King Richard broke the back of the Moslem hordes. If it weren't for Richard's patience, he would never have made Saladin knuckle under. He sustained countless skirmishes over the long march to Arsoup in an endeavor to bring his enemy close for successful in-fighting. His passive tactics bear witness to Ascalon, Gaza, Blanche-Garde, Lyda, Ramich and all the other abandoned fortresses that became his on the long march...But I see I am boring you."

Kenneth said, "All I want to know is how I can keep from going through anything like this again."

"Well, if you are set on giving the ring another try, I would suggest concentrating on real estate. Make a tidy sum for yourself. And leave the girls alone."

From then on Kenneth was careful about the ring. Emily's interest remained constant, but he gave her no encouragement; neither did he spurn her, aware of the direction in which his guilt feelings might lay. Merriel Mae told him one day at the water cooler she was sorry about the other night she'd make sure it would never happen again. He thanked her, told her he would let her know. The pursuit of money was much safer than the pursuit of women. Trefelgen was right about that. And he sold property on Cherry Street that had been on the books for months, put over deals that involved a dozen houses in an old tract, set the office record for four closings in one day.

Once he bought a turtle—a sawtooth slider—and set it loose in the park lagoon when he found it in his pocket and at the instant of its discovery remembering buying it and being so specific about its type. He then recalled that he had not mentioned these aberrations to Trefelgen, decided it was just as well.

Another time he took off his shoes and threw them into the river and drove home in his stockinged feet wondering now why in the hell did I do that I wish I knew when these spells were coming.

It was near the end of the second week that Merriel Mae came out to tell him T.W. wanted to see him at once, and when he went in the Old Man thrust out his wet palm, gave him a smile and said, "Ken, I've been following your progress and I want you to know we've all been pleasantly surprised."

He said thanks and squeezed the fingers.

T.W. cleared his throat. "I want you to give a little sales talk at the next staff. Some of the boys need to be shored up and you're just the man to do it. Let them know it can be done if only they'd get down to following your example."

"Be glad to, Mr. Babcock."

"T.W. to you from now on."

"Yes, T.W."

"One other thing. You've heard me talk about the Anletter property. Lord knows we've had it long enough. Confidentially, Gus Anletter will accept seventy-five thousand, and it so happens I have a prospect at the original figure." He happily rubbed his hands together. "Man's name is Dempster. Luther Dempster. He's coming down this afternoon, thought you might show the place to him." He clamped his lips together and said tightly, "There'll be twenty-five hundred and a partnership if you swing it."

It took Kenneth no time at all to say, "Make it five thousand and you'll have a sale, T.W."

"You press me," T.W. said, mopping his forehead with a monogrammed handkerchief, "but you've got yourself a deal."

Played right, Kenneth said to himself, there's no end to the possibilities of the ring and I'm never giving it up do you hear that, Eric Trefelgen?

"What are you grinning about?"

"I like this business, T.W."

He let Dempster look at the property and it all went like clockwork. His prospect seemed blind to the cracking plaster, the threadbare rugs, the wretched state of the roof, the fact that the cornices were so loose they were ready to fall.

Since he had the ring there was very little required of Kenneth, except to suggest closing the deal, so he let Anletter emphasize the Opal's virtues and forget to mention its drawbacks, and he watched Dempster nod in approval.

Dempster asked to see the heating system, which was ponderous, hideous and archaic, and Anletter was silent because there were no virtues in the boiler room. But to the owner's amazement, Dempster seemed pleased with it.

Anletter was even more surprised when Dempster agreed to a meeting of all concerned the next morning in the office of Kramer and Willowby, and wrote out a token check to show his sincerity. But Kenneth wasn't surprised at all.

Dempster's attorney was there the next day, and T.W. was beside himself in the outer office because he'd heard the attorney would try to argue Dempster out of it. But the man, a gargantua with briefcase, failed to render any objection during the course of the transaction.

"You were right, Ken," T.W. whispered. "I don't see how you do it."

"It's easy," Kenneth said, "if you know how."

Emily had been there to help with the paperwork, and after everything had been done and every last paper signed, she walked with him back toward the office, trudging along, folders under her arm, saying nothing.

"Quite a deal, eh?" Kenneth said finally, looking sidelong at her, disturbed by her silence.

"I suppose so. But I feel sorry for Mr. Dempster."

"Why, for heaven's sake?"

"That building's ready to fall down."

"It's just a business deal, Emily. Things like this happen every day. Maybe he's got a motive—you know, tearing it down for a parking lot or something. Maybe there's oil under it. He may be smarter than we think."

She stopped and he turned to look at her. She said, "You know that's not true, Kenneth Severn. Suddenly you've become some kind of super salesman and you talk people into things. Everyone's talking about it. But I don't see how you can be proud of tricking somebody into buying a pile of junk—"

"I didn't trick him." But the words were like fire in his throat.

"Pressured him, then."

"I didn't pressure him either." He could hardly get the words out.

Emily seemed ready to cry, and suddenly what she was became clear to him, the voice of his inner feelings, and he felt an ominous chilling of his blood. He knew he must convince her, as he must convince himself, that it hadn't been wrong, that it was only what T.W. might have done, had tried to do. It was routine. It was natural.

"Look, Emily," he said gently, putting a hand out to her.

"Get away from me," she cried, evading the outstretched hand and walking swiftly away.

"Emily!" He started after her.

Suddenly she turned and crossed the street. Conscious of his wanting to reach her, she broke into a run, her blonde hair flying.

"Emily!"

There was plenty of time to cross because the car was more than half a block away, but once he set foot in the street it increased speed and the driver hunched over the wheel like a demon.

Kenneth uttered a hoarse cry, sprinted for the other curb. But the car was even faster. It caught him long before he reached it, crunching his bones, crumpling him against the front end, tossing him to the pavement like a dummy when the driver braked screeching to a halt.

"I didn't mean to do it," the driver wailed. "I didn't mean to do it! The car just *went*." And he commenced an agitated shaking.

Eric Trefelgen entered his laboratory, turned on the lights, sat down on the stool before his workbench and sighed. To his right and left were thousands of scarab rings, none quite as polished and pretty as the one he'd given Kenneth. He reached up over the bench to the master control panel where a red light had winked out some time ago, pulled a switch, and then reached for the nearest ring, prying off the simulated green stone scarab, setting a loupe in his eye and probing the delicate circuitry within.

There had been good response to control—the box of cigars, the five dollar bills, the turtle, the shoes. There was no question in his mind about this part of it. But what about the conscience circuit? Each control needed some inhibition. But how to divorce it successfully from the will when it wasn't needed?

He scraped a little with the needle probe along a point deep in the almost microscopic array of wires. He made several other adjustments.

After a while he slipped the scarab cover on and started polishing the silver part of the ring, whistling a little tune. It was early.

He liked to think he had the patience of King Richard.

■

The Invisible Enemy

For an hour they had been circling the spot at 25,000 feet while technicians weighed and measured the planet and electronic fingers probed where no eye could see.

And for an hour Harley Allison had sat in the computer room accepting the information and recording it on magnetic tapes and readying them for insertion into the machine, knowing already what the answer would be and resenting what the commander was trying to do.

It was quiet in the ship except for the occasional twitter of a speaker that recited bits of information which Allison dutifully recorded. It was a relief from the past few days of alarm bells and alerts and flashing lights and the drone of the commander's voice over the intercom, even as that had been a relief from the lethargy and mindlessness that comes with covering enormous stellar distances, for it was wonderful to see faces awaken to interest in things when the star drive went off and to become aware of a changing direction and lessening velocity. Then had eyes moved from books and letters and other faces to jump to the growing pinpoints of the Hyades on the scanners.

It was only then that Allison punched the key that released the ship from computer control and gave it to manual, and in the ensuing lull the men of the *Nesbitt* heard for the first time why they had come so far across space.

The heretofore secret orders were read by Commander William Warrick himself.

Then the men had sat down to controls unmanned for so long. They sought out first the star among the hundreds in the system. Then they found its fourth planet.

Finally they located the small spaceship they were hunting. It lay on its side on the desert surface of the planet.

There was laughter and the scrape of feet in the hall and Allison looked up to see Wendell Hallom enter the computer room, followed by several others.

"Well, looks like the rumors were right," Hallom said, eyes squinting up at the live screen above the control panel. The slowly rotating picture showed the half-buried spaceship and the four pillars of the force field about it tilted at ridiculous angles. "I suppose you knew all about this."

"I didn't know any more than you, except we were headed for the Hyades," Allison said. "I just work here, too, you know."

"I wish I was home," Tony Lazzari said, rolling his eyes. "I don't like the looks of that yellow sand. I don't know why I ever joined this man's army."

"It was either join or go to jail," Gordon Bacon said.

"I ought to punch you right in the nose." Lazzari moved toward Bacon, who thumbed his nose at him. "In fact, I got a good mind to turn it inside out."

Allison put a big hand on his shoulder, pulled him back. "Not in here you don't. I got enough troubles. That's all I'd need."

"Yeah," Hallom said. "Relax, kid. Save your strength. You're going to need it. See that pretty ship up there with nobody on it?"

"You and the commander," Bacon said. "Why's he got it in for you, Allison?"

"I wouldn't know," Allison said, smiling thinly. "I've got a wonderful personality. I don't understand it."

Hallom snorted. "Allison's in the Computer Corps, ain't he? The commander thinks that's just like being a passenger along for the ride. And he don't like it."

"That's what happens when you get an old-line skipper and try to help him out with a guy with a gadget," Bacon observed.

"It wouldn't be so bad," Homer Petry said at the door, "if it had been tried before."

"Mr. Allison," a speaker blared.

"All right, you guys," Allison said. "Clear out." He depressed a toggle. "Yes, Lieutenant?"

"You have everything now, Allison. Might as well run it through."

"The commander can't think of anything else?"

There was a cough. "The commander's standing right here. Shall I ask him?"

"I'll run this right through, Lieutenant."

Commander William Warrick was a fine figure of a man: tall, militant, graying, hatchet-nosed. He was a man who hewed so close to the line that he never let humanity get between, a man who would be perpetually young, for even at fifty there was an absence of paunch, though his eyes held a look of a man who had many things to remember.

He stood for a while at one end of the control room without saying anything, his never-absent map pointer in his right hand, the end of it slapping the open palm of his left hand. His cold eyes surveyed the men who stood crowded shoulder-to-shoulder facing him.

"Men," he said, and his deep voice was resonant in the room, "take a good look at the screen up there." The eyes of nearly fifty men shifted to the giant screen beside and above him. "That's the *Esther*." The ship was on gyro, circling the spot, and the screen showed a rotating ship on the sand.

"We'll be going down soon and we'll get a better look. But I want you to look at her now because you might be looking at the *Nesbitt* if you're not careful."

The commander turned to look at the ship before going on. "The *Esther* is a smaller ship. It had a complement of only eight men. Remember the tense there. *Had.* They disappeared just as the men in the two ships before them did, each carrying eight men—the *Mordite* and the *Halcyon*. All three ships were sent to look for Traveen Abbott and Lew Gesell, two explorers for the Federation who had to their credit successful landings on more than ninety worlds. They were cautious, experienced and wise. Yet this planet swallowed them up, as it did the men of the three ships that followed."

Commander Warrick paused and looked at them severely. "We're fifty men and I think we have a better chance than an eight-man crew, not just because there are more of us but because we have the advantage of knowing we're against something really deadly. In case you haven't already deduced our mission, it is simply to find out what it is and destroy it."

The insignia on the commander's collar and sleeve glittered in the light from the ever-changing screen as the ship circled the site of the *Esther*.

"This is a war ship. We are armed with the latest weapons. And—" his eyes caught Allison's "—we even have a man from the Computer Corps with us, if that can be counted as an advantage."

Allison, who stood at the rear of the room behind the assembled sol-dier-technicians, reddened. "The tapes got us here, Commander."

"We could have made it without them," the commander said without ire. "But we're here with or without tape. But just because we are we're not rush-ing down there. We know the atmosphere is breathable, the gravity is close to Earth's and there are no unusually dangerous bacteria. All this came from the *Esther* prior to the…incident, whatever it was. But we checked again just to make sure. The gravity is nine-tenths that of Earth's, there is a day of twenty-four and a half hours, temperature and humidity tropical at this parallel, the atmosphere slightly less rich in oxygen, though not harmfully so—God only knows how a desert planet like this can have oxygen with so little vegetation and no evident animal life. There is no dangerous radiation from the surface or from the sun. Mr. Allison has run the assembled data through his ma-chine—would you care to tell the men what the machine had to say, Allison?"

Allison cleared his throat and wondered what the commander was driv-ing at. "The planet could sustain life, if that's what you mean, Commander."

"But what did the machine say about the inhabitants, Mr. Allison?"

"There wasn't enough data for an assumption."

"Thank you. You men can get some idea of how the Computer Corps helps out in situations like this."

"That's hardly fair, Commander," Allison protested. "With more data—"

"We'll try to furnish you with armfuls of data." The commander smiled broadly. "Perhaps we might let you collect a little data yourself."

There was laughter at this. "So much for the Computer Corps. We could go down now, but we're circling for eighteen more hours for observa-tion. Then we're going down. Slowly."

The ship came out of the deep blue sky in the early morning and the commander was a man of his word. The *Nesbitt* moved down slowly, begin-ning at sunup and ending in the sand within a few hundred feet of the *Esther* in an hour.

"You'd think," Lazzari said as the men filed back into the control room for another briefing, "that the commander has an idea he can talk this thing to death."

"I'd rather be talked to death by the commander than by you," Hallom said. "He has a pleasanter voice."

"I just don't like it, all that sand down there and nothing else."

"We passed over a few green places," Allison corrected. "A few rocky places, too. It's not all sand."

"But why do we have to go down in the middle of it?" Lazzari insisted.

"That's where the other ships went down. Whatever it is attacked them on the sand."

"If it was up to me, I'd say: Let the thing be, whatever it is. Live and let live. That's my motto."

"You're just lazy," said Petry, the thin-faced oldster from Chicago. "If we was pickin' apples you'd be askin' why. If you had your way you'd spend the rest of your life in a bunk."

"Lazy, hell!" Lazzari snorted. "I just don't think we should go poking our nose in where somebody's going to bite it off."

"That's not all they'll bite off, Buster," said Gar Caldwell, a radar and sonics man from Tennessee.

Wang Lee, force-field expert, raised his thin oriental eyebrows and said, "It is obvious we know more than our commander. We know, for example, *it* bites. It follows then that it has teeth. We ought to report that to the commander."

The commander strode into the room, map pointer under his arm, bearing erect, shoulders back, head high. Someone called attention and every man stiffened but Allison, who leaned against the door. Commander Warrick surveyed them coldly for a moment before putting them at ease.

"We're dividing into five teams," he said. "Four in the field and the command team here. The rosters will be read shortly and duplicate equipment issued. The lieutenants know the plans and they'll explain them to you. Each unit will have a g-car, force-field screen, television and radio for constant communication with the command team. There will be a blaster for each man, nuclear bombardment equipment for the weapons man, and so on."

He put his hands on his hips and eyed them all severely. "It's going to be no picnic. It's hot as hell out there. A hundred degrees in the daytime and no shade. It's eighty at night and the humidity's high. But I want you to find out what it is before it finds out what you are. I don't want any missing men. The Federation's lost three small ships and twenty-four men already. And Mr. Allison—"

Allison jerked from the wall at the unexpected calling of his name. "Yes, Commander?"

"You understand this is an emergency situation?"

"Well, yes, Commander."

The commander smiled slyly and Allison could read something other than humor behind his eyes.

"Then you must be aware that, under Federation regulations governing ships in space, the commander exercises unusual privileges regarding his crew and civilians who may be aboard."

"I haven't read the regulation, Commander, but I'll take your word for it that it exists."

"Thank you, Mr. Allison." The lip curled ever so slightly. "I'd be glad to read it to you in my quarters immediately after this meeting, except there isn't time. For your information in an emergency situation, though you are merely attached to a ship in an advisory capacity, you come under the jurisdiction of the ship's commander. Since we're short of men, I'm afraid I'll have to make use of you."

Allison balled two big, brown hands and put them behind his back. They had told him at Computer Corps school he might meet men like Commander Warrick—men who did not yet trust the maze of computer equipment that only a few months ago had been made mandatory on all ships of the *Nesbitt* class. It was natural that men who had fought through campaigns with the old logistics and slide-rule tactics were not going to feel immediately at home with computers and the men that went with them. It wasn't easy trusting the courses of their ships or questions of attack and defense to magnetized tape.

"I understand, Commander," Allison said. "I'll be glad to help out in whatever way you think best."

"Good of you, I'm sure." The commander turned to one of the lieutenants near him. "Lieutenant Cheevers, break out a blaster for Mr. Allison. He may need it."

When the great port was opened, the roasting air that rushed in blasted the faces of the men loading the treadwagons. Allison, the unaccustomed weight of the blaster making him conscious of it, went with several of them down the ramp to look out at the yellow sand.

Viewing it from the surface was different from looking at it through a scanner from above. He squinted his eyes as he followed the expanse to the horizon and found there were tiny carpets of vegetation here and there, a few larger grass islands, a wooded area on a rise far away on the right, mountains in the distance on the left. And above it all was a deep blue sky with a blazing white sun. The air had a burned smell.

A tall lieutenant—Cork Rogers, who would lead the first contingent—moved down the ramp into the broiling sun and gingerly stepped into the sand. He sank into it up to his ankles. He came back up, shaking his head. "Even the sand's hot."

Allison went down, the sun feeling like a hot iron on his back, bent over and picked up a handful of sand. It was yellower than Earth sand and he was surprised to find it had very little weight. It was more like sawdust, yet it was granular. He looked at several tiny grains closely, saw that they were hollow. They were easily crushed.

"Why was I born?" Lazzari asked no one in particular, his arms loaded with electrical equipment for the wagon. "And since I was, how come I ever got in this lousy outfit?"

"Better save your breath," Allison said, coming up the ramp and wiping his hands on his trousers.

"Yeah, I know. I'm going to need it." He stuck his nose up and sniffed. "They call that air!"

In a few minutes, the first treadwagon loaded with its equipment and men in their tropicals purred down the ramp on its tracks and into the sand. It waited there, its eye tube already revolving slowly high on its mast above the weapons bridge. The soldier on the bridge was at ready, his tinted visor pulled down. He was actually in the small g-car which could be catapulted at an instant's notice.

Not much later there were four treadwagons in the sand and the commander came down the ramp in his light tropicals, a faint breeze tugging at his sleeves and collar.

He took the salute of each of the officers in turn—Lieutenant Cork Rogers of Unit North, Lieutenant Vicky Noromak of Unit East, Lieutenant Glen Foster of Unit West and Lieutenant Carl Quartz of Unit South. They raised the green and gold of the Federation flag as he and the command team stood at attention behind him.

Then the commander's hand whipped down and immediately the purrs of the wagons became almost deafening as they veered from one another and started off through the sand, moving gracefully over the rises, churning powder wakes and leaving dusty clouds.

It was quiet and cool in the control room. Commander Warrick watched the four television panels as they showed the terrain in panorama from outpositions a mile in each direction from the ship. On all of them there were these same things: the endless, drifting yellow sand with its frequent carpets of grass, the spaceship a mile away, the distant mountain, the green area to the right.

Bacon sat at the controls for the panels, Petry at his side. Once every fifteen seconds a radio message was received from one of the treadwagon units: "Unit West reporting nothing at 12:18:15." The reports droned out over the speaker system with monotonous regularity. Petry checked off the quarter minutes and the units reporting.

Because he had nothing better to do, Allison had been sitting in the control room for four hours and all he had seen were the television panels and all he had heard were the reports—except when Lieutenant Cheevers and three other men returned from an inspection of the *Esther*.

"Pile not taken, eh?" The commander pursed his lips and ran a forefinger along his jaw. "Anything above median level would have taken the pile. I can't see it being ignored."

The lieutenant shook his head. "The *Esther* was relatively new. That would have made her pile pretty valuable."

"I can't figure out why the eight men on the *Esther* couldn't handle the situation. They had the *Mordite* and the *Halcyon* as object lessons. They must have been taken by surprise. No sign of a struggle, eh, Cheevers?"

"None, sir. We went over everything from stem to stern. Force field was still working, though it had fallen out of line. We turned it off."

"No dried blood stains? No hair? No bones?"

"No, sir."

"That's odd, don't you think? Where could they have gone?" The commander sighed. "I expect we'll know soon enough. As it is, unless something is done, the *Esther* will sink farther into this sand until she's sunk out of sight with the other two ships." He frowned. "Lieutenant, how would you like to assume command of the *Esther* on our return? It must still be in working order if the pile is there. I'll give you a crew."

Cheevers grinned. "I'd like it, sir."

"Look good on your service record, eh, Corvin?" The commander then saw Allison sitting at the rear of the room watching the panels. "What do you make of all this, Allison?"

"I hardly know what to think, Commander."

"Why don't you run a tape on it?"

"I wish I could, but with what little we know so far it wouldn't do any good."

"Come, now, Allison, surely a good man like you—you're a computer man, remember?—surely you could do something. I've heard of the wonders of those little machines. I'll bet you could run that through the machine and it would tell us exactly what we want to know."

"There's not enough data. I'd just get an ID—Insufficient Data—response as I did before."

"It's too bad, Allison, that the computer people haven't considered that angle of it—that someone has to get the data to feed the machine, that the Federation must still rely on guts and horse sense and the average soldier-technician. I'll begin thinking computers are a good thing when they can go out and get their own data."

That had been two hours ago. Two hours for Allison to cool off in. Two hours to convince himself it had been best not to answer the commander. And now they all sat, stony-faced and quiet, watching the never-ending sweep of the eye tubes that never showed anything different except the changing shadows as the planet's only sun moved across the sky. Yellow sand and carpets of green, the ship, the mountain, the wooded area...

It was the same on the next four-hour watch. The eye tubes turned and the watchers in the ship watched and saw nothing new, and radio reports droned on every fifteen seconds until the men in the room were scarcely conscious of them.

And the sun went down.

Two moons, smaller than Earth's single moon, rode high in the sky, but they didn't help as much as infrared beams from the treadwagons, which rendered the panel pictures as plain as day. And there was nothing new.

The commander ordered the units moved a mile farther away the second day. When the action was completed, the waiting started all over again.

It would not be fair to say *nothing* was new. There was one thing—tension. Nerves that had been held ready for action began demanding it. And with the ache of taut nerves came impatience and an over-exercising of the imagination. The quiet, the heat, humidity and monotony of nothing the second day and night erupted in a blast from Unit East early on the morning of the third day. The nuclear-weapons man in the g-car had fired at something he saw moving out on the sand.

At the site Technician Gar Caldwell reported by radio while Lieutenant Noromak and another man went through the temporarily damped force field to investigate. There was nothing at the target but some badly burned and fused sand.

Things went back to normal again.

Time dragged through the third day and night, and the hot breezes and high humidity and the waiting rubbed already-raw nerves.

On the morning of the fourth day Homer Petry, who had been checking off the radio reports as they came in, suddenly announced: "No radio report from Unit West at 8:l4:45!"

Instantly all eyes went to the Unit West panel.

The screen showed a revolving panorama of shimmering yellow sand and blue sky.

Lieutenant Cheevers opened the switch. "Unit West! Calling Unit West!"

No answer.

"What the hell's the matter with you, Unit West!"

The commander yelled, "Never mind, Lieutenant! Get two men and shoot over there. I'll alert the other units."

Lieutenant Cheevers picked up Allison, who happened to be in the control room at the time, and Hallom. In a matter of moments the port dropped open with the lieutenant at the controls and the two men digging their feet in the side stirrups and their hands clasping the rings for this purpose on either side. The small g-car soared out into the sweltering air screaming toward Unit West.

The terrain rushed by below them as the car picked up still more speed and Allison, not daring to move his head too far from the protective streamlining lest it get caught in the hot air stream, saw the grass-dotted, sunbaked sand blur by.

Then the speed slackened and, raising his head, he saw the treadwagon and the four force-field pillars they were approaching.

But he saw no men.

The lieutenant put the car in a tight turn and landed it near the wagon. The three grabbed their weapons, jumped from the car and ran with difficulty through the sand to the site.

The force field blocked them.

"What the hell!" Cheevers kicked at the inflexible, impenetrable shield and swore some more.

The treadwagon was there in the middle of the square formed by the force-field posts and there was no one in it. The eye tube was still rotating slowly and noiselessly, weapons on the bridge beneath still pointed menacingly at the empty desert, the g-car was still in its place, and the Federation flag fluttered in the slight breeze.

But there was nothing living inside the square. The sand was oddly smooth in many places where there should have been footprints and Allison wondered if the slight breeze had already started its work of moving the sand to obliterate them. There were no bodies, no blood, no signs of a struggle.

Since they couldn't get through the barrier, they went back to the g-car and went over it, landing inside the invisible enclosure, still alert for any emergency.

But nothing attacked because there was nothing there. Only the sand, the empty treadwagons, the weapons, the stores.

"Poor Quartz," Cheevers said.

"What, sir?" Hallom asked.

"Lieutenant Quartz. I knew him better than any of the others." He picked up a handful of sand and threw it angrily at the wagon's treads.

Allison saw it hit, watched it fall, then noticed the tread prints were obliterated inside the big square. But as he looked out across the waste to the ship he noticed the tread prints there were quite clear.

He shivered in the hot sun.

The lieutenant reported by the wagon's radio and after they had collected and packed all the gear, Allison and Hallom drove the treadwagons back to the ship.

"I tell you it's impossible!" The commander's eyes were red-rimmed and bloodshot and he ran sweating hands through wisps of uncombed hairs. "There must have been something!"

"But there wasn't, sir," Cheevers said with anguish. "And nothing was overlooked, believe me."

"But how can that be?" The commander raised his arms in the air, let them fall. "And how will it look in the record? Ten men gone. Just like that." He snapped his fingers. "The Federation won't like it—especially since it is exactly what happened to the others. If only there had been a fight! If there were a chance for reprisal! But this—" He waved an arm to include the whole planet. "It's maddening!"

It was night before the commander could contain himself enough to talk rationally about what had happened and to think creatively of possible action.

"I'm not blaming you, Lieutenant Cheevers, or anybody," he said, slouched in his desk chair and idly eyeing the three remaining television screens that revealed an endless, turning desert scene. "I have only myself to blame for what happened." He snorted. "I only wish I knew what happened." He turned to Cheevers, Allison and Hallom, who sat on the other side of the desk. "I've done nothing but think about this thing all day. I don't know what to tell those fellows out there, how they can protect themselves from this thing. I've examined the facts from every angle, but I always end up where I started." He stared at Cheevers. "Let's hear your idea again, Cheevers."

"It's like I say, sir. The attack could have come from the air."

"Carried away like eagles, eh? You've still got that idea?"

"The sand was smooth, Commander. That would support the idea of wings of birds setting the air in motion so the sand would cover up the footprints."

The commander bit his lower lip, drummed on the desk with his fingers and stared hard at Cheevers. "It is possible. Barely possible. But it still doesn't explain why we see no birds, why we saw no birds on the other viewers during the incident, why the other teams saw no birds in flight. We've asked, remember? Nobody has seen a living thing. Where then are we going to get enough birds to carry off ten men? And how does this happen with no bloodshed? Surely one of your men could have got one shot, could have wounded *one* bird."

"The birds could have been invisible, sir," Hallom said hesitantly.

"Invisible birds!" The commander glared. Then he shrugged. "Hell, I suppose anything is possible."

"That's what Allison's machine says."

"I ran the stuff through the computer," Allison said.

"I forgot there was such a thing. So that's what came out, eh?"

"Not exactly, Commander." Allison withdrew a roll of facsimile tape. "I sent through what we had. There are quite a few possibilities." He unrolled a little of it. "The men could still exist at the site, though rendered invisible and mute—"

"Nuts!" the commander said. "How the hell—!"

"The data," Allison went on calmly, "was pretty weird itself and the machine lists only the possibilities, taking into consideration everything, no matter how absurd. Other possibilities are that we are victims of hypnosis and that we are to see only what *they*—whoever *they* are—want us to see; that the men were surprised and spirited away by something invisible, which would mean none of the other units would have seen or reported it or that the men themselves would not have seen the—let's say 'invisible birds'; that the men sank into the sand somehow by some change in the composition of the ground itself, or were taken there by something, that there was a change in time or space—"

"That's enough!" the commander snapped. He rose, eyes blazing. "I can see we're going to get nothing worthwhile from the Computer Corps. 'Change in time' hell! I want a straight answer, not a bunch of fancies or something straight from a fairy tale. The only thing you've said so far I'd put any stock in is the idea of the birds. And the lieutenant had that idea first. But as far as they're being invisible is concerned, I hardly think that's likely."

"But if it had been just birds," Allison said, putting away the roll of tape, "there would have been resistance and blood would have been spilled somewhere."

Commander Warrick snorted. "If there'd been a fight we'd have seen some evidence of it. It was too quick for a fight, that's all. And I'm warning the other units of birds and of attack without warning."

As a result, the three remaining units altered the mechanism of their eye tubes to include a sweep of the sky after each 360-degree pan of the horizon.

The fourth night passed and the blazing sun burst forth the morning of the fifth day with the situation unchanged except that anxiety and tension were more in evidence among the men than ever before. The commander ordered sedatives for all men coming off watches so they could sleep.

The fifth night passed without incident.

It was nearly noon on the sixth day when Wang Lee, who was with Lieutenant Glen Foster's Unit West, reported that one of the men had gone out of his head.

The commander said he'd send over a couple men to get him in a g-car.

But before Petry and Hallom left, Lee was on the radio. "It's Prince, the man I told you about. Maybe you can see the screen. He's got his blaster out and insists we turn off the force field."

The television screen showed the sky in a long sweep past the sun down to the sand and around, sweeping past the figure of a man, obviously Prince, as it panned the horizon.

"Lieutenant Foster's got a blaster on him," Lee went on.

"Damn it!" Sweat popped out on the commander's forehead as he looked at the screen. "Not enough trouble without that." He turned to

Cheevers. "Tell Foster to blast him before he endangers the whole outfit."

But the words were not swift enough. The screen went blank and the speaker emitted a harsh click.

It was late afternoon when the treadwagon from Unit West purred to a stop beside the wagon from Unit South and Petry and Bacon stepped out of it.

"There she is," Cheevers told the commander at his side on the ramp. "Prince blasted her but didn't put her out of commission! Only the radio—you can see the mast has been snapped off. No telling how many men he got in that blast before…"

"And now they're all gone. Twenty men." The commander stared dumbly at the wagon and his shoulders slouched a little now. He looked from the wagon to the horizon and followed it along toward the sun, shading his squinting red eyes. "What is it out there, Cheevers? What are we up against?"

"I wish I knew, sir."

They walked down the ramp to the sand and waded through it out to the treadwagon. They examined it from all sides.

"Not a damn bloodstain anywhere," the commander said, wiping his neck with his handkerchief. "If Prince really blasted the men there ought to be stains and hair and remains and stench and—well, *something*."

"Did Rogers or Noromak report anything while I was gone?"

"Nothing. Not a thing…Scene look the same as before?"

"Just like before. Smooth sand inside the force field and no traces, though we did find Prince's blaster. At least I think it's his. Found it half-buried in the sand where he was supposed to be standing. We can check his serial number on it."

"Twenty men!" the commander breathed. He stared at the smooth sweep of sand again. "Twenty men swallowed up by nothing again." He looked up at the cloudless sky. "No birds, no life, no nothing. Yet something big enough to—" He shook his fist at the nothingness. "Why don't you show yourself, whoever you are—whatever you are! Why do you sneak and steal men!"

"Easy, Commander," Cheevers said, alarmed at the commander's red face, wide eyes and rising voice.

The commander relaxed, turned to the lieutenant with a wry face. "You'll have a command some day, Corvin. Then you'll know how it is."

"I think I know, sir," he said quietly.

"You only think you know. Come on, let's go in and get a drink. I need one. I've got to send in another report."

If it had been up to Allison, he would have called in the two remaining units—Unit East, Lieutenant Noromak's outfit, and Unit North, Lieutenant Rogers' group—because in the face of what had twice proved so undetectable and unpredictable, there was no sense in throwing good men after those who had already gone. He could not bear to think of how the men felt who manned the remaining outposts. Sitting ducks.

But it was not up to him. He could only run the computer and advise. And even his advice need not be heeded by the commanding officer whose will and determination to discover the planet's threat had become something more to pity than admire because he was willing to sacrifice the remaining two units rather than withdraw and consider some other method of attack.

Allison saw a man who no longer looked like a soldier, a man in soiled uniform, unshaven, an irritable man who had spurned eating and sleeping and had come to taking his nourishment from the bottle, a man who now barked his orders in a raucous voice, a man who could stand no sudden noises and, above all, could not tolerate any question of his decisions. And so he became a lonely man because no one wanted to be near him and he was left alone to stare with fascination at the two remaining TV panels and listen to the half-minute reports…and take a drink once in a while.

Allison was no different from the others. He did not want to face the commander. But he did not want to join the muttering soldiers in crew quarters either. So he kept to the computer room and, for something to do, spliced the tapes he had made from flight technician's information for their homeward flight. It took him more than three hours and when he was finished he put the reels in the flight compartment and, for what he thought surely must have been the hundredth time, took out the tapes he had already made on conditions and factors involved in the current emergency. He rearranged them and fed them into the machine again, then tapped out on the keys a request for a single factor that might emerge and prove helpful.

He watched the last of the tape whip into the machine, heard the gentle hum, the click of relays and watched the current indicators in the three different stages of the machine, knew that inside memory circuits were giv-

ing information, exchanging data, that other devices were examining results, probing for other related information, extracting useful bits, adding
this to the stream, to be rejected or passed, depending upon whether it
fitted the conditions.

At last the delivery section was energized, the soft *ding* of the response
bell and the lighted green bar preceded a moment when the answer facsimile tape whirred out and even as he looked at it he knew, by its length,
that it was as evasive and generalized as the information he had asked it to
examine.

He had left the door to the computer room open and through it suddenly came the sound of hoarse voices. He jumped to his feet and ran out
and down the hall to the control room.

The two television panels showed nothing new, but there was an excited radio voice that he recognized as Lieutenant Rogers'.

"He's violent, Commander, and there's nothing we can do," the lieutenant was saying. "He keeps running and trying to break through the force
field—oh, my God!"

"What is it?" the commander cried, getting to his feet.

"He's got his blaster out and he's saying something."

The commander rushed to the microphone and tore it from Cheevers'
hands. "Don't force him to shoot and don't you shoot, Lieutenant. Remember what happened to Unit West."

"But he's coming up to the wagon now—"

"Don't lose your head, Rogers! Try to knock him out—but don't use
your blaster!"

"He's entering the wagon now, Commander."

There was a moment's silence.

"He's getting into the g-car, Commander! We can't let him do that!"

"Knock him out!"

"I think we've got him—they're tangling—several men—he's knocked
one away—he's got the damned thing going!"

There was a sound of clinking metal, a rasp and scrape and the roar of
the little g-car.

"He got away in it! Maybe you can pick it up on the screen."

The TV screen moved slowly across the sky and swept by a g-car that
loomed large on it.

"Let him go," the commander said. "We'll send you another. Anybody
get hurt?"

"Yes, sir. One of the men got a bad cut. They're still working on him on the sand. Got knocked off the wagon and fell into the sand. I saw his head was pretty bloody a moment ago before the men gathered around him and...My God! No! *No!*"

"What?"

"*They're coming out of the ground—*"

"What?"

There were audible hisses and clanks and screams and...and suddenly it was very quiet.

"Lieutenant! Lieutenant Rogers!" The commander's face was white. "Answer me, Lieutenant, do you hear? Answer me! You—you can't do this to me!" He almost wept.

But the radio was dead.

But above, the television screen showed a panorama of endless desert illuminated by infrared and as it swept by one spot Allison caught sight of the horrified face of Tony Lazzari as the g-car soared by.

Allison pushed the shovel deep into the sand, lifted as much of it as he could get in it, deposited it on the conveyor. There were ten of them digging in the soft yellow sand in the early morning sun, sweat rolling off their backs and chins—not because the sand was heavy or that the work was hard but because the day was already unbearably hot—digging a hole that couldn't be dug. The sand kept slipping into the very place they were digging. They had only made a shallow depression two or three feet deep at the most and more than twenty feet wide.

They had found nothing.

Commander Warrick, who stood in the g-car atop Unit North's treadwagon with Lieutenant Noromak and Lieutenant Cheevers at his side, had first ordered Unit East to return to the ship, which Allison considered the smartest thing he had done in the past five days. Then a group of ten, mostly men who had not been in the field, were dispatched in Unit South's old wagon, with the officers in the g-car accompanying them, to Unit North.

There was no sign of a struggle, just the smooth sand around the wagon, the force field still intact and functioning.

Then the ten men had started digging.

"All right," the commander called from the wagon. "Everybody out. We'll blast."

They got out of the hole and on the other side of the wagon while the commander ordered Cheevers to aim at the depression.

The shot was deafening, but when the clouds of sand had settled, the depression was still there with a coating of fused sand covering it.

Later, when the group returned to the ship, three g-car parties were sent out to look for Lazzari. They found him unconscious in the sun in his g-car in the sand. They brought him back to the ship where he was revived.

"What did you see?" the commander asked when Lazzari regained consciousness.

Lazzari just stared.

Allison had seen men like this before. "Commander," he said, "this man's in a catatonic state. He'd better be watched because he can have periods of violence."

The commander glared. "You go punch your computer, Mr. Allison. I'll handle Lazzari."

And as the commander questioned the man, Lazzari suddenly started to cry, then jerked and, wild-eyed, leaped for the officer.

They put Lazzari in a small room.

Allison could have told the commander that was a mistake, too, but he didn't dare.

And, as the commander was planning his next moves against the planet's peril, Lazzari dashed his head against a bulkhead, fractured his skull, and died.

The funeral for Lazzari, the commander said, was to be a military one— as military as was possible on a planet revolving around a remote star in the far Hyades. Since rites were not possible for the twenty-nine others of the *Nesbitt* who had vanished, the commander said Lazzari's would make up for the rest.

Then for the first time in a week men had something else to think about besides the nature of things on the planet of the yellow sand that had done away with two explorers, the crews of three ships and twenty-nine Federation soldier-technicians who had come to do battle.

New tropicals were issued, each man showered and shaved, Lieutenant Cheevers read up on the burial service, Gordon Bacon practiced Taps on his bugle, Homer Petry gathered some desert flowers in a g-car, and Wendell Hallom washed and prepared Lazzari for the final rites which were to be held within a few hundred feet of the ship.

Though Allison complied with the directives, he felt uneasy about a funeral on the sand. He spent the hour before the afternoon services in the computer room, running tapes through the machine again, seeking the factor responsible for what had occurred.

He reasoned that persons on the sand were safe as long as the onslaught of the *things* out of the ground was not triggered by some action of men in the parties.

He did not know what the Unit South provocation had been—the radio signals had just stopped. He did know the assault on Unit West occurred after Prince's blast at the men on the treadwagon (though the blast in the sand at Unit North had brought nothing to the surface—if one were to believe Lieutenant Rogers' final words about things coming out of the ground). And the attack at Unit North was fomented by Lazzari's taking off in the g-car and throwing those battling him to the sand.

Allison went so far as to cut new tapes for each incident, adding every possible detail he could think of. Then he inserted these into the machine and tapped out a question of the advisability of men further exposing themselves by holding a burial service for Lazzari in the sand.

In a few minutes the response whirred out.

He caught his breath because the message was so short. Printed on the facsimile tape were these words:

Not advised.

Heartened by the brevity of the message and the absence of all the ifs, ands and buts of previous responses, he tapped out another question: Was there danger to life?

Agonizing minutes. Then:

Yes.

Whose life?

All.

Do you know the factor responsible for the deaths?

Yes.

He cursed himself for not realizing the machine knew the factor and wished he had asked for it instead. With his heart tripping like a jackhammer, Allison tapped out: What is the triggering factor?

When the answer came he found it ridiculously simple and wondered why no one had thought of it before. He stood staring at the tape for a long time knowing there could now be no funeral for Tony Lazzari.

He left the computer room, found the commander talking to Lieutenant Cheevers in the control room. Commander Warrick seemed something of his old self, attired in a natty tropical, clean shaven and with a military bearing and a freshness about him that had been missing for days.

"Commander," Allison said. "I don't mean to interrupt, but—we can't have the funeral."

The commander turned to him with a look full of suspicion. Then he said, "Allison, this is the one and only trip you will ever make with me. When we get back it will be either you or me who gets off this ship for the last time. If you want to run a ship you have to go to another school besides the one for Computer Corps men."

"I've known how you feel, Commander," Allison said, "but this is important."

"The General Staff ought to know that you can't mix army and civilian. I shall make it a point to register my feeling on the matter when we return."

"You can tell them what you wish, Commander, but it so happens that I've found out the factor responsible for all the attacks."

"And it so happens," the commander said icily, "that the lieutenant and I are reviewing the burial rites. A strict military burial has certain formalities which cannot be overlooked, though I don't expect you to understand that. There is too little time to go into any of your fancy theories now."

"This is no theory, Commander. This is fact."

"Did your computer have anything to do with it?"

"It had everything to do with it. I'd been feeding the tapes for days—"

"While we're on the subject, Allison, we're not using computer tapes for our home journey. We're going the whole way manually. I'm awaiting orders now to move off this Godforsaken world, in case you want to know. I'm recommending it as out-of-bounds for all ships of the Federation. And I'm also recommending that computer units be removed from the *Nesbitt* and from all other ships."

"You'll never leave this planet if you have the funeral," Allison said heatedly. "It will be death for all of us."

"Is that so?" The commander smiled thinly. "Courtesy of your computer, no doubt. Or is it that you're afraid to go out on the sand again?"

"I'm not afraid of the sand, Commander. I'll go out any time. But it's the others I'm thinking of. I won't go out to see Lazzari buried because of the blood on his head and neither should anyone else. You see, the missing factor—the thing that caused all the attacks—is blood."

"Blood?" The commander laughed, looked at Cheevers, who was not laughing, then back to Allison. "Sure you feel all right?"

"The blood on Lazzari, Commander. It will trigger another attack."

"What about the blood that's in us, Allison? That should have prevented us from stepping out on the sand without being attacked in the first place. Your reasoning—or rather your computer's reasoning—is ridiculous."

"It's fresh blood. Blood spilled on the sand."

"It seems to me you've got blood on the brain. Lazzari was a friend of yours, wasn't he?"

"That has nothing to do with it."

The commander looked at him hard and long, then turned to the lieutenant. "Cheevers, Allison doesn't feel very well. I think he'd better be locked up in the computer room until after the funeral."

Allison was stunned. "Commander—!"

"Will you please take him away at once, Lieutenant? I've heard all I want from him."

Sick at heart, Allison watched the commander walk out of the control room.

"You coming along, Allison?" Cheevers asked.

Allison looked at the lieutenant. "Do you know what will happen if you go out there?" But there was no sympathy or understanding in the eyes of the officer. He turned and walked down the hall to the computer room and went in.

"It doesn't make any difference what I think," Cheevers said, his hand on the knob of the door, his face not unkind. "You're not in the service. I am. I have to do what the commander says. Someday I may have a command of my own. Then I'll have a right to my own opinion."

"You'll never have a command of your own, after today."

"Think so?" It seemed to Allison that the lieutenant sighed a little. "Goodbye, Allison."

It was an odd way to put it. Allison saw the door close and click shut. Then he heard the lieutenant walk away. It was quiet.

Anguish in every fiber, Allison clicked on the small screen above the computer, turned a knurled knob until he saw the area of the intended burial. He hated to look at what he was going to see. The eyes of the wide, shallow grave stared at him from the view plate.

In a few minutes he saw Bacon carrying a Federation flag move slowly into view, followed by six men with blasters at raise, then Hallom and his bugle, Lieutenant Cheevers and his book, the stretcher bearing Lazzari with three pallbearers on either side, and the rest of the men in double ranks, the officers leading them.

Go ahead, Commander. Have your military field day because it's one thing you know how to do well. It's men like you who need a computer.

The procession approached the depression, Bacon moving to one side, the firing party at the far side of the shallow, Lieutenant Cheevers at the near end, making room for the pallbearers who moved into the depression and deposited their load there. The others moved to either side of the slope in single file.

Make it slick, Commander. By the numbers, straight and strong, because it's the last thing you'll ever do.

The men suddenly stiffened to attention, uncovering and holding their dress hats over their left breasts.

Bacon removed the Federation flag from its staff, draped it neatly over Lazzari. Cheevers then moved to the front and conducted the services, which lasted for several minutes.

This is the end, Commander....

Allison could see Commander Warrick facing the firing party, saw the blast volleys. But he was more interested in Lazzari. Two soldiers were shoveling the loose sand over him. Hallom raised his bugle to his lips.

Then *they* came.

Large, heavy, white porpoise-like creatures they were, swimming up out of the sand as if it were water, and snatching men in their powerful jaws, rending and tearing—clothes and all—as they rose in a fury of attacks that whipped up sand to nearly hide the scene. There were twenty or more and then more than a hundred rising and sinking and snapping and slashing, sun glistening on their shiny sides, flippers working furiously to stay atop the sand.

This, then, was the sea and these were the fish in it, fish normally uninterested in ordinary sweating men and machines and treadwagons, but hungry for men's blood or anything smeared with it—so hungry that a drop of it on the sand must have been a signal conducted to the depths to attract them all.

And when the men were gone there were still fish-like creatures burrowing into the sand, moving through it swiftly half in and half out like sharks, seeking every last vestige of—blood.

Then, as suddenly as they had come, the fish were gone.

Then there was nothing but smooth sand where before it had been covered by twenty men with bowed heads…except one spot which maximum magnification showed to be a bugle half-buried in the sand.

Allison did not know how long he sat there looking at the screen, but it must have been an hour because when he finally moved he could only do so with effort.

He alone had survived out of fifty men and he—the computer man. He was struck with the wonder of it.

He rose to leave the room. He needed a drink.

Only then did he remember that Cheevers had locked him in.

He tried the door.

It opened!

Cheevers *had* believed him, then. Somehow, this made the whole thing more tragic. There might have been others who would have believed, too, if the commander had not stood in the way.

The first thing Allison did was close the great port. Then he hunted until he found the bottle he was looking for. He took it to the computer room with him, opened the flight compartment, withdrew the tapes, set them in their proper slots and started them on their way.

Only when he heard the ship tremble alive did he take a drink.

A long drink.

There would have to be other bottles after this one.

There *had* to be.

It was going to be a long, lonely ride home.

And there was much to forget.

■

Brknk's Bounty

I never thought I'd like circus life, but a year of it has changed me. It's in my blood now and I suppose I'll never give it up—even if they'd let me.

This job is better than anything I could get in the newspaper racket. I work all summer, it's true, but I get the winter off, though some of the offers for winter work are mighty tempting. Maybe if I hadn't been kicked off the paper, I'd be city editor now, knocking my brains out. Who knows? But maybe I'd just be a rewrite man, or in the slot, writing heads, or copy reading. But the thought of newspaper work after all this appalls me.

Trlk, the Sybillian, should be thanked for the whole thing, I suppose, though it would be a grudging thank you I'd give him, considering all the trouble he caused. Still…

I first saw him on a July morning at the beginning of the vacation schedule, when four of us on the local side were trying to do five people's work.

My first inkling anything was wrong came when I returned from the courthouse beat and stuck a sheet of paper in the typewriter to write the probate court notes.

I struck the keys. They wouldn't go all the way down. I opened the cover plate, looked in to see what was wrong. I saw nothing, so I tried again. Oscar Phipps, the city editor, was giving me the eye. I figured maybe he was pulling a trick on me. But then I knew *he* hadn't. He wasn't the type.

The back space, tabular, margin release, shift and shift lock worked perfectly. But the keys only went down a short way before they stopped. All except one key. The cap *D*.

I hit the *D*. It worked fine the first time, but not the second. I tried all the keys again. This time only the *i* worked. Now I had *Di*. I went ahead testing. Pretty soon I had

Dimly

Then came a space. A few letters more and it was

Dimly drouse the dreary droves

Phipps had one eyebrow raised. I lifted the cover plate again. Quickly. There I saw a fuzzy thing. It whisked out of sight. I snapped the plate down and held it down. The party I had been on the night before hadn't been that good and I had had at least three hours' sleep.

I tried typing again. I got nothing until I started a new line. Then out came

Primly prides the privy prose

I banged up the plate, saw a blur of something slinking down between the type bar levers again. Whatever it was, it managed to squeeze itself out of sight in a most amusing way.

"Hey!" I said. "I know you're down there. What's the big idea?"

Fuzzy squeezed his head up from the levers. The head looked like that of a mouse, but it had teeth like a chipmunk and bright little black beads for eyes. They looked right at me.

"You go right ahead," he said in a shrill voice. "This is going to be a great poem. Did you get all that alliteration there in those two lines?"

"Listen, will you get out of there? I've got work to do!"

"Yes, I think I've hit it at last. It was that four-stress iambic that did it. It *was* iambic, wasn't it?"

"Go away," I said miserably.

Fuzzy pulled the rest of himself out of the bars and stood on hind feet. He crossed his forepaws in front of him, vibrated his long, furry tail, and said definitely, "No."

"Look," I pleaded, "I'm not Don Marquis and you're not Archie and I have work to do. Now will you please get out of this typewriter?"

His tiny ears swiveled upward. "Who's Don Marquis? And Archie?"

"Go to hell," I said. I slammed the cover down and looked up into the cold eyes of Oscar Phipps, who was standing next to my desk.

"Who, may I ask," he said ominously, "do you think you're talking to?"

"Take a look." I lifted the plate once again. Fuzzy was there on his back, his legs crossed, his tail twitching.

"I don't see anything," Phipps said.

"You mean you can't see Fuzzy here?" I pointed to him, the end of my finger an inch from his head. "Ouch!" I drew my hand away. "The little devil bit me."

"You're fired, Mr. Weaver," Phipps said in a tired voice. "Fired as of right now. I'll arrange for two weeks' severance pay. And my advice to you is to stay off the bottle or see a psychiatrist—or both. Not that it'll do you any good. You never amounted to anything and you never will."

I would have taken a swipe at Fuzzy, but he had slunk out of sight.

During the two erratic years I had been on the newspaper, I had passed the city park every morning on my way to work, feeling an envy for those who had nothing better to do than sit on the benches and contemplate the nature of the universe. Now I took myself there and sat as I had seen others do, hoping to feel a kinship with these unfortunates.

But all I did is feel alone, frustrated, and angry at Phipps. Maybe I had been too convivial, maybe I had enjoyed night life too much, maybe I hadn't given the paper my all. But I wasn't ready for the booby hatch even if I had seen a fuzzy little thing that could talk.

I drew a copy of *Editor and Publisher* from my pocket and was scanning the "Help Wanted: Editorial" columns when out of the corner of my eye I saw a blob of black moving along the walk.

Turning handsprings, balancing himself precariously on the end of his vibrating tail, running and waving his forepaws to get my attention was Fuzzy.

I groaned. "Please go away!" I covered my eyes so I wouldn't have to look at him.

"Why?" he piped.

"Because you're a hallucination."

"I'm not a hallucination," he said indignantly. "I'm real flesh and blood. See?" He vibrated his tail so fast, I could hardly see it. Then it stopped and stood straight out. "Lovely, isn't it?"

"Look," I said, leaning far off the bench to speak to him, "I can prove you're a hallucination."

"You *can?*" he quavered. "How?"

"Because Phipps couldn't see you."

"That square? Hah! He would not have believed it if he had seen me."

"You mean you—"

He disappeared and reappeared like a flashing neon sign. "There!" he said triumphantly.

"Why didn't you let him see you then?" I asked, a little angry but pleased nonetheless with his opinion of Phipps. "Because you didn't, you cost me my job."

He waved a forepaw deprecatingly. "You didn't want to stay on that hick sheet anyway."

"It was a job."

"Now you've got a better one."

"Who's kidding whom?"

"Together we'll write real literature."

"I don't know anything about literature. My job is writing the news."

"You'll be famous. With my help, of course."

"Not with that 'dimly drouse' stuff."

"Oh, that!"

"Where did you come from, Fuzzy?"

"Do I ask you where you come from?"

"Well, no—"

"And my name's not Fuzzy. It's Trlk, pronounced Turlick and spelled T-r-l-k."

"My name's Larry Weaver, pronounced Lar-ree—"

"I know. Look, you got a typewriter?"

"A portable. At the apartment."

"That will do."

"Aren't you taking things for granted? I haven't said yet whether I liked the idea."

"Do you have any choice?"

I looked at him, a couple of ounces of harmless-looking fur that had already cost me my immediate future in the newspaper business.

"I guess not," I said, hoping I could find a way to get rid of him if things didn't work out right.

And so began a strange collaboration, with Trlk perched on my shoulder dictating stories into my ear while I typed them. He had definite ideas about writing and I let him have his way. After all, I didn't know anything about literature.

Sometimes, when he'd get stuck, he'd get down and pace the living room rug. Other times he'd massage his tail, which was as long as he, smoothing it with his tongue and meticulously arranging every hair on it.

"It's lovely, don't you think?" he often asked.

And I'd say, "If you spent as much time working on this story as you do admiring your tail, we'd get something done."

"Sorry," he'd say, hopping on my shoulder again. "Where were we?" I'd read the last page and we'd be off again.

One day, Trlk crawled on a shelf to watch me shave, whiffed the shaving lotion bottle, became excited and demanded I put a drop of it in front of him. He lapped it up, sank blissfully back on his tail and sighed.

"Wonnerful," he squeaked. "Shimply wonnerful." He hiccuped.

I let him sleep it off, but was always careful with the lotion after that.

Days stretched into weeks, my money was running low and the apartment superintendent was pressing me for payment of the month's rent. I kept telling him I'd pay as soon as the first checks came in.

But only rejection slips came. First one, then two, then half a dozen.

"They don't even read them!" Trlk wailed.

"Of course they read them," I said. I showed him the sheets. They were wrinkled from handling.

"The post office did that," he countered.

I showed him coffee spots on one page, cigarette burns on another.

"Well, maybe—" he said, but I don't think anything would have convinced him.

When the last story came back, Trlk was so depressed I felt sorrier for him than I did for myself.

It was time. We had been working hard. I got out a bottle.

I poured a little lotion for Trlk.

The next afternoon we tackled the problem in earnest. We went to the library, got a book on writing and took it home. After reading it from cover to cover, I said, "Trik, I think I've found the trouble with your stories."

"What is it?"

"You don't write about things you know, things that happened to you, that you have observed." I showed him where it advised this in the book.

His eyes brightened. We went right to work.

This time the stories glowed, but so did my cheeks. The narratives all involved a man who lived in a hotel room. They recounted the seemingly endless love affairs with his female visitors.

"Why, Trlk!" I exclaimed. "How come you know about things like this?"

He confessed he had lived with such a man, a free-lance writer who never made the grade with his writing, but who had plenty of girlfriends who paid the freight.

"He had a way with women," Trlk explained.

"He certainly had," I said, reading again the last page he had dictated.

"He finally married an older woman with money. Then he gave up trying to write."

"I don't blame him," I said wistfully.

"I had to find another writer. This time I decided to try a newspaper. That's where I ran into you."

"Don't remind me."

Things got better after that. We began to get a few checks from magazines. They were small checks, but they paid a few bills.

The big blow fell, however, when Mr. Aldenrood, the superintendent, came roaring upstairs one day clutching a sheaf of papers.

"This stuff!" he screamed, waving the sheets before me. "The kids found it in the waste paper. They're selling them a dime a sheet around the neighborhood."

"They're worth more than that," I said, regretting that Trlk and I hadn't burned our rough drafts.

"You're going to move," Mr. Aldenrood said, "at the earliest possible instant." His face was apoplectic. "I'm giving you notice right now—thirty days!" He turned and went out, muttering, "The idea of anybody committing to paper—" and slammed the door.

Two days later, I was seated at the typewriter smoking a cigarette and waiting for Trlk as he paced back and forth on the rug, tiny paws clasped behind his back, talking to himself and working out a story angle at the same time, when suddenly there appeared on the carpet next to him a whole host of creatures just like him.

I nearly gulped down my cigarette.

Trlk let out a high-pitched screech of joy and ran over to them. They wound their long tails around each other, clasped and unclasped them, twined them together. It seemed a sort of greeting. Meanwhile, they kept up a jabber that sounded like a 33 1/3 rpm record being played 78 rpm.

Finally, the biggest one detached himself from the group and gave Trlk a tongue-lashing that would have done justice to a Phipps. Trlk hung his head. Every time he tried to say something, the big one would start in again.

At length the leader turned to me. "My name is Brknk, pronounced burk-neck and spelled b-r-k-n-k."

"And I'm Larry Weaver," I said, hoping they weren't relatives who were going to stay. "That's pronounced Lar-ree—"

"I know. We're from Sybilla III. Tourists. We include Earth in our itinerary. It has some of the quaintest customs of all the inhabited planets we visit. We're terribly sorry for all the inconveniences our wayward Trlk here has caused you."

"It was nothing," I said with a lightness I didn't feel.

"Trlk had threatened to run off many times. He has a craze for self-expression and your literature fascinates him. He has an insatiable thirst—"

"I know."

He turned to Trlk. "It's against the rules of the Galactic Tours to make yourself visible to any of the inhabitants along the way. You know that. And it's a prime offense to interfere with their lives. Do you realize how many rules you have broken, how long we have been looking for you?"

"He did the best he could," I said hopefully. "As a matter of fact, we were having considerable success with his—a—literary project."

"I understand you lost your job because of him. Is that right?"

"Yes, but I encouraged him." I hoped there was some way I could ease the sentence.

"Trlk has committed grievous wrongs, Mr. Weaver. We must make it up to you."

"Oh?" Here was an angle I hadn't expected.

"What can we do for you?"

I considered a moment. "You mean a wish or something?"

Brknk laughed. "Nothing like that. We're not magicians."

"Well, I could stand a little cash."

"I'm sorry," he said, and he did look pained. "We can't interfere in business. We don't have any of your currency and we are forbidden to duplicate or steal it."

He frowned and studied me. Suddenly his face brightened. He bawled orders and several smaller Sybillians rushed forward and started scampering all over me. One of them nipped a piece of flesh out of my arm.

"Ouch!" I yelped, rubbing the spot. "What are you doing?"

"You humans are a proud race," Brknk explained. "I'll give you reason to be prouder than the rest. We'll change your metabolism, your endocrine balance, toughen your muscle fibers a thousandfold. We'll make you the strongest man on Earth!"

"Look," I said, "I don't want to be the strongest man on Earth."

"Well, how about the world's champion boxer? We can speed up your reflexes at least ten times."

I shook my head. "I don't want that either. Sounds too much like work. Besides, I never liked getting into fights."

Brknk scowled, called a huddle. They buzzed at each other, their tails vibrating like mad. One of them finally yipped and everybody spun around.

Brknk beamed. "We've got it!"

"What is it?"

A little Sybillian I hadn't noticed jabbed something in my arm. I winced and he nearly fell off. He retreated with injured pride.

"Come along, Trlk," Brknk said.

"What's supposed to happen?" I asked.

"It will be a glorious surprise," Brknk assured me. "You'll never regret it. The only thing I ask is that you never tell anyone about us."

I promised.

Trlk looked up at me. I noticed the beginning of tears in his eyes. I reached down and patted him gently on the head.

"So long, little fellow," I said. "It's been fun."

"Goodbye," he said sorrowfully.

They vanished.

Nothing happened for several days, so I bought a copy of *Editor and Publisher* and was writing for my first job when I felt a tender spot on my tail bone. When I examined it I saw a protuberance there.

There was no denying it. The Sybillians had given me what they treasured most.

I was growing a tail—a long, hairy tail.

As I say, I have come to like circus life.

At first I tried to get doctors to cut it off, but they were too curious for that. Then I thought of jumping in the river or putting a bullet through my head.

But after I saw what the scientists were making of it, when I viewed my picture in all the papers, and when I saw the awe with which I was regarded by everyone, I changed my mind.

Now I make a cool twenty-five thousand a year without lifting a finger.

Just my tail.

I've become rather fond of it. I've even learned how to vibrate it.

But I've never told anyone about the Sybillians. They wouldn't believe it.

Not old Phipps, anyway.

Someday I'll go and vibrate my tail right in his face. I'd never amount to anything, eh? Let's see *him* grow a tail!

■

Counterweight

Sure, I'm a Nilly, and I've died seven times, always in the blackness of the outer reaches, and I'm not alone, although there aren't very many of us, never were.

It made sense. Interstellar was new and they wanted him on the ship because he was a trained observer. They wanted facts, not gibberish. But to ask a man to give up two years of his life—well, that was asking a lot. Two years in a sardine can. Still, it had an appeal Keith Ellason knew he couldn't deny, a newsman's joy of the clean beat, a planetary system far afield, a close-up view of the universe, history in the making.

Interstellar Chief Rexroad knocked the dottle from his pipe in a tray, saying, "Transworld Press is willing to let you have a leave of absence, if you're interested."

He knew Secretary Kripps from years of contacting, and now Kripps said, "Personally, I don't want to see anybody else on the job. You've got a fine record in this sort of thing."

Keith Ellason smiled thinly. "You should have called me for the first trip."

Kripps nodded. "I wish we had had you on the *Weblor I*."

"Crewmen," Rexroad said, "make poor reporters."

The *Weblor I* had made the first trip to Antheon five years before with a thousand families, reached the planet with less than five hundred surviving colonists. Upon the return to Earth a year later, the crew's report of suffering and chaos during the year's outgoing transit was twisted, distorted and fragmentary. Ellason remembered it well. The decision of Interstellar was that the colonists started a revolution far out in space, that it was fanned by the ignorance of Captain Sessions in dealing with such matters.

"Space affects men in a peculiar way," Kripps said. "We have conquered the problem of small groups in space—witness the discovery of Antheon, for example—but when there are large groups, control is more difficult."

"Sessions," Rexroad said, "was a bully. The trouble started at about the halfway point. It ended with passengers engaging in open warfare with each other and the crew. Sessions was lucky to escape with his life."

"As I recall," Ellason said, "there was something about stunners."

"Yes." Kripps rubbed his chin. "No weapons were allowed on the ship, but you must remember the colonists were selected for their individuality, intelligence and resourcefulness. They utilized these very attributes to set up weapons shops to arm themselves."

"The second trip is history," Rexroad said. "And a puzzle."

Ellason nodded. "The ship disappeared."

"Yes. We gave control to the colonists."

"Assuming no accident in space," Kripps said, "it was a wrong decision. They probably took over the ship."

"And now," Ellason said, "you're going to do it again."

Rexroad said gravely, "We've got the finest captain in Interplanetary. Harvey Branson. No doubt you've heard of him. He's spent his life in our own system, and he's hand-picking his own crew. We have also raised prerequisites for applicants. We don't think anything is going to happen, but if it does we want to get an impersonal, unprejudiced view. That's where you come in. You do the observing, the reporting. We'll evaluate it on your return."

"If I return."

"I suppose that's problematical," Kripps said, "but I think you will. Captain Branson and his fifty crewmen want to return as badly as you do." He grinned. "You can write that novel you're always talking about on your return trip on the *Weblor II*."

Being a Nilly is important, probably as important as running the ship, and I think it is this thought that keeps us satisfied, willing to be what we are.

The *Weblor II* had been built in space, as had its predecessor, the *Weblor I*, at a tremendous cost. Basically, it was an instrument which would open distant vistas to colonization, reducing the shoulder-to-shoulder pressure of a crowded system. A gigantic, hollow spike, the ship would never land anywhere but would circle Antheon as it circled Earth, shuttling its cargo and passengers to the promised land, the new frontier. A spaceborne metropolis, it would be the home for three thousand persons outward bound, only the crew on the return trip. It was equipped with every conceivable facility and comfort—dining rooms, assembly hall, individual and family compartments, recreation areas, swimming pool, library, theater. Nothing had been overlooked.

The captain's briefing room was crowded, the air was heavy with the breathing of so many men, and the ventilators could not quite clear the air of tobacco smoke that drifted aimlessly here and there before it was caught and whisked away.

In the tradition of newspaperman and observer, Keith Ellason tried to be as inconspicuous as possible, pressing against a bulkhead, but Captain Branson's eyes sought his several times as Branson listened to final reports from his engineers, record keepers, fuel men, computer men, and all the rest. He grunted his approval or disapproval, made a suggestion here, a restriction there. There was no doubt Branson was in charge, yet there was a human quality about him that Ellason liked. The captain's was a lean face, well tanned, and his eyes were chunks of blue.

"Gentlemen," Branson said at last, as Ellason knew he would, "I want to introduce Keith Ellason, whose presence Interstellar has impressed upon us. On loan from Transworld, he will have an observer status." He introduced him to the others. All of them seemed friendly; Ellason thought it was a good staff.

Branson detained him after the others had gone. "One thing, Mr. Ellason," he said. "To make it easier for you, I suggest you think of this journey strictly from the observer viewpoint. There will be no story for Transworld at the end."

Ellason was startled. While he had considered the possibility, he had not dwelt on it. Now it loomed large in his mind. "I don't understand, Captain Branson. It seems to me—"

"Let me put it differently. Let me say that you will not understand why I say that until the journey ends." He smiled. "Perhaps I shouldn't have mentioned it."

Ellason left the captain's quarters with an odd taste in his mouth. Now why had Branson said that? Why hadn't Rexroad or Kripps said something, if it was important?

He made himself comfortable in his seven-foot-by-seven-foot cubicle, which is to say he dropped on his bed, found it more comfortable than he thought it would be, put his arms behind his head, stared at the ceiling. Metal walls, no windows, one floor vent, one ceiling vent, and a solitary ceiling molding tubelight. This would be his home for a year, just as there were homes like it for three thousand others, except that the family rooms would be larger. His quarters were near the front of the spike near the officers' quarters.

He felt rather than heard the dull rumble. It was a sound he knew would be with him for two years—one year going and one year returning. He looked at his watch, picked up his notebook and made an entry. The ship would right now be slipping ever so slowly away from Earth. He got up. He'd have to go forward to the observation dome to see that. Last view of Earth for two years.

The penetration of space by large groups is the coming out from under the traditions of thousands of years, and as these planet-originated rules fall away, the floundering group seeks a new control, for they are humanity adrift, rudderless, for whom the stars are no longer bearings but nonexistent things, and values are altered if they are not shown the way.

The theft of Carver Janssen's attache case occurred on the thirty-first day out. In Ellason's mind the incident, though insignificant from the standpoint of the ship as a whole, could very well be the cause of dissension later on. His notes covering it were therefore very thorough.

Janssen's case contained vegetable and flower seeds—thousands of them, according to the Captain's Bulletin, the ship's daily newsletter which went to all hands and passengers. In the Bulletin the captain appealed to the thief to return the case to Mr. Janssen. He said it was significant that all en route had passed stability tests and that it was to the ship's discredit that someone with criminal tendencies should have been permitted to step aboard.

Ellason had to smile at that. What did Captain Branson think of those colonists who killed each other on the *Weblor I*? They had passed stability tests, too. This then was what happened when you took three thousand strangers and stuck them in a can for a year.

When Ellason saw Branson about it, the captain said, "Of course I realize it takes only a little thing like this to set things off. I know people get tired of seeing each other, playing the same tapes, looking at the stars from the observation dome, walking down the same corridors, reading the same books, eating the same meals, though God knows we try to vary it as much as we can. Space brings out rough edges. But the point is, we know all this, and knowing it, we shouldn't let it happen. We've got to find that thief."

"What would he want seeds for? Have you thought of that?"

"Of course. They'd have real value on Antheon."

Ellason sought out Carver Janssen. He was a middle-aged man with a tired face and sad eyes. He said, "Now what am I going to Antheon for? I could only take along so much baggage and I threw out some comfort items to make room for the seeds. I'm a horticulturist, and Interstellar asked me to go along. But what use am I now? Where am I going to get seeds just like that? Do you know how long it took me to collect them? They're not ordinary seeds, Mr. Ellason."

There was an appeal from Janssen in the next day's newsletter describing the seeds, telling of their value, and requesting their return in the interests of the Antheon colony and of humanity.

On the thirty-fourth day a witness turned up who said he saw a man emerging from Janssen's compartment with the black case. "I didn't think anything of it at the time," Jamieson Dievers said.

Branson asked him to describe the man.

"Oh, he was about six feet tall, stocky build, and he wore a red rubber mask that covered his head completely."

"Didn't you think that was important?" Branson asked in an outraged voice. "A man wearing a red mask?"

Dievers shrugged. "This is space, isn't it? They say funny things happen out here. I didn't know but maybe he was part of the ship or something."

Although Dievers' account appeared in the newsletter, it was largely discounted.

"If it is true," Branson told Ellason, "the theft must be the work of a psychotic. But I don't believe Jamieson Dievers. It may well be he's the psychotic." He snorted. "Red rubber mask! I think I'll have Dievers sent through psychiatry."

Attendant to taking notes on this incident, Ellason noted a strange thing. Janssen lived in that part of the ship known as the First Quadrant, and those who lived in that quadrant, more than seven hundred men, women and children, felt that the thief must surely live in Quadrant Two or Four. Elias Cromley, who had the compartment next to Janssen's, sounded the consensus when he said, "Surely a man wouldn't steal from his own quadrant, now would he, Mr. Ellason?"

And so, Ellason observed in his notebook, are wars created.

Seen in space, stars are unmoving, silent, sterile bright eyes ever watchful and accusing. To men unused to it, such a sight numbs, compresses, stultifies. He introduces a countermeasure, proof he exists, which is any overt act, sometimes violent.

On the forty-fifth day June Failright, pert young wife of one of the passenger meteorologists, ran screaming down one of the long corridors of the Third Quadrant. She cried out that she had been assaulted. She told the captain she had been attacked in her compartment while her husband was in the ship's library. She was taken to one of the ship's doctors who confirmed it.

She said the culprit was a husky man wearing a red rubber mask, and though her description of what he did did not appear in the story in the newsletter, it lost no time in penetrating every compartment of the ship.

Ellason was present when a delegation from the Third Quadrant called on Captain Branson demanding action.

Branson remained seated behind his desk, unperturbed, saying, "I have no crewmen to spare for police duty."

To a man the delegation commenced speaking vehemently, to be quieted by Branson's raised hand. "I sympathize," Branson said, "but it is up to each quadrant to deal with its problems, whatever they may be. My job is to get us to Antheon."

"I suppose," Branson said, when the group left in a surly mood, "that you wonder at my reluctance, Mr. Ellason. But suppose I assign the crew to patrol duties, the culprit isn't caught and further incidents occur. What then? My crew is inefficient. It soon becomes their fault. And soon the colonists will begin thinking these things might be the crew's doing in the first place."

"Yes," Ellason said, "but suppose the intruder is a crewman?"

"I know my men," Branson said flatly.

"You could have a shakedown for the mask and the seed case."

"Do you think it is a member of the crew?" Branson's eyes were bright. "No, I trust my men. I won't violate that trust."

Ellason left the captain feeling vaguely uneasy. If he were Branson, he'd initiate an investigation, if nothing else than to prove the crew guiltless. Why couldn't Branson see the wisdom of setting an example for the colonists?

As a Nilly, I know that space breeds hate. There is a seed of malevolence in every man. It sometimes blossoms out among the stars. On the Weblor II *it was ready for ripening.*

Raymond Palugger was killed in the ship's hospital on the sixty-first day. Palugger, a Fourth Quadrant passenger, had complained of feeling ill, had been hospitalized with a diagnosis of ileus. He had put his money belt in the drawer of the small stand beside his bed. A man in a red mask was seen hurrying from the hospital area, and a staff investigation revealed that Palugger had died trying to prevent the theft of his belt.

Captain Branson did not wait for the newsletter. He activated the ship's speaker system, reported that Palugger had a fortune in credits in the belt, had died of a severe beating. He said that since the incident occurred in the staff section of the ship his crew would be forced to submit to a thorough inspection in an effort to find the mask, the seed case, the money and the man.

"I will not countenance such an act by a crewman," Branson said. "If and when he is found, he will be severely dealt with. But he might not be a member of the crew. I am ordering an assembly of all passengers at nine tomorrow morning in the auditorium. I will speak to you all then."

Faces were angry, tongues were sharp at the meeting, and eyes were suspicious and tempers short. Above it all was the overpowering presence of Captain Branson speaking to them.

"It is not my desire to interfere in passenger affairs," he said. "Insofar as the ship is concerned, it is my duty to make certain no crewman is guilty. This I am doing. But my crew is not and cannot be a police force for you. It is up to you people to police and protect yourselves."

"How can we protect ourselves without stunners?" one colonist called out.

"Has Red Mask a gun?" Branson retorted. "It seems to me you have a better weapon than any gun or number of guns."

"What's that?" another voice asked dryly.

"Yourselves, your numbers. It seems to me this ship is only so wide, so long, so deep. If every inch is searched, you'll find your man."

The colonists quieted. Benjamin Simpson, one of the older men, was elected president of the newly formed Quadrant Council. One man from each of the quadrants was named to serve under him. Each of these men in turn selected five others from his own group.

Those assembled waited in the hall while each team of six inspected the compartments of the others. These compartments were then locked, everyone returned to his compartment, and the larger search was conducted. It took twenty hours.

No mask was found. No mask, no case, no money, no man.

The captain reported that his search had been equally fruitless. At another assembly the following day it was decided to make the inspection teams permanent to await further moves on the part of Red Mask. The Quadrant Council held periodic meetings to set up a method of trial for him when he was caught. It was all recorded in the newsletter and by Keith Ellason.

We Nillys know about hate and about violence. We know too that where there is hate there is violence and where there is violence there is death.

During sleep time on the seventy-ninth day Barbara Stoneman, awakened by a strange sound, sat up in the bed of her compartment to find a man in a red mask in her room. She screamed and her cries brought neighbors into the corridor. The flight of the man was witnessed by many, and several men tried to stop him. But the intruder was quick, light on his feet, and fast. He escaped.

The Quadrant Council confronted the captain, demanding weapons.

"Are you out of your minds?" Branson said.

Tom Tilbury, Fourth Quadrant leader, said, "We want to set up a police force, Captain. We want stunners."

"There's no law against it," Branson said, "but it's a rule of mine that no weapons are to be issued en route."

"If we had had a gun, we'd have got Red Mask," Tilbury said.

"I might have a murder on my conscience if you had."

Tilbury said, "We've thought of that. Suppose you supply us with half-power stunners? That way we can stun but not kill."

They got their guns. Now there were twenty-four policemen on duty in the corridors—eight on at a time. Ellason observed that for the first time the passengers seemed relaxed.

Let Red Mask move against armed men, they said.

Yeah, let him see what happens now.

Red Mask did.

On the one hundred and first day he was seen in a corridor in Quadrant Four, and Emil Pierce, policeman on duty, managed to squeeze off several shots at his retreating figure. He was seen again on the one hundred and twentieth day, on the one hundred and thirty-fifth day, and the one hundred and fifty-seventh. He was seen, shot at, but not felled. He was also unable to commit any crime.

We've got him on the run, the colonists said.

He's afraid to do anything now that we've got police protection, they said smugly.

The Quadrant Council congratulated itself. The passengers were proud of themselves. A special congratulatory message from Captain Branson appeared one day in the Bulletin newsletter.

The colonists settled down to living out their days until the landing on Antheon.

But on the one hundred and seventieth day calamity struck. From somewhere Red Mask appropriated a stunner, made his way down one whole corridor section in Quadrant Two, put occupants to sleep as he went, taking many articles of value and leaving disorder behind.

Ellason interviewed as many victims as he could, noted it all in his book. Some of the things taken were keepsakes, photographs and items of personal value. He seemed to concentrate on things that were irreplaceable, and it seemed to be the work of a madman. If Red Mask wanted to make everyone furious, he certainly succeeded.

"What does he want that stuff for?" Casey Stromberg, a passenger doctor, asked. "I can see him taking my narcotics, my doctor's kit, but my dead wife's picture—that I don't understand."

It was the same with the others. "The man's insane, Mr. Ellason. Positively insane." Many people said it.

The council issued orders that all passengers from now on would be required to lock their compartments at all times. More guns were obtained from the captain. More policemen were appointed.

Ellason was busy noting it all in his book. It became filled with jottings about innocent people being accidentally stunned when trigger-happy policemen thought their movements suspicious, about one man's suspicion of another and the ensuing search of compartments, people who saw Red Mask here, saw him there. Hardly a day went by without some new development.

"Oh, yes, Mr. Ellason, we're going to get him," Tilbury, now chief of police, said, cracking his knuckles, his eyes glowing at the thought. "We're bound to get him, don't you see? We've got things worked out. To the finest detail. He won't be able to get through our fingers now. Just let him make so much as a move. He'll see."

"And what will you do when you get him?"

"Kill him," Tilbury said, licking his lips, his eyes glowing more fiercely than ever.

"Without a trial?"

"Oh, there'll be a trial, Mr. Ellason, but you don't think any jury'd let him live after all the things he's done, do you?"

Red Mask was stunned in Quadrant Four in a corridor by a police-man named Terryl Placer on the two hundred and first day. The criminal was carried to the assembly room surrounded by guards, for he surely would have been mauled, if not killed, by angry colonists who crowded around. In the assembly hall his mask was whipped off. The crowd gasped. Nobody knew him.

Ellason's first thought was that he must be a stowaway, but then he remembered the face, and Captain Branson, who came to have a look at him, said he was, sadly, a member of the crew, his name was Harrel Critten and he was a record keeper third class.

"Well, Critten," Branson roared at him, "what have you got to say for yourself?"

"Go to hell," Critten said quietly. As if it were an afterthought, he spat at him.

Branson looked as if he were going to kill him himself right then and there.

It was a long trial—from the two hundred and twentieth to the two hundred and forty-first day—and there didn't seem to be much doubt about the outcome, since Critten didn't help his own cause during any of it.

Lemuel Tarper, who was appointed prosecutor, asked him, "What did you do with the loot, Critten?"

Critten looked him square in the eye and said, "I threw it away, out one of the escape chutes. Does that answer your question?"

"Threw it away?" Tarper and the crowd were incredulous.

"Sure," Critten said. "You colonists got the easy life as passengers, just sitting around getting fat. I had to work. I had to keep records for you lazy bastards."

The sentence was, of course, death.

They executed Harrel Critten on the morning of the two hundred and seventieth day with blasts from six stunners supplied with full power. It was witnessed by a great crowd in the assembly hall. A detail from the ship's crew disposed of his body in one of the chutes.

It was all duly recorded in Keith Ellason's notebooks.

Dying is easy for a Nilly. Especially if it's arranged for beforehand, which it always is.

The *Weblor II* was only one day out of orbit when Captain Branson sent for Ellason and introduced him to the executed man.

"Hello," Critten said, grinning.

"I figured as much," Ellason said. "I've been doing a lot of thinking."

"You're perhaps a little too good as an observer," Branson said. "Or maybe it was because you really weren't one of the colonists. But no matter, Critten did a good job. He was trained by an old friend of mine for this job, Gelthorpe Nill. Nill used to be in counter-espionage when there were wars."

"You were excellent," Ellason said.

"Can't say I enjoyed the role, but I think it saved lives."

"Let me get this straight. Interstellar thought that it was idleness and boredom that caused the killings on the *Weblor I*, so they had you trained to be a scapegoat. Is that right?"

Critten nodded. "When great numbers are being transported, they are apt to enlarge on each little event because so little happens. It was my job to see that they directed none of their eventual venom against each other or the crew but toward me."

Branson smiled. "It made the time pass quickly and interestingly for the passengers."

"To say nothing of me," Critten said.

"And you, Mr. Ellason, were along to observe it all. Interstellar wanted an accurate picture of this. If it worked, they told me they'd use it on other trips to Antheon."

Ellason nodded. "No time for brooding, for differences of opinion on small matters. Just time to hate Mr. Critten. Unanimously."

"Probably," Critten said, "you are wondering about the execution."

"Well, yes."

"We removed the charges before the guns were used."

"And Carver Janssen's case?"

"He'll get it back when he's shuttled to Antheon. And all the other items will be returned. They're all tagged with their owners' names. Captain Branson will say they were found somewhere on the ship. You see, I was a liar. I was going to use it anyway."

"I see. How about that assault on June Failright?"

Critten grinned again. "She played right into our hands. I had to make plenty of noise to get her attention, and she ran out into the hall claiming I'd attacked her, which I did not. She was certainly amazed when the ship's physicians agreed with her. Of course Captain Branson told them to do that."

"And the murder?"

"I'm no murderer. Raymond Palugger died in the hospital all right, but he died from his illness on the operating table. We turned it into an advantage for me, made it look black."

Ellason nodded. "And by that time everybody was seeing a Red Mask everywhere and the colonists organized."

"Gave them something to do," Branson said.

"Every time things got dull, I livened them up. I got a stunner, robbed along the corridor. That really stirred them. Lucky nobody got hurt during any of it, including that Stoneman woman. I was trying to rob her when she woke up."

Branson cleared his throat. "Ah, Ellason, about that story. You understand you can't write it, don't you?"

Ellason said regretfully that he could see no point in it.

"People must never know," Branson went on. "The colonists will never know any different. There will be other ships outward bound."

Critten sighed. "And I'll have to be caught again."

Yes, we're anonymous, nameless, we Nillys, for that's what we call each other, and are a theme, with variations, in the endless stretches of deep space, objects of hatred and contempt, professional heels, dying once a trip when the time is ripe, antidote to boredom, and we'll ply our trade, our little tragedies, on a thousand ships bringing humanity to new worlds.

■

Death In Transit

Clifton stood at the bottom of the shaft, his face white, his eyes wide, his stance against the bulkhead that of a man who needed only a slight push to slump to the floor.

"Karen," he murmured. "Karen."

He had been standing there a long time.

He was staring at his dead wife, a heap of broken bones and blood on the floor. But he was not seeing her—at least not as she was now. He was seeing her the way his mind kept bringing her back to him: the white evenness of her teeth when she smiled, the fury of her bright blue eyes when she was angry, the way she had uncomplainingly slept on the wrinkled sheets of the bed he had made when she had been ill ten years before, and the way they had laughed about that when she reminded him of it years later. He moved to stand erect, wondering why he should have thought about that at a time like this, and then, as he looked at her again and saw what the fall had done to her, he clenched his hands in anger.

They had said it couldn't happen! But they had been wrong. Man's wisdom was not infinite after all. All the man-years of thought, all the endless whirring and clicking of the computers and calculators—all of it had not taken into account what might happen to Karen.

His hands fell open. He knew that actually, they had never been wrong. If he had found her right away, he could have put her back together. He could have utilized the synthesizer for anything really bad, like a shattered bone. The needles of the organic analyzer would have told him what else he had to do.

But Karen had been dead for hours when he found her. Too long. The damage was irreparable, permanent. She was beyond recall. He might conceivably have animated her muscles, her glands, got her blood to flowing again. But her brain would have remained a vacuous, inert thing. You had to get reconstruction going in a matter of minutes when the brain, the anatomy's most perishable component, was involved. And in some cases he had known, the memories were never fully restored.

Why couldn't it have been a tumor? A deficiency disease? A nervous breakdown? Insanity…There was nothing the medocenter couldn't handle. The machines were right there on the ship ready to be used—but Karen had to fall down the ventilator shaft, opening the door and walking into it as if it were her bedroom, and falling all the way down and breaking half the bones in her body.

And he had found her too late. Hours too late.

"Too late," he said, and he nodded his head in agreement. Then he was engulfed in sudden pity and remorse and a feeling of loss, as if she had snatched a vital part of him in her going. But hadn't she? Hadn't she taken her laughter with her, the laughter that had brightened his days? The things they had shared…

He glared at her, suddenly angry that she should have done this to him, and he glared at the shaft and blew out his cheeks and clenched his hands again and roared a great cry that echoed deafeningly in the smallness of the shaft.

Then he shouted obscenities at the ship and the stars and the hundred people who lay as if dead in neat rows in the sleep locker and he pounded the walls until blood from his hands left imprints there.

But no one heard. There was no one to hear. Only the sleepers who lived their days with his years.

"Why?" he shouted, while his tears fell. And he thought: I haven't cried since I was a kid. Then, saying her name again and again, he knelt by her side to feel the silkiness of her jet-black hair.

There had been no death aboard a Star Transit ship since the very beginning. From the first day of the Great Emigration more than a hundred years before, when the first captain and his wife stepped aboard to pilot the precious cargo of sleeping humans ten or more years across the vast stellar reaches to colonies on planets in a half-dozen far-distant star systems, there had been no recorded death.

But now there would always be Karen.

He should have told them she walked in her sleep. But the Medical Examiners would have shrugged as they had with everything else he had told them. The medocenters would take care of it. You couldn't cure sleepwalking with the devices in the medocenter. But they would have taken care of anything that happened as a result—if he had reached her in time. It was unforeseen, this business of her walking into the shaft. No one was to blame. No one, that is, except himself.

Clifton looked up from beside his wife to the circle of light at the top of the shaft. "All right," he called out, "I'm to blame, do you hear? I did it. She could be alive except for me."

There was no answer to his self-indictment.

"And where does it leave me?" he shouted bitterly. "I'm the one who has to live and I've got nine years to go. Nine years to Ostarpa and the small colony there. What am I supposed to do?"

He never remembered later how long he stood in the shaft shouting until he was hoarse, only recalling that at one point the walls seemed to close in on him and the ship seemed filled with an oppressive strangeness, and he was clawing his way up the ladder to the top. And there were blurred images of walls and rooms as he ran about the ship, and he remembered his jerking open the liquor cabinet and the stupor that followed.

It was days later when he sobered and, insulated by the intervening unreality, managed to dispose of her body in a waste chute.

Then he moved to the office and saw that it was the three hundredth and seventy-first day and looked at the log to see that he had stopped making entries on the three hundred and sixty-third day. He examined the other books. Karen's precise handwriting had recorded her final readings on that day, too. Now he would have to do her work as well as his own.

Clifton sighed, sat at his desk and, in a steady hand, wrote in the log:

Karen rose in her sleep, walked to and fell down the right aft third level ventilating shaft and was killed. Reached her approximately three hours after the incident. She could not be saved.

Clifton West, Captain

Skipping to the three hundred and seventy-first day, he wrote:

Sent Karen's body out the ventral waste chute.

He sat studying the words, then added:

Am alone on the ship.

Instantly he wished he had not written that, but was not moved to cross the words out. It was true enough. He was alone. Would be alone nine more years.

But suppose something should happen to him? Who would land the ship? And what would happen to the sleepers?

He did not want to think about it. The medocenter would take care of everything. He didn't walk in his sleep. His duty was to get the hundred humans through to Ostarpa and then they all would become part of the colony there, except of course he'd be ten years older than the sleepers upon awakening. He looked at the day gauge on the wall. Just three thousand three hundred and thirty-two days short of Ostarpa.

Three thousand three hundred and thirty-two days without Karen! An eternity of talking to himself and listening only to the sound of his own feet as he walked about the ship. A lifetime for remembrance, just as he remembered now how eager they both had been to make the trip, how she had shared the rigorous training. It had been a chance of a lifetime: ten years of being together! Time to meditate, to ponder the problems of life, of all humanity, of each other. They had thought soberly of it as an opportunity to make something of themselves—write a great play, solve a great problem. But they had never gotten around to that. The first year had been only the sheer delight of each other's company. He wondered if it would have ever changed. How fast it had gone!

And now it was over and the nine years ahead loomed like a dark tunnel, large and forbidding.

Clifton slammed the palms of his hands on the desk. Enough of that. He was captain of the ship and he had duties. He could not spend his time in the past. There were things to do. He must keep himself occupied. He must not think of her.

But he did.

Even though the days stretched into weeks he still found his steps faltering every time he walked past rooms where he had often looked for her. For one thing there was the stereo room where Karen loved to spend leisure hours. He never saw much in stereo, but she seemed to enjoy it. And there was the music tape room, the massage parlor, the baths. She seemed to have a need of them. But all Clifton had ever needed was her.

He passed the jammed clothes locker, filled with enough apparel to last her ten years. He could not force himself to open it, though Karen seldom had opened it herself. She had made most of her own clothes, taking the material out of the huge storage bins.

He found himself one day in her sewing room, a room she had converted from a nursery, storing the nursery stuff until such a time as it was needed and installing her sewing machine and getting to work. They had joked about how, when they landed on Ostarpa, all the clothes in the locker would be still intact because she so enjoyed fashioning her own. Once he had asked her what was to become of them.

"We'll start a dress shop, darling," Karen had said quickly, as if she had already thought about it, which was the way she answered everything. "The sleeper women will want several changes right away."

"You know," he replied, "I think I'll be your manager, set you up. Karen West, Ostarpa's great dress designer. You'll have business and we'll make a fortune."

"I'm not that good," she said. But her face glowed with joy.

Even as he stood there he could hear the words as if they were said a moment ago and he felt as if he should at any moment hear the click of her heels across the floor, and when she'd enter the room, she'd say, "Clifton, what in the world are you doing here?"

The Transit Service had been right. No man was an island. A man might be for a day, perhaps, or a week or even longer. But not for ten years. That's why the service had insisted a man and his wife, proven psychologically compatible, serve together as co-captains of each transit liner.

So it wasn't right that he should spend the next nine years a lonely man. Karen was gone, but what about those hundred people in the sleep locker? He needed someone, a companion, someone to talk to, someone to take Karen's place. Not a woman, of course. That would not be right. Especially after Karen. There could be no other woman like Karen. Besides, suppose they didn't like each other?

"No," he said, standing in the sewing room and shaking his head, "it must not be a woman."

Then he brought himself back to reality. No sleeper had ever been awakened before the liner reached its destination. "And no sleeper is going to be awakened this trip," he said firmly.

Sure, he had the power to wake any or all of them in an emergency, but could his own personal emergency constitute grounds for that? Hardly.

But suppose something happens to me? he reminded himself again. Who's going to carry on?

Then he set his lips close together, turned on his heel and left the sewing room. "Nothing," he said aloud, "is going to happen to you. That's why they put medocenters on these ships." And he went to the place and spent the afternoon being checked over.

He found himself in perfect health. For some reason he was disappointed.

The weeks passed slowly, but they did pass, and Clifton busied himself with exhaustive checks throughout the entire ship, interested himself in the stereos (they weren't so bad now that he had nothing else to do), music tapes (he weeded out the ones he didn't like), massages (he was pleased to discover they left him with a glow), books (funny how hard it was to read after the ease of stereos), mathematics (how much he'd forgotten), a few languages (German was still his hardest), moods of writing (he just did not have the knack), painting (he was always drawing machinery, and wondering why)—and found the image of Karen's laughing blue eyes still there at the edge of his mind, though curiously distant, as if it were one of the stereos he had seen.

Then the hunger started.

He sat for long hours in the chill of the sleep locker and envied the sleepers there, row on row, all of them without a worry, without thought, trustful of him, confident he would get them through, none of them knowing Karen was dead and not caring, and he had an urge to wake them all and throw a furious party to end all parties.

And sometimes he'd have a party there all by himself.

And then he grew to hate them. When he did, he went to the medocenter and this was erased and he was made whole again.

But the hunger got worse.

"Karen, Karen!" And he finally wondered if it was really Karen he wanted. And the medocenter only made his hunger worse and he cursed the efficiency of it.

Then one day he got out the file of sleepers, went through it from Abelard, Johannes, to Yardley, Greta, put the pictures in the stereo and saw what the sleepers looked like and wondered which of them would prove the most companionable. Which man, that is, for a woman...well, it just would not be right to awaken a woman. It would not look right in the log, for one thing, and he was sure all he needed was another person to talk to and it might as well be a man. After all, man is a gregarious animal. If he had someone to talk to it would be—well, more normal.

He turned back through the file for Hedstrom, George, a pleasant-looking fellow of thirty—which would make him five years Clifton's junior—and in passing he came upon the picture of Portia Lavester again. He slipped the picture in the stereo and spent a long time looking at it. Quite a girl. Blonde. Unlike Karen in that respect. And she wore her hair longer. Her eyes weren't as blue as Karen's. But her skin was darker. Sun? Karen didn't like the sun. It made her freckled. But this girl must have lived in it. The stereo was inadequate, however. It didn't tell how she laughed. Did she laugh? Was it pleasing?

He put it down and looked at the record. Portia Lavester. Twenty years old. Five feet three. Weight 109. He looked at the picture again. The weight was well distributed.

He shuffled the picture back in the pile, tried to concentrate on Hedstrom, George. A logical choice among the single men. Mechanical background. He peeked at the Lavester record again. The girl was a home economics expert. She'd do well on Ostarpa. Or on the ship.

Clifton sighed and shoved the file away. Only then did he realize how much he had missed Karen's cooking. The ship's electronic cookery was all right, but it left much to be desired. It had no personal touch.

But to get back to Hedstrom. How would the fellow act if he awakened him? Immediately he thought of the girl and wondered what she would be like.

"Stop it!" he admonished himself. "She's much too young." And he started going through looking at the other single women. The girl Lavester was clearly the nicest. Again he studied her.

And again he forced himself to go back to the man. Finally he decided to do nothing at present, left the office and started his rounds, determined to think of other things.

Eventually he found himself in the sleep locker looking for number 33, Portia Lavester's compartment. He saw it and discovered it was no different from number 57, the compartment of George Hedstrom. The same black oblong box with the ribbon of red plastic where it was sealed near the top. It would be easy to activate the rollers, move it out of line and out to the medocenter, rip off the plastic and charge the contents with life. He wiped away a few dust motes and found that to him the box suddenly seemed different from the others.

He was sweating.

Later in the tape room he listened to music and pondered the question. Suppose he awakened her and she proved to be anything but what he wanted? Sure, she was good looking, but what about her age? Her mannerisms?

Would his fifteen years turn her against him? There were nine years left to Ostarpa; a lot could happen in nine years and she would eventually discover he was no ogre. She might even learn to love him. Why, she might even take Karen's place!

He clicked off the music with a trembling hand, went to the bar, drew a double shot and ice.

Karen, Karen! Why did it have to happen to you?

Forgive me, darling, for what I am about to do.

Clifton watched the lard-like flesh become suffused with pink, saw the surge of color in the lips, the catch of breath and the resultant swell of breast. Then the eyelids flickered.

A moment later Portia Lavester was staring at him, and even as she did so Clifton could see that she did not understand what had happened. But when the vacant eyes came alive, the girl sat up, crossed her hands to her bare, hunched shoulders and looked around frantically.

"Don't be frightened," Clifton said, smiling. "You're still on the ship. You've just been awakened."

"Thanks," she said without gratitude, "but I wasn't frightened. I was looking for something to put on."

"Oh." Clifton had forgotten about that. Now he blushed and opened a nearby drawer and withdrew a white gown. "Take this. It will have to do until I get you something else."

She took it and held it to her nakedness, eyeing him coldly. He turned, heard her drop quietly to the floor. "Where are the others?" she asked, and he could hear the rustle of the gown as she put it around her. "And where can I pick up my clothes?"

He turned to look at her, found her at the side of the room in front of its only mirror, inspecting her face and pushing her lush hair this way and that and grimacing. "How long ago did we land? What's Ostarpa like?"

She was lovely and not unlike Karen in manner and it was going to be harder for him than he thought.

"Was I the first or the last? Or was I in the middle? Just like me to be in the middle." She laughed a little and he was glad to hear her, though her laughter was a little lower in pitch than Karen's. And then her eyes found his in the mirror and they widened. She turned. "Why don't you say something? Is anything wrong?" Now she was frightened.

She was very young and he was glad to hear her voice and he wanted to tell her so, but he knew she wouldn't understand. So he said only, "I want to talk to you."

"What's happened?" Her eyes were panicky.

"There are no others," he blurted out.

"No others?" Her voice was shrill.

He shook his head. "I awakened you because my wife died and I needed someone." It was blunt, but he wanted to be honest with her. "The others are still asleep out there."

She stared with round eyes and a round, open mouth, and her hands fell away from her face and were lost when the gown's long sleeves fell over them.

"I—I had to hear someone talk again," Clifton said haltingly. "I went through the file. I studied all the sleepers. I decided on you. I'm sorry if—"

"How long?" she murmured, lips hardly moving.

"Long?" he answered. "What do you mean?" And then he understood. "We're a little more than a year from Earth."

Her moan startled and unnerved him. Her eyes closed and she slumped to the floor.

When she did not move, he went to her, lifted her head. At once her eyelids fluttered and she saw him and then her face darkened and she lashed out with tiny fists, scratching and crying.

"It's not as bad as all that!" he cried, half-angry with her now, trying to stop her, clutching her flailing arms. He drew away quickly when she bit him.

"You—you *beast!*" she wailed. "You spoiled everything. *Everything.* Everything had been so carefully planned."

"I know, I know," he soothed.

"Oh," she quavered, and she fell to the floor again, sobbing.

Clifton got up, surveyed her weeping figure, a mound of white on the floor. Well, he thought, at least this is a change for me. And he felt rather foolish about what he had done. If only it had been a man; he could reason with a man. He turned in disgust and walked from the medocenter. She would change. After all, nine years is a long time. No woman could cry nine years. He smiled a little. Fiery little thing, isn't she? he told himself as he started his tour of the ship.

He didn't find her in the medocenter when he returned. The white gown was not there either. It was a long time before he found her lying atop one of the compartments in the sleep locker. She was still clad in the gown, a gaunt, spiritless figure, her eyes staring at the low ceiling.

"Miss Lavester," he said, "I know it was a shock to wake up this side of Ostarpa, but believe me, I intended no harm. If only you knew the loneliness—" and he could not go on, remembering the emptiness of the days just past.

She said nothing, only blinking her eyes, pale blue eyes in a white face.

"If I'd known how upset you'd be, I'd never have awakened you," Clifton said bitterly. "If I could put you back to sleep now I would." Her face turned toward his, eyes icy in a withering glance. She rose, a firm press of breast against the white gown as she slid off the compartment. Clifton's heart quickened. But she ignored him and walked away. She looks like Karen sleepwalking, he thought.

The next day he found her in the stereo room, dressed in one of Karen's gowns from the clothes locker, a thin, pale blue dress that accentuated her small waist and blonde hair. She looked ever so much like Karen. He wondered where she had slept, if she had eaten.

"Portia," he said, sitting in a nearby chair. She only sat, a still figure, staring ahead, her hair brushed back in a long sweep, glossy and smooth, and Clifton thought: My God, but she's a beautiful thing.

"Portia," he repeated, "I want to talk to you." What could he do with this girl? Was there no way to break through to her?

Portia gave him a hateful glance and rose. He watched her and his hunger was more than he could stand.

"Please," he said desperately, "don't leave."

She turned at the doorway and looked at him coldly.

"You don't know what it means to lose your wife and have no one to talk to and have to decide what to do." He looked down at his hands embarrassedly. Why was he finding it so hard to talk to her? He felt his face coloring. "I think I'd have gone mad if I hadn't awakened you. It wasn't snap judgment, Portia. I didn't just pull your number out of a hat. You see—" He looked up. She wasn't there.

He saw her in the hallway, her head down, contemplative and walking slowly, and catching up to her and walking beside her, he explained, "Suppose I'd have an accident like Karen did? Then none of you would ever land on Ostarpa. Somebody had to be awakened. Can't you understand that, Portia?" She gave no hint she knew he was there.

He watched her in the massage room, unable to take his eyes off her as the soft, flexible arms stroked her flesh, and he said softly, "You say I spoiled everything, but I'd like you to think about that. On Ostarpa you'd have to go to work right away, be given your duty number just like you had on Earth. On the ship you've got nine years to play with, nine years of carefree life. You can do what you want and nobody's going to say or do a thing to tell you to stop, have you thought of that?" The moving arms were silent and smooth and so was Portia.

He followed her to the bath but could not bring himself to enter there. He stayed beyond the filmy curtain and talked to her. "Sure, I know it was a surprise, awakening you like that, and I know you had in mind waking on Ostarpa, but being on the ship, the two of us, with all our wants taken care of—it has its advantages."

And in the bar, with her eyes averted, drinking with her, he explained, "Oh, I'll admit there are records to keep. But I missed a few days after Karen died. Taking the whole ten years into account, that won't make much difference. But suppose I became ill for a few days. Somebody's got to be on hand to see I get treatment at the medocenter. That's why you've got to come around, why you've got to start thinking about this thing."

And finally, in the navigation room, he told her, "You can't go on like this. You've got to learn all about this ship. Why, if something happened to me, who'd awaken the sleepers? You will have to do that, Portia. You'd be the only one left. You've just got to be ready to take over, that's all there is to it. And don't think it's too hard. The ship does most of it. Automatic. Just a lever here, a button there. I'll teach you all about it. Even landing the ship. You won't find it hard, once you put your mind to it."

Through it all she remained aloof and unspeaking, a beautiful, silent thing with two accusing orbs for eyes, a lovely mouth with generous lips much given to a look of disdain.

Until one day.

It was totally unexpected. Portia had taken over Karen's bedroom next to his, closing and locking the intervening door as if forever. He had gone to sleep in his room, with her still distant and uncommunicative in hers.

He awakened to the smell of coffee and a cooking breakfast. He sat up quickly, wondering if Karen's death and the events that followed it had been a bad dream, and when he assured himself that they had not, wondering if he had at last lost his mind.

Clifton quickly dressed and entered the kitchen.

Portia was there.

She smiled at him.

She said, "Good morning, Clifton." Just like Karen.

He stood speechless, staring.

"Breakfast is about ready."

"Wh—what's come over you?" he said numbly, both pleased and dumfounded, his eyes relishing the lovely figure in one of Karen's sheerest nightgowns.

"You were right," she said, tossing her head to bring the blonde hair away from her face and smiling. Her teeth were every bit as even and white as Karen's. "I just realized it. As you said, there are nine years ahead of us. I might as well make the best of it."

"I'm glad," he said warmly, and the memory of what she had been like during the days before were eclipsed by what she was now. "I was hoping you'd come around."

"Come, sit down," she said, indicating the place set for him, the gleaming silver, the neat napkin, the steaming coffee in the cup. "Don't let it get cold."

"Karen used to say that." And then he thought: That's a mistake; I mustn't mention Karen ever again. But Portia seemed not to have noticed. And she seemed so much like her now.

"I got tired of eating by myself," Portia said, sitting opposite him at the table. And she stole a sly look as she said, "And I'm afraid I acted badly."

"Not at all," Clifton said gallantly. "I understand how you felt. It's just taken a little time, that's all." He started eating, but his eyes were on her and the transformation of eyes that were no longer cold, lips that weren't scornful any more.

"Pity the poor sleepers," she said, laughing. "They can't enjoy a breakfast like this."

"Do you suppose," he said, endeavoring to keep the talk in the same vein, "that any might rise up when they smell that coffee?" He inhaled ecstatically. "Hmm. There's nothing like it."

"I hope I never make it that strong." And she laughed again.

With a shock he found his knee touching hers. He drew away, wondering if it had been accidental. Later, when he tried to kiss her, she turned away, murmuring, "Not yet, Cliff. Give me time. It's so—so sudden."

He obeyed, turned his attention to other things. He could afford to wait. After all, there were nine years. A day or so—what did it matter?

It was more than a week before he managed to kiss her for the first time. And then it was nothing like Karen's kisses. But immediately he felt he was asking too much of Portia too soon. There'd be time for teaching.

They lost themselves in the intricacies of the ship, covering its complete operation, the records that had to be kept, the functions of each section, the matter of awakening the sleepers—which, Clifton explained, was quite simple, since the medocenter did most of the work, but still demanded certain procedures and precautions and delicate adjustments. He even taught her how to use the communications system that would become operable within a few months of Ostarpa. In all, they spent a good two months studying together every facet of the ship.

"It's so complicated," she said in an awed voice. She squeezed his hand she had taken to holding. "But you're an awfully good teacher, Cliff."

"And you're the loveliest student I ever had," he said, squeezing back and drawing closer to kiss her.

"Cliff!" she said, drawing away and laughing. "You're always joking. I'll bet I'm the only student you ever had."

"Well," he said lamely, "I hate to admit it, but you are."

Then they both laughed.

At length they finished everything he could show her on the ship. Then he brought up what had been on his mind ever since awakened her.

"Portia," he said gravely, "I'm captain of this ship and have invested in me the right to perform marriage."

Portia smiled. "You're always saying things so seriously, Cliff. So—so pontifically. Is that the word?"

"I'm serious, Portia."

"I know." She laughed a little more, then straightened her face. "I didn't mean to offend you."

"You're always laughing at me. Why?"

"I don't mean to."

"I want to marry you, Portia."

"I know." And instantly her eyes were grave. "I've known for a long time."

"I've wanted you since the day you first looked at me."

"I've known that, too."

"It was all I could do to—"

"You've been more than kind, Cliff."

"When, darling? When can I marry you?"

She looked up. "Tomorrow?"

His heart leaped. "Marry you tomorrow?"

She nodded. "Tomorrow."

Was there something odd in her look? He couldn't decide.

When Clifton went to bed that night his heart sang. The years ahead no longer seemed appalling and interminable. How they'd spend them! The sewing room…it could always be changed back into a nursery. Portia had shown no interest in sewing, so he'd just store Karen's stuff. Perhaps somebody would find use for it when they landed on Ostarpa. It wasn't unusual for captains and their wives to have a half-dozen kids during transit.

He went to sleep with the sound of children's feet echoing about the halls and corridors of the ship. And when he dreamed of the marriage, it was, oddly, Karen he was marrying.

He was awakened with a start. On this morning there was no welcome aroma of coffee. At first he thought perhaps he was too early. But it was time. Portia was probably so excited she was all off schedule.

Clifton was careful on this morning. He took his bath, toweled himself until his skin tingled, used his deodorant sparingly, gave himself a close shave. The part in his hair was never straighter.

Dressing himself in a clean, pressed suit, he strolled from his bedroom. Portia was not in the kitchen. He walked to her bedroom. The bed had been made. But no Portia.

Where the devil had she gone?

He started walking about the ship, searching first here and then there. Of course not in stereo. Not this day. Massage? No. Bath? Not there. Tape? Same.

She was nowhere to be found. Then he recalled the funny look in her face the previous night. It meant *something*.

Suicide? Frantic now, he went to both waste chutes. Neither gave evidence of having been opened. Still…

An hour later he returned, a bewildered and disconsolate man, to his office.

Portia was there.

With her was a man.

He was George Hedstrom.

Clifton could only sink back against the wall and look at the two of them, the Portia he had never seen so radiant, George, a dark, handsome fellow who wore a quizzical look. Clifton was shocked to see they were holding hands.

"Captain," George said in a friendly way, rising his full six feet, "Portia tells me—"

"I'm sorry, Cliff," Portia interrupted. "George is my fiance. We were to be married on Ostarpa, but as long as you—"

Tomorrow, she had said.

The two figures blurred before him, the room reeled and Clifton clutched the doorway for support. Karen, Karen! I've been bewitched. This girl—I thought she was you…I should have known.

"Let me help you."

Clifton struck out at the dark head, hit it somewhere.

Karen, Karen! Can you hear me?

He stumbled out of the room and down the corridor.

Karen, Karen! Where are you?

He found the ventral waste chute. He was in it, heard the door click behind him. Now they'd never get him out, never take him away from his Karen.

The sides of the chute were closing in. It was hot. But it was cool where Karen was.

"Wait, Karen!" he cried. And as he inched his way down the chute he hoped he wasn't too late, hoped she'd forgive him.

There was the outer door. On the other side was coolness and Karen. Dear, beautiful, lovely Karen. The *real* Karen.

With a surge of joy he held to the smooth sides of the shaft and raised his foot.

He plunged it down unerringly against the door. It burst open with a deadly whoosh of air.

The door clicked closed.

The chute was empty.

∎

The Ultroom Error

HB73782. Ultroom error. Tendal 13. Arvid 6. Kanad transfer out of 1609 complete. Intact. But too near limit of 1,000 days. Next Kanad transfer ready. 1959. Reginald, son of Mr. and Mrs. Martin Laughton, 3495 Orland Drive, Marionville, Illinois, U.S.A. Arrive his 378th day. TB73782.

Nancy Laughton sat on the blanket she had spread on the lawn in her front yard, knitting a pair of booties for the PTA bazaar. Occasionally she glanced at her son in the playpen, who was getting his daily dose of sunshine. He was gurgling happily, examining a ball, a cheese grater and a linen baby book, all with great interest.

When she looked up again she noticed a man walking by—except he turned up the walk and crossed the lawn to her. He was a little taller than her husband, had piercing blue eyes and a rather amused set to his lips.

"Hello, Nancy," he said.

"Hello, Joe," she answered. It was her brother who lived in Kankakee.

"I'm going to take the baby for a while," he said.

"All right, Joe."

He reached into the pen, picked up the baby. As he did so the baby's knees hit the side of the playpen and young Laughton let out a scream—half from hurt and half from sudden lack of confidence in his new handler. But this did not deter Joe. He started off with the child.

Around the corner and after the man came a snarling mongrel dog, eyes bright, teeth glinting in the sunlight. The man did not turn as the dog threw himself at him, burying his teeth in his leg. Surprised, the man dropped the screaming child on the lawn and turned to the dog.

Joe seemed off-balance and he backed up confusedly in the face of the snapping jaws. Then he suddenly turned and walked away, the dog at his heels.

"I tell you, the man said he was my brother and he made me think he was," Nancy told her husband for the tenth time. "I don't even have a brother."

Martin Laughton sighed. "I can't understand why you believed him. It's just—just plain nuts, Nancy!"

"Don't you think I know it?" Nancy said tearfully. "I feel like I'm going crazy. I can't say I dreamt it because there was Reggie with his bleeding knees, squalling for all he was worth on the grass—Oh, I don't even want to think about it."

"We haven't lost Reggie, Nancy. Remember that. Now why don't you try to get some rest?"

"You—you don't believe me at all, do you, Martin?"

When her husband did not answer, her head sank to her arms on the table and she sobbed.

"Nancy, for heaven's sake, of course I believe you. I'm trying to think it out, that's all. We should have called the police."

Nancy shook her head in her arms. "They'd—never—believe me either," she moaned.

"I'd better go and make sure Reggie's all right." Martin got out of his chair and went to the stairs.

"I'm going with you," Nancy said, hurriedly rising and coming over to him.

"We'll go up together."

They found Reggie peacefully asleep in his crib in his room upstairs. They checked the windows and tucked in the blankets. They paused in the room for a moment and then Martin stole his arm around his wife and led her to the door.

"As I've said, sergeant, this fellow hypnotized my wife. He made her think he was her brother. She doesn't even have a brother. Then he tried to get away with the baby." Martin leaned down and patted the dog. "It was Tiger who scared him off."

The police sergeant looked at the father, at Nancy and then at the dog. He scribbled notes in his book.

"Are you a rich man, Mr. Laughton?" he asked.

"Not at all. The bank still owns most of the house. I have a few hundred dollars, that's all."

"What do you do?"

"Office work, mostly. I'm a junior executive in an insurance company."

"Any enemies?"

"No…Oh, I suppose I have a few people I don't get along with, like anybody else. Nobody who'd do anything like this, though."

The sergeant flipped his notebook closed. "You'd better keep your dog inside and around the kid as much as possible. Keep your doors and windows locked. I'll see that the prowl car keeps an eye on the house. Call us if anything seems unusual or out of the way."

Nancy had taken a sedative and was nearly asleep by the time Martin finished cleaning the .30-.30 rifle he used for deer hunting. He put it by the stairs, ready for use, fully loaded, leaning it against the wall next to the telephone stand.

The front door bell chimed. He answered it. It was Dr. Stuart and another man.

"I came as soon as I could, Martin," the young doctor said, stepping inside with the other man. "This is my new assistant, Dr. Tompkins."

Martin and Tompkins shook hands.

"The baby—?" Dr. Stuart asked.

"Upstairs," Martin said.

"You'd better get him, Dr. Tompkins, if we're to take him to the hospital. I'll stay here with Mr. Laughton. How've you been, Martin?"

"Fine."

"How's everything at the office?"

"Fine."

"And your wife?"

"She's fine, too."

"Glad to hear it, Martin. Mighty glad. Say, by the way, there's that bill you owe me. I think it's thirty-two dollars, isn't that right?"

"Yes, I'd almost forgotten about it."

"Why don't you be a good fellow and write a check for it? It's been over a year, you know."

"That's right. I'll get right at it." Martin went over to his desk, opened it and started looking for his checkbook. Dr. Stuart stood by him, making idle comments until Dr. Tompkins came down the stairs with the sleeping baby cuddled against his shoulder.

"Never mind the check now, Martin. I see we're ready to go." He went to his assistant and took the baby. Together they walked out the front door.

"Goodbye," Martin said, going to the door.

Then he was nearly bowled over by the discharge of the .30-.30. Dr. Stuart crumpled to the ground, the baby falling to the lawn. Dr. Tompkins whirled and there was a second shot. Dr. Tompkins pitched forward on his face.

The figure of a woman ran from the house, retrieved the now-squalling infant and ran back into the house. Once inside, Nancy slammed the door, gave the baby to the stunned Martin and headed for the telephone.

"One of them was the same man!" she cried.

Martin gasped, sinking into a chair with the baby. "I believed them," he said slowly and uncomprehendingly. "They made me believe them!"

"Those bodies," the sergeant said. "Would you mind pointing them out to me, please?"

"Aren't they—aren't they on the walk?" Mrs. Laughton asked.

"There is nothing on the walk, Mrs. Laughton."

"But there *must* be! I tell you I shot these men who posed as doctors. One of them was the same man who tried to take the baby this afternoon. They hypnotized my husband—"

"Yes, I know, Mrs. Laughton. We've been through that." The sergeant went to the door and opened it. "Say, Homer, take another look around the walk and the bushes. There's supposed to be two of them. Shot with a .30-.30."

He turned and picked up the gun and examined it again. "Ever shoot a gun before, Mrs. Laughton?"

"Many times. Martin and I used to go hunting together before we had Reggie."

The sergeant nodded. "You were taking an awful chance, shooting at a guy carrying your baby, don't you think?"

"I shot him in the leg. The other—the other turned and I shot him in the chest. I could even see his eyes when he turned around. If I hadn't pulled the trigger then…I don't want to remember it."

The patrolman pushed the door open. "There's no bodies out here but there's some blood. Quite a lot of blood. A little to one side of the walk."

The policemen went out.

"Thank God you were still awake, Nancy," Martin said. "I'd have let them have the baby." He reached over and smoothed the sleeping Reggie's hair.

Nancy, who was rocking the boy, narrowed her eyes.

"I wonder why they want our baby? He's just like any other baby. We don't have any money. We couldn't pay a ransom."

"Reggie's pretty cute, though," Martin said. "You've got to admit that."

Nancy smiled. Then she suddenly stopped rocking.

"Martin!"

He sat up quickly.

"Where's Tiger?"

Together they rose and walked around the room. They found him in a corner, eyes open, tongue protruding. He was dead.

"If we keep Reggie in the house much longer he'll turn out to be a hermit," Martin said at breakfast a week later. "He needs fresh air and sunshine."

"I'm not going to sit on the lawn alone with him, Martin. I just can't, that's all. I'd be able to think of nothing but that day."

"Still thinking about it? I think we'd have heard from them again if they were coming back. They probably got somebody else's baby by this time." Martin finished his coffee and rose to kiss her goodbye. "But for safety's sake I guess you'd better keep that gun handy."

The morning turned into a brilliant, sunshiny day. Puffs of clouds moved slowly across the summer sky and a warm breeze rustled the trees. It would be a crime to keep Reggie inside on a day like this, Nancy thought.

So she called Mrs. MacDougal, the next-door neighbor. Mrs. MacDougal was familiar with what had happened to the Laughtons and she agreed to keep an eye on Nancy and Reggie and to call the police at the first sign of trouble.

With a fearful but determined heart Nancy moved the playpen and set it up in the front yard. She spread a blanket for herself and put Reggie in the pen. Her heart pounded all the while and she watched the street for any strangers, ready to flee inside if need be. Reggie just gurgled with delight at the change in environment.

This peaceful scene was disturbed by a speeding car in which two men were riding. The car roared up the street, swerved toward the parkway, tires screaming, bounced over the curb and sidewalk, straight toward the child and mother. Reggie, attracted by the sudden noise, looked up to see the approaching vehicle. His mother stood up, set her palms against her cheeks and shrieked.

The car came on, crunching over the playpen and killing the child. The mother was hit and instantly killed, the force of the blow snapping her spine and tossing her against the house. The car plunged on into a tree, hitting it a terrible blow, crumpling the car's forward end so it looked like an accordion. The men were thrown from the machine.

"We'll never be able to prosecute in this case," the state's attorney said. "At least not on a drunken-driving basis."

"I can't get over it," the chief of police said. "I've got at least six men who will swear the man was drunk. He staggered, reeled and gave the usual drunk talk. He reeked of whiskey."

The prosecutor handed the report over the desk. "Here's the analysis. Not a trace of alcohol. He couldn't have even had a small glass of near beer. Here's another report. This is his physical exam made not long afterwards. The man was in perfect health. Only variations are he had a scar on his leg where something, probably a dog, bit him once. And then a scar on his chest. It looked like an old gunshot wound, they said. Must have happened years ago."

"That's odd. The man who accosted Mrs. Laughton in the afternoon was bitten by their dog. Later that night she said she shot the same man in the chest. Since the scars are healed, it obviously could not be the same man. But there's a real coincidence for you. And speaking of the dogbite, the Laughton dog died that night. His menu evidently didn't agree with him. Never did figure what killed him, actually."

"Any record of treatment on the man she shot?"

"The *men*. You'll remember, there were two. No, we never found a trace of either. No doctor ever made a report of a gunshot wound that night. No hospital had a case either—at least not within several hundred miles—that night or several nights afterward. Ever been shot with a .30-.30?"

The state's attorney shook his head. "Would I be here if I had?"

"I guess not. The pair must have crawled away to die God knows where."

"Getting back to the man who ran over the child and killed Mrs. Laughton. Why did he pretend to be drunk?"

It was the chief's turn to shake his head. "Your guess is as good as mine. There are a lot of angles to this case none of us understand. It looks deliberate, but where's the motive?"

"What does the man have to say?"

"I was afraid you'd get to that," the chief said, his neck reddening. "It's all been rather embarrassing to the department." He coughed self-consciously. "He's proved a strange one all right. He says his name is John Smith and he's got cards to prove it, too—for example, a Social Security card. It looks authentic, yet there's no such number on file in Washington, so we've discovered. We've had him in jail for a week and we've all taken turns questioning him. He laughs and admits his guilt—in fact, he seems amused by most everything. Sometimes all alone in his cell he'll start laughing for no apparent reason. It gives you the creeps."

The state's attorney leaned back in his chair. "Maybe it's a case for an alienist."

"One jump ahead of you. Dr. Stone thinks he's normal, but won't put down any I.Q. Actually, he can't figure him out himself. Smith seems to take delight in answering questions—sort of anticipates them and has the answer ready before you're half through asking."

"Well, if Doctor Stone says he's normal, that's enough for me." The prosecutor was silent for a moment. Then, "How about the husband?"

"Laughton? We're afraid to let him see him. All broken up. No telling what kind of a rumpus he'd start—especially if Smith started his funny business."

"Guess you're right. Well, Mr. Smith won't think it's so funny when we hang criminal negligence or manslaughter on him. By the way, you've checked possible family connections?"

"Nobody ever saw John Smith before. Even at the address on his driver's license. And there's no duplicate of that in Springfield, in case you're interested."

The man who had laughingly told police his name was John Smith lay on his cot in the county jail, his eyes closed, his arms folded across his chest. This gave him the appearance of being alert despite reclining. Even as he lay, his mouth held a hint of a smile.

Arvid 6—for John Smith *was* Arvid 6—had lain in that position for more than four hours, when suddenly he snapped his eyes open and appeared to be listening. For a moment a look of concern crossed his face and he swung his legs to the floor and sat there expectantly. Arvid 6 knew Tendal 13 had materialized and was somewhere in the building.

Eventually there were some sounds from beyond the steel cell and doorway. There was a clang when the outer doorway was opened and Arvid 6 rose from his cot.

"Your lawyer's here to see you," the jailer said, indicating the man with the briefcase. "Ring the buzzer when you're through." The jailer let the man in, locked the cell door and walked away.

The man threw the briefcase on the jail cot and stood glaring.

"Your damned foolishness has gone far enough. I'm sick and tired of it," he declared. "If you carry on any more we'll never get back to the Ultroom!"

"I'm sorry, Tendal," the man on the cot said. "I didn't think—"

"You're absolutely right. You didn't think. Crashing that car into that tree and killing that woman—that was the last straw. You don't even deserve to get back to our era. You ought to be made to rot here."

"I'm *really* sorry about that," Arvid 6 said.

"You know the instructions. Just because you work in the Ultroom don't get to thinking human life doesn't have any value. We wouldn't be here if it hadn't. But to unnecessarily kill—" The older man shook his head. "You could have killed yourself as well and we'd never get the job done. As it is, you almost totally obliterated me." Tendal 13 paced the length of the cell and back again, gesturing as he talked.

"It was only with the greatest effort I pulled myself back together again. I doubt that you could have done it. And then all the while you've been sitting here, probably enjoying yourself with your special brand of humor I have grown to despise."

"You didn't have to come along at all, you know," Arvid 6 said.

"How well I know! How sorry I am that I ever did! It was only because I was sorry for you, because someone older and more experienced than you was needed. I volunteered. Imagine that! I volunteered! Tendal 13 reaches the height of stupidity and volunteers to help Arvid 6 go back six thousand years to bring Kanad back, to correct a mistake Arvid 6 made!" He snorted. "I still can't believe I was ever that stupid. I only prove it when I pinch myself and here I am.

"Oh, you've been a joy to be with! First it was that hunt in ancient Mycenae when you let the lion escape the hunters' quaint spears and we were partly eaten by the lion in the bargain, although you dazzled the hunters, deflecting their spears. Then your zest for drink when we were with Octavian in Alexandria that led to everybody's amusement but ours when we were ambushed by Anthony's men. And worst of all, that English barmaid you became engrossed with at our last stop in 1609, when her husband mistook me for you and you let him take me apart piece by piece—"

"All right, all right," Arvid 6 said. "I'll admit I've made some mistakes. You're just not adventurous, that's all."

"Shut up! For once you're going to listen to me. Our instructions specifically stated we were to have as little as possible to do with these people. But at every turn you've got us more and more enmeshed. If that's adventure, you can have it." Tendal 13 sat down wearily and sank his head in his hands. "It was you who conceived the idea of taking Reggie right out of his playpen. 'Watch me take that child right out from under its mother's nose' were your exact words. And before I could stop you, you did. Only you forgot an important factor in the equation—the dog, Tiger. And you nursed a dogbite most of the afternoon before it healed. Then you had to take your spite out on the poor thing by suggesting suffocation to it that night.

"And speaking of that night, you remember we agreed I was to do the talking. But no, you pulled a switch and captured Martin Laughton's attention and I was forced to play a minor role. What happened for my pains? I got shot in the leg and you got a hole in your chest. We were both nearly obliterated that time and we didn't even come close to getting the kid.

"Still you wanted to run the whole show. 'I'm younger than you, I'll take the wheel.' The next thing I know I'm floating in space halfway to nowhere with two broken legs, a spinal injury and a concussion—"

"These twentieth-century machines aren't what they ought to be," Arvid 6 said.

"You never run out of excuses, do you, Arvid? Remember what you said in the Ultroom when you pushed the lever clear over and transferred Kanad back six thousand years? 'My hand slipped.' As simple as that. 'My hand slipped.' It was so simple everyone believed you. You were given no real punishment. In a way it was a reward—at least to you—getting to go back and rescue the life germ of Kanad out of each era he'd be born in."

Tendal 13 turned and looked steadily and directly at Arvid 6. "Do you know what I think? I think you deliberately pushed the lever over as far as it would go *just to see what would happen*. That's how simple I think it was."

Arvid 6 flushed, turned away and looked at the floor.

"What crazy things have you been doing since I've been gone?" Tendal 13 asked.

Arvid 6 sighed. "After what you just said I guess it wouldn't amuse you, although it has me. They got to me right after the accident, before I had a chance to collect my wits, dematerialize or anything—you said we shouldn't dematerialize in front of anybody."

"That's right."

"Well, I didn't know what to do. I could see they thought I was drunk, so I was. But they had a blood sample before I could manufacture any alcohol in my blood, although I implanted a memory in them that I reeked of it." He laughed. "I fancy they're thoroughly confused."

"And you're thoroughly amused, no doubt. Have they questioned you?"

"At great length. They had a psychiatrist in to see me. He was a queer fellow with the most stupid set of questions and tests I ever saw."

"And you amused yourself with him."

"I suppose you'd think so."

"Who did you tell them you are?"

"John Smith. A rather prevalent name here, I understand. I manufactured a pasteboard called a Social Security card, and a driver's license—"

"Never mind. It's easy to see you've been your own inimitable self. Believe me, if I ever get back to the Ultroom I hope I never see you again. And I hope I'll never leave there again though I'm rejuvenated through a million years."

"Was Kanad's life germ transferred all right this time?"

Tendal 13 shook his head. "I haven't heard. The transfers are getting more difficult all the time. In 1609, you'll remember, it was a case of pneumonia for the two-year-old. A simple procedure. It wouldn't work here. Medicine's too far along." He produced a notebook. "The last jump was three hundred and forty-two years, a little more than average. The next ought to be around 2250. Things will be more difficult than ever there, probably."

"Do you think Kanad will be angry about all this?"

"How would you like to have to go through all those birth processes, to have your life germ kicked from one era to the next?"

"Frankly, I didn't think he'd go back so far."

"If it had been anybody but Kanad nobody'd ever have thought of going back after it. The life germ of the head of the whole galactic system who came to the Ultroom to be transplanted to a younger body—and then sending him back beyond his original birth date—" Tendal 13 got up and commenced his pacing again. "Oh, I suppose Kanad's partly to blame, wanting rejuvenating at only three hundred years. Some have waited a thousand or more or until their bones are like paper."

"I just wonder how angry Kanad will be," Arvid 6 muttered.

> *HB92167. Ultroom error. Tendal 13. Arvid 6. Kanad transfer out of 1959 complete. Next Kanad transfer ready. 2267. Phullain 19, son of Orla 39 and Rhoda 5. 22H Level M, Hemisphere B, Quadrant 3, Sector L. Arrive his 329th Day. TB92167.*

Arvid 6 rose from the cot and the two men faced each other.

"Before we leave, Arvid," Tendal 13 started to say.

"I know, I know. You want me to let you handle everything."

"Exactly. Is that too much to ask after all you've done?"

"I guess I have made mistakes. From now on you be the boss. I'll do whatever you say."

"I hope I can count on that." Tendal 13 rang the jail buzzer. The jailer unlocked the cell door.

"You remember the chief said it's all right to take him with me, Matthews," Tendal 13 told the jailer.

"Yes, I remember," the jailer said mechanically, letting them both out of the cell.

They walked together down the jail corridor. When they came to another barred door the jailer fumbled with the keys and clumsily tried several with no luck.

Arvid 6, an amused set to his mouth and devilment in his eyes, watched the jailer's expression as he walked through the bars of the door. He laughed as he saw the jailer's eyes bulge.

"Arvid!"

Tendal 13 walked briskly through the door, snatched Arvid 6 by the shoulders and shook him.

The jailer watched stupefied as the two men vanished in the middle of a violent argument.

■

A Tribute to Jerry Sohl

by Richard Matheson

My relationship with Jerry was something less—and more—than that of writer to writer—although Jerry was certainly a writer—as I will explain at the conclusion of this salute to an old friend.

To begin with we both loved classical music. I remember once, at his house, that we played a game using an LP record on which a large number of classic moments were performed. It was neck-and-neck between us. I barely managed to win and I do mean barely; Jerry had a profound knowledge of all classical music from the eighteenth century to the present.

Considering that we both played the piano—a description tantamount to me stating that Einstein and I both were familiar with the multiplication tables—we came up with the notion of playing two-piano music. Not duets, but two separate pianos. I had, for some reason I cannot remember, two baby grands in our house. They were never used to mutual advantage, however, until Jerry and I commenced to play two-piano compositions.

As I have indicated, Jerry far outshone me on the keyboard. I had to practice thirty minutes each day to keep up with him—which I barely managed to do.

And we got pretty damned good, too. I think the high point was the playing of *Variations on a Theme by Haydn* composed by Brahms. Not an easy composition to play—but we finally got it down and it sounded—and *felt*—marvelous.

There were other two-piano pieces we played as well—some easy, some difficult—but it was a wonderful experience getting together one night a week to bang out our double-keyboard harmonizing. And, as stated, we got pretty good too.

Jerry played the hard parts.

Then there was golf—which leads me to my final remark about Jerry as a writer.

We played on a regular basis—at three or four different courses. As with our piano playing, Jerry's ability at golf far outshone mine. As I recall, we didn't keep score, but simply enjoyed the activity, the fresh air, the companionship. Probably Jerry allowed the non-scoring out of pity for my lesser golf ability.

The day emblazoned on my memory occurred in 1963 at Elkins Ranch which is, I believe, north of Fillmore. We rode there in Jerry's car; he drove.

We played the first nine holes, then repaired to the small sandwich shop on the course to get ourselves some lunch.

We discovered, to our dazed shock, that, while we were playing the first nine holes, President Kennedy had been assassinated in Dallas.

I doubt very much if we ever had lunch. Certainly, all desire to play golf was obliterated by the horrible news. So we tossed our clubs in the trunk of Jerry's car and he started to drive us back to Thousand Oaks where my car was parked at his house.

The road back to Fillmore from Elkins Ranch was, to my recollection, only two lanes; it was definitely not a freeway or even a highway.

We had not been driving through this canyon road for more than ten or fifteen minutes when this giant truck appeared behind us.

Its driver didn't honk his horn and God knows he didn't slow down. He tailgated us closely, and the faster Jerry drove to get away from him, the faster he went until we were speeding through this winding canyon road at speeds in excess of sixty miles an hour; maybe seventy.

We were frightened and enraged at the same time. Cursing at the truck driver as though he could hear our rage. But there was no escaping him. He sped closer behind us as though intending to knock us off the road and kill us.

Which I am convinced he would have done if Jerry hadn't spotted a dirt area beside the road and quickly steered into it. At the speed we were going, braking hard caused the car to fishtail, then spin in circles, coming to a hard, jerking halt.

We screamed out curses at the truck driver who went roaring by, unmoved by our fury, our fear and our narrow escape.

We sat in heavy-breathing, sweating silence.

Then it happened.

If I had been with anyone else, what I did would have undoubtedly repelled them. They would likely have said, "How can you *think* that way? What the hell is *wrong* with you? President Kennedy has just been killed by an assassin. A crazy truck driver has just come damn close to killing *you*. And you can do *this?*"

For what I had done was pick up an envelope—a letter of Jerry's—and written something on it. My mind, still traumatized by the assassination and the brush with death, took the occasion to comment, "Hey, that's a good idea for a story." And I wrote down something to the effect of a man being chased by a truck driver. Seven years later, it became my story, then my teleplay, entitled *Duel*.

Jerry asked me what I was writing down and I told him. Which is where the final observation on Jerry now takes place.

First and foremost, Jerry was a writer. He knew exactly how my writer's mind was functioning—because he had the same sort of mind—in spades.

So, despite the double trauma we had just undergone, Jerry understood perfectly the bizarre machinations of a writer's psyche. And it amused us both simultaneously. What kind of monsters *were* we who could experience that double trauma and immediately follow it up by getting an idea for a story?

We both burst into dark laughter.

Such is the writers' mentality we shared.

■

Television
Rarities

The Ghost In the Zone

by Marc Scott Zicree

Recently, while having dinner with my friend Armin Shimerman—who has gained pop-culture immortality on two fronts by playing both Quark on *Deep Space Nine* and the Principal on *Buffy*—I questioned what he looked for in playing a character, what gained him the greatest insight.

"I ask myself, 'What's his secret?' " Armin responded.

Jerry Sohl had one hell of a secret…and I'm the one who discovered it.

It was simply this: the most famous thing he wrote in his long career, the one that millions of folks would instantly recognize, virtually no one knew he wrote.

This is how famous it is, after forty years. I can type one line from it, and odds are it will give you a dazzling memory burst, a cascade of images scorched permanently into your brain.

"My name is Talky Tina, and I'm going to kill you."

You know what it is, of course. Anyone who's ever seen it would. The "Living Doll" episode of *Twilight Zone*, in which evil stepfather Telly Savalas (long before his *Kojak* fame) finds himself pitted against a most vengeful, lethal doll.

A doll, by the way, that was voiced by June Foray, the voice of Rocky the Flying Squirrel and—even more germane—the Chatty Cathy doll that this episode was satirizing.

If you've seen "Living Doll"—even forty years ago, even as a child, *especially* as a child—I need say no more. It is one of the high points of television history, a story unlike any other, a perfect gem.

But if you revisit the episode today, you'll see that the writing credit reads "by Charles Beaumont." Besides Rod Serling, creator of *The Twi-*

light Zone with ninety-two of the total one hundred and fifty-six episodes to his credit, Beaumont was the most prolific of the *Zone* writers—with titles including "The Howling Man" and "Miniature"—and was a major fantasist in TV, books and film. He was also a larger-than-life figure who raced sports cars, hopped planes to Europe at the drop of a hat and numbered among his friends and co-conspirators great writers of the day including Ray Bradbury and Ian Fleming.

Beaumont lived and wrote full-out, every joy, idea and emotion whitehot and immediate, as though he didn't have time to waste, or rest, or stop. As though tomorrow might come for others, but not him.

And in that, he was right.

I began researching my book *The Twilight Zone Companion* in 1977, when I was twenty-two. I already knew the show backwards and forwards, knew all the great episodes by Serling and Beaumont and Richard Matheson and George Clayton Johnson.

I also knew that Matheson and Beaumont and Johnson had been fast friends, part of a large circle of writers with the charismatic Beaumont at its center.

The first person I interviewed for the *Companion* was George and, when I asked who I should talk to next, he said, "Jerry Sohl."

I was surprised. I knew of Sohl from novels like *Costigan's Needle* and his *Star Trek* episode "The Corbomite Maneuver," but I knew of no connection to *The Twilight Zone.*

"Talk to him," George said. "He'll have a story to tell."

When I first sat down with Jerry Sohl, he was initially reluctant to speak, as if he were opening a long-closed vault, summoning up ghosts.

He had good reason to be reluctant—he was a member of the Writer's Guild, and what he was about to confess was a violation of their rules.

But fourteen years after the fact, it was time to shine light into the vault, to put the ghosts to rest…and to lay claim to what was rightfully his.

Sohl told me that in 1963 his friend Charles Beaumont began exhibiting disturbing symptoms that included difficulty with memory and slurred speech. At first, it was ascribed to Beaumont's increasingly heavy drinking (of course, everyone back then drank pretty hard). But as the signs of deterioration increased—including accelerated aging—it was clear the cause was far more dire.

In 1965, Beaumont was diagnosed with presenile dementia, caused by one of two little-known and incurable maladies, either Pick's or

Alzheimer's disease. Only an autopsy would show which. (Curiously, with hindsight, Beaumont's symptoms, notably the rapid aging, didn't fit either diagnosis. Both Matheson and Johnson believe Beaumont—who consumed massive amounts of Bromo Seltzer to alleviate his chronic, blinding headaches—was actually a victim of long-term bromide poisoning.)

But in 1963, no one yet knew precisely what was wrong with "Chuck," especially Beaumont himself. At the height of his career, he could still get writing assignments but was finding it increasingly difficult—ultimately impossible—to write them. And with deadlines for short stories, articles in *Playboy*, movies and TV shows looming, he increasingly turned to others to write them, loyal friends such as William F. Nolan, OCee Ritch, John Tomerlin.

And Jerry Sohl.

Sometimes Beaumont shared credit, such as with John Tomerlin on *Twilight Zone*'s "Number Twelve Looks Just Like You."

But more often than not, his friends were ghost writers on the work.

Sohl told me that his first collaboration with Beaumont was during *Twilight Zone*'s fourth season, on an episode entitled "The New Exhibit." A Hitchcockian murder mystery set in a wax museum (and starring *Psycho*'s Martin Balsam), it was well-suited to Sohl, who had written for the Hitchcock show.

The way they worked together was that Beaumont would pitch the idea to *Zone*'s producers, get the assignment, then he and Sohl would meet in a coffee shop and quickly bang out the storyline. Sohl would then go off and write the script.

He wrote "Living Doll" in a single day.

He also wrote "Queen of the Nile," in which a woman—just like the title character in Beaumont's classic *Zone* episode "Long Live Walter Jameson"—aspires to immortality.

Looking back, Sohl told me, he was a fool to ghost those scripts. He got no pension benefits, no health plan. But on the other hand, he didn't have to deal with the producers, the network, the bullshit. "I just got to write."

And at long last, everyone would know it.

When *The Twilight Zone Companion* came out in 1982, I credited Jerry with the teleplays he had written. And when we held the publication party, he came—in public at last—along with Matheson and George Clayton Johnson, to finally receive accolades for the wonderful work he had done.

Charles Beaumont died in 1967 at the age of thirty-eight, looking like a ninety-year-old man (William Nolan commented that, like his character Walter Jameson, Beaumont "just dusted away"), and Jerry Sohl is gone, now literally a ghost.

But the work lives on, and in the *Companion* and the on-screen material I wrote for the *Twilight Zone* DVDs, the ghost is finally visible and the secret is out.

Jerry Sohl had one last secret, however—or more accurately, two.

It turns out that he wrote two additional scripts for *Twilight Zone*, scripts that were bought but—for various reasons of production and whim—were not made.

"Pattern for Doomsday" and "Who Am I?"

Like many of the classic episodes of *Twilight Zone*, they deal with themes of alienation, of identity, of fear and loss and death.

Two fantastic tales that until now remained sealed in the vault, unknown, forgotten, denied.

A final gift from a ghost.

Enjoy.

■

The Twilight Zone
Pattern For Doomsday

FADE IN:

EXT. WHITE HOUSE—LONG SHOT—DAY—STOCK

A bright summer day in Washington, D.C.

                                                  DISSOLVE THROUGH TO:

INT. WHITE HOUSE—CONFERENCE ROOM—FULL SHOT

A desk is to the right of a projection screen that has been set up, and beribboned GENERAL SINCLAIR, a dignified career soldier in his fifties, stands between them facing the eight people who sit before him: four MEN and four WOMEN. A slide projector has been set up on a small table at the rear of the room; it is attended by a PROJECTIONIST.

                          SINCLAIR
          ...its progress has been closely watched and
          measured for the past month, as is the case
          in all unidentified objects sighted in space...
          May we have the slide, please.

The room darkens. A photograph of a section of the night sky is projected on the screen.

FULL SHOT—PROJECTED SLIDE ON SCREEN

Sinclair movies INTO FRAME with a pointer.

>   SINCLAIR
>   This is a routine photograph taken a little
>   over a month ago—October 3, 1974, to be
>   exact—using the 200-inch Hale telescope
>   on Mount Palomar.
>   (using pointer)
>   This short white line in the star field is the
>   first picture taken of Wanderer.

PAN SHOT—LISTENERS' FACES

Each is different: each listens in his own way. They are: HARVEY
WINTERROTH, 28, wrapt; LILI WONG, 32, wide-eyed but serene;
DR. PHILLIP JEWELL, 50, frowning concentration; DEE CLARK, 34,
adjusting her glasses to see better; REGINA WALSH, 28, a Negro, calm
but attentive; JODY HALLAM, 40, chewing gum absently; FRANCIE
BLAZE, 30, reeking of sex and trying to assimilate the words; and DR.
RUSSELL CONRAD, 35, making notes on a pad.

>   SINCLAIR'S VOICE
>   Next slide…This photograph, taken only
>   three weeks ago, clearly indicated Wanderer
>   was headed for the solar system. Next
>   slide…It was this one that conclusively
>   proved what astronomers were beginning
>   to fear—

REACTION SHOT—GROUP

As Sinclair imparts the grave news.

>   SINCLAIR'S VOICE
>   —that Wanderer was on a collision course
>   with earth.

Gasps, startled looks to one another, growing uneasiness.

MED. SHOT—SINCLAIR AND SCREEN

He taps the desk with the pointer to restore order.

>   SINCLAIR
>   Next slide.

Pictured is a stellar object much like the moon, except it is irregular and jagged.

>   SINCLAIR
>   (con't)
>   This picture was taken two days ago. It
>   allowed astronomers to actually measure
>   Wanderer...It is about two thousand
>   miles in diameter, a little less than the moon.

CLOSE SHOT—HALLAM

Chewing his gum savagely, then with a cynical smile:

>   HALLAM
>   Hey, General—is this really on the level?

SHOT—SINCLAIR

Facing him grimly.

>   SINCLAIR
>   I wish I could report otherwise, but the
>   fact is—may we have the lights, please—

He looks at his watch as the room brightens.

>   SINCLAIR
>   (con't)
>   —the time of the collision is in fifty-three
>   hours, forty minutes.

GROUP—FAVORING HALLAM

Murmurs of concern, restlessness, anxious faces now.

> HALLAM
> Couldn't we blast it with an H-bomb or
> something?

Sinclair ENTERS FRAME to answer.

> SINCLAIR
> Efforts are being made to destroy or deflect
> it, but scientists have told us there isn't much
> hope for success.

> CONRAD
> General, if, as you say, astronomers have
> known about it for some time, why is it the
> public hasn't been alerted?

> SINCLAIR
> Simply to avoid panic. The various heads
> of state have agreed on this.

> HALLAM
> But what about us? Why were we dragged
> here if this thing's going to hit the earth?

> MISS BLAZE
> When they came for me I thought for sure I
> was done for, but now I find out it's the world
> that's going to get it.

> WINTERROTH
> What about it, General? What do you expect
> *us* to do?

A door opens o.s. They look toward it, react with surprise.

                          SINCLAIR
               Mr. President.

Several start to get to their feet.

ANGLE PAST GROUP TO DOOR

The President moves to Sinclair's side; two aides stay at the door.

                          PRESIDENT
               Please remain seated.
                    (to Sinclair)
               Have you finished your briefing?

                          SINCLAIR
               Yes, sir.

The President faces them solemnly.

                          PRESIDENT
               Of the general population, you eight people
               are the only ones who are aware of the
               approaching disaster. I will tell you why.

GROUP

They listen with varying degrees of intensity and anxiety.

                          PRESIDENT'S VOICE
               It has taken ten years for the United States
               to build and perfect its first large,
               nuclear-powered spaceship, the *Varuna I*.
               It was to be used for the exploration of space.

SHOT—PRESIDENT

Choosing his words carefully, effectively.

          PRESIDENT
     That ship now stands on its launching pad in
     New Mexico, ready for its first and last mission:
     that of transporting human life to a new planet
     where it may be safely perpetuated and grow.

GROUP

Absorbed, hanging onto every word. The CAMERA MOVES IN on
Hallam, who has forgotten to chew his gum; his mouth hangs open a little.

          PRESIDENT'S VOICE
     You have been selected to be those people.

Hallam's mouth closes with a snap and a sly smile of satisfaction with his
good fortune blossoms on his face.

          SERLING'S VOICE
     Portrait of a man who has been granted a
     reprieve from certain death…

SHOT—SERLING

          SERLING
     …He is Jody Hallam, gambler, con man,
     a man who lives by his wits and a man who
     wants, above all else, to go on living. At
     the moment the odds look good to Mr.
     Hallam, but he is about to discover that the
     laws of chance are not always the same in
     The Twilight Zone.

                FADE OUT

FADE IN:

INT. WHITE HOUSE—CONFERENCE ROOM—FULL SHOT—DAY

The President holds up a hand to quiet the colonists, who are talking to each other in low voices. They quiet.

> PRESIDENT
> Before I leave you, I want you to know that
> if the people of the United States—in fact,
> the people of the world—were aware that
> in you rests the heritage of all humanity,
> their prayers for success would go with you
> as mine do.

The President steps to them, offers his hand to Dr. Conrad, who gets up, the others rising, too. The CAMERA MOVES IN.

> PRESIDENT
> Good luck to you.

> CONRAD
> Thank you, sir.

> PRESIDENT
> (to all)
> Could I have your names and where you're
> from?

> CONRAD
> I'm Dr. Conrad—Russell Conrad. I'm a
> psychologist from Denver, Colorado.

SHOT—MISS BLAZE

Miss Blaze flashes the President a big smile as he moves to her.

> MISS BLAZE
> Francie Blaze. Los Angeles, California.
> (uncertainly)
> I, uh, entertain.

The President nods, shakes hands, moves on, the CAMERA FOLLOW-
ING to Hallam, who grins.

>   HALLAM
>   Jody Hallam, Mr. President. My home's in
>   Chicago, I guess you'd say. I'm a
>   speculator.

>   MISS WALSH
>   Regina Walsh, Kansas City, Missouri…I'm
>   a singer.

>   MISS CLARK
>   Dee Clark, Spokane, Washington.
>   Bacteriologist.

>   JEWELL
>   (harshly)
>   Phillip Jewell, New York City.
>   (blurting it out)
>   Mr. President, I'm not sure I approve of all
>   this. I—

>   PRESIDENT
>   You're *Dr.* Jewell?

>   JEWELL
>   Yes.

>   PRESIDENT
>   I've read many of your books on philosophy.

>   JEWELL
>   Thank you. But about what's happening
>   here—

>   PRESIDENT
>   General Sinclair will discuss it with you, Doctor.

Jewell fumes silently as the President moves on.

> MISS WONG
> Lili Wong, San Francisco. I'm an artist.

> WINTERROTH
> (tightly)
> Harvey Winterroth, Traverse City, Michigan.
> Auto mechanic.

ALL

As the President steps back.

> PRESIDENT
> Believe me, the hopes and aspirations of the
> world go with you all…Goodbye.

He turns, moves to his aides, one of whom opens the door. They go out.
CAMERA MOVES IN on the group. Hallam has resumed chewing his
gum excitedly, Miss Walsh dabs at her eyes, Miss Blaze gets out a compact
and proceeds to powder her face, Conrad lights a cigarette, and Winterroth
stares at the door the President has just gone through.

> WINTERROTH
> I never thought I'd ever get to see the President,
> but there I was shaking his hand and talking
> to him!

MED. SHOT—JEWELL

Frowning, getting to his feet.

> JEWELL
> (combatively)
> General, I demand to know just how eight
> people can be selected as representative of the
> human race.

Sinclair moves INTO FRAME to answer him.

> SINCLAIR
> It was not the whim of one man, Doctor. It
> was a matter of electronic selectivity. A computer
> was programmed with all the prerequisites—
> ecological, physiological and psychological.

> JEWELL
> Who did the programming?

> SINCLAIR
> A large staff of experts.

> JEWELL
> Based on what requirements?

> SINCLAIR
> Intelligence for one thing. Fertility for another.
> That is why you had that examination.

> JEWELL
> How many people were considered?

> SINCLAIR
> The entire population, Doctor.

Winterroth ENTERS FRAME.

> WINTERROTH
> General, how come the President isn't going
> along? I should think—

> SINCLAIR
> He is married, which was one of the
> disqualifying factors.
> (to all)
> For those of you who are interested, the stringent

requirements, which even included cellular structures and the proper genes, are listed in a brochure I have here.

He moves off for the desk, some of the others following.

TWO SHOT—HALLAM AND BLAZE

They are seated, Hallam still wearing a dazed smile as a result of his good fortune, Miss Blaze applying lip rouge.

> HALLAM
> You know something? I've been lucky all my life. When other kids got the measles, me, I didn't get it.

> MISS BLAZE
> Not me. I always got everything.

> HALLAM
> Oh, I wasn't one hundred percent lucky, but when I lost it was always because somebody else was doing the dealing.
> (chuckles)
> Man, I tell you I sure wised up in a hurry. I've been handling the deal ever since.

> MISS BLAZE
> I thought you looked like a sharpie. I can spot one a mile away.

> HALLAM
> (affronted)
> Hey now, look, baby, don't get me wrong. I don't do anything crooked.

> MISS BLAZE
> I know. You just help the cards along a little.

> HALLAM
> The suckers get greedy, that's all. So they
> overplay, they get restless. Is that my fault?
> Can I help it if they want to make it all in one
> night?
> (beat)
> Look, I ask you, who's the smart one, me
> or them?

> MISS BLAZE
> You heard what the general said about brains.
> We'll see how you make out where we're
> going.

> HALLAM
> (fiercely)
> Listen: Jody Hallam *always* makes out. You
> remember that.

> MISS BLAZE
> Just don't expect any favors from me.

> HALLAM
> Ha! Who needs it?

He gets up disgustedly.

ANGLE PAST GROUP IN F.G.

and TOWARD Hallam as he gets up to join them, followed by Miss
Blaze, CAMERA TIGHTENING the SHOT. Sinclair has the brochure
on the desk before him.

> SINCLAIR
> ...after that it was all put on a memory drum,
> it was collated, there was a small tabulator
> run—

JEWELL
So we have a machine to blame.

CONRAD
Blame? You should be happy the machine
picked you!

JEWELL
Should I? Then why do I feel as if I'm
deserting humanity in its hour of need?

They are all silent for a moment.

MISS WALSH
General, when will the *Varuna* leave earth?

SINCLAIR
(looking at watch)
It less than twenty-four hours. You will be
flown there.

MISS CLARK
What about food on the ship?

SINCLAIR
There will be breads, soups, meats—even
ice cream. Enough for a lifetime, if necessary.
You won't be hungry.

WINTERROTH
How can they get that much food on one ship?

SINCLAIR
It will be made from continuously growing tanks of
chlorella, a fast-growing single-celled plant.

WINTERROTH
A plant!

> MISS CLARK
> It isn't unpalatable.

ANOTHER ANGLE—FAVORING HALLAM

He stuffs another piece of gum in his mouth.

> HALLAM
> Hey General, what planet are we supposed
> to be landing on?

> SINCLAIR
> Mars, Venus, if they're habitable.

> HALLAM
> How about if they're not?

> SINCLAIR
> The ship's nuclear power pack could take
> you all the way to Alpha Centauri, if necessary.
> That's the nearest star system with planets.

TWO SHOT—HALLAM AND MISS BLAZE

She gets caught up in the possibilities.

> MISS BLAZE
> Maybe there'll be people there—humans
> like us. I read a story once—

> HALLAM
> You could go into your dance, knock their
> eyes out.

> MISS BLAZE
> (suddenly sobering)
> Who's kidding who? I was never a very
> good dancer. I was never very good at

anything, really, but I got along because
there were people who would—pay for it.
            (beat; with resolve)
No. I'll start over. I'll be *me* this time. I'll
be what *I* want to be, not what *they* want
me to be.

                    HALLAM
            I wouldn't count on it, baby.

MED. SHOT—SINCLAIR

Miss Wong joins him.

                    MISS WONG
            I have a question…Who's going to take us
            to Mars or wherever we're going?

                    SINCLAIR
            There is a crew of two. Captain Gerald Vickers
            will be in charge. The crewman is Lt. Robert
            McKenna. You will meet them when we—

A phone RINGS. Sinclair turns to it.

                    SINCLAIR
                    (con't)
            Excuse me.

ANGLE TO DESK

Sinclair moves to it, picks up the phone.

                    SINCLAIR
            Sinclair…Yes…Right away.
                    (puts phone down)
            A limousine is ready to take you to the
            airport.

The colonists cluster around him.

> CONRAD
> No calls, I suppose…to say goodbye
> to someone, I mean.

> SINCLAIR
> I'm sorry, Doctor, no calls…Now, if you
> will all come with me, please.

He starts off. They follow.

DISSOLVE

EXT. SHOT—ARMY JET TRANSPORT IN FLIGHT—STOCK

It moves with unerring swiftness above the clouds.

DISSOLVE THROUGH TO:

EXT. SPACEPORT—FULL SHOT—DAY

The *Varuna I* stands in the far b.g. In the f.g. is a heavy wire fence and gate and TWO armed GUARDS in uniform. Beyond them is the large operations building. The o.s. SOUND of an automobile engine is HEARD. It moves INTO FRAME and the gate is opened by one of the guards, who salutes as the limousine moves by, the gate closing behind it. CAPTAIN GERALD VICKERS, 35, and LIEUTENANT JOHN MCKENNA, 25, move from the operations building toward the car.

ANGLE TO CAR

The colonists and Sinclair get out, the DRIVER moving the car off. They are joined by Vickers and McKenna, who salute. Sinclair returns it, turns to the colonists.

> SINCLAIR
> This is your pilot, Captain Vickers, and his
> assistant, Lt. McKenna…Mr. Hallam, Miss
> Walsh, Miss Wong, Miss Blaze, Dr. Conrad,
> Miss Clark, Dr. Jewell, Mr. Winterroth.

There are handshakes. Hallam gravitates to the f.g., Miss Walsh following. He looks o.s., then at her.

> HALLAM
> Well, there she is. Take a good look. That
> ship's going to be home for a long time.

> MISS WALSH
> It's a beautiful ship.

Miss Blaze joins them. In the b.g. Vickers looks toward her.

> MISS BLAZE
> It looks so small!

Vickers smiles, moves to her, Conrad following.

> VICKERS
> It's not small at all, Miss Blaze. Just enough
> room for eight people.

Conrad darts Vickers a sharp look.

MED. SHOT—SINCLAIR

Surrounded by other colonists, approached by another OFFICER, who salutes.

> OFFICER
> General, a Priority A communication from
> Washington.

Sinclair salutes perfunctorily, takes the message, the officer saluting, moving off as Sinclair reads, his face darkening. He looks around at the colonists.

> SINCLAIR
> You might as well know that the armed
> missiles three countries sent up to intercept
> Wanderer have exploded on its surface.
> (beat)
> There was no appreciable deviation from
> its established course.

Jewell moves to the forefront, frowning.

> JEWELL
> That means there is no last great hope for
> earth.

> SINCLAIR
> I would say, Doctor, that your group is
> that hope.

TWO SHOT—CONRAD AND VICKERS

Something bothers Conrad; he looks at Vickers.

> CONRAD
> Captain Vickers—something you said a
> moment ago—

> VICKERS
> What is it, Doctor?

> CONRAD
> You said there was room for only eight
> people aboard the ship…Does that include
> you and Lt. McKenna?

Vickers glances at Sinclair o.s.

SHOT—SINCLAIR

He has heard the exchange, looks around.

> SINCLAIR
> Let me have your attention....I have an
> announcement to make. If you will follow
> me, please.

He turns away.

GROUP

Turning to follow him uneasily, glancing at each other and toward the ship.

INT. OPERATIONS BUILDING—ANGLE DOWN HALLWAY

Sinclair leads the group TOWARD CAMERA, which FOLLOWS HIM to a door labeled BRIEFING ROOM. He opens the door; the others start in. They look at him; his face is blank.

INT. BRIEFING ROOM—FULL SHOT

The usual furnishings, a blackboard, chairs, telephone, desk, etc. Through the windows we can see the *Varuna I* on her pad. Vickers, Sinclair and McKenna move to the front of the room.

ANGLE TO SINCLAIR

The colonists move toward the chairs but do not sit, but look to Sinclair uneasily.

> SINCLAIR
> Sit down, please.

They all sit, McKenna and Vickers taking chairs behind the desk. They become quiet.

> SINCLAIR
> (con't)
> When this group was organized by Presidential order, two reserves were included.

PAN SHOT—COLONISTS

They listen, fearing the worst.

> SINCLAIR'S VOICE
> The reason for this was that there was no way of telling if you were all alive and well, or even if you could be found after being chosen. There was also the risk of accident. The reserves were simply a preparation for a contingency that did not occur.

SHOT—JEWELL

Forthright, direct.

> JEWELL
> Who are the reserves?

SHOT—SINCLAIR

> SINCLAIR
> They were not specified.

SHOT—JEWELL

> JEWELL
> Then I volunteer to stay behind.

SHOT—HALLAM

He wets his lips nervously.

> SINCLAIR'S VOICE
> I cannot accept your offer, Doctor.

SHOT—MISS WONG

> MISS WONG
> I will give up my place…I have friends who
> will die…

Turning from Miss Wong o.s. to Sinclair o.s.

> SINCLAIR'S VOICE
> I cannot accept your offer either, Miss Wong.

Hallam's hopes fade a little.

> SINCLAIR'S VOICE
> (con't)
> It was provided in a case like this that the
> matter be decided by chance.

Hallam's face brightens. He springs to his feet, draws a deck of cards out
of his pocket.

> HALLAM
> I'll handle this, General. It so happens I
> have a deck of cards with me.
> (starting off)
> The high cards go.

SHOT—MISS BLAZE

> MISS BLAZE
> (scornfully)
> Don't make me laugh.

ANGLE TO DESK

As Hallam walks to the desk, taking the cards out of their package; he reeks of confidence.

> HALLAM
> It's the only fair way, Aces and Kings
> sure winners.

> SINCLAIR
> Mr. Hallam...

> HALLAM
> (shuffling)
> Deuces and treys on the losing end...
> Understand?
> (spreading them)
> I'll lay them out here and you can come
> up and—

Sinclair moves to him, slaps his hand down on the cards angrily.

> SINCLAIR
> We are *not* using cards, Mr. Hallam.
> We're using straws.

Hallam is completely unperturbed, smiles and takes out a paper book of matches.

> HALLAM
> As you say, General...Makes it simpler
> yet. I have a book of matches here. You
> can see I'm tearing them out one by one.
> I'll make two short ones.

> SINCLAIR
> Sit down, Mr. Hallam.

> HALLAM
> (hurt)

No matches either? Well…

                SINCLAIR
          I said sit down.
                (as Hallam leaves)
          Captain Vickers has already prepared the
          straws…Captain?

Vickers opens a drawer, takes out a book from which protude eight identical slivers of wood. He gets to his feet.

ANGLE TO MISS BLAZE

Vickers moves to her first.

                VICKERS
          Miss Blaze.

She wets her lips, takes one, looks at it, lets out her breath with relief.

SHOT—CONRAD

He takes one, looks at it, his face registering nothing.

SHOT—JEWELL

He grabs one, doesn't look at it.

SHOT—MISS WONG

She frowns, hesitates, then takes one.

SHOT—WINTERROTH

He reaches out a trembling hand.

INSERT—BOOK

Winterroth's hand wavers, he plucks one.

BACK TO WINTERROTH

He looks at his choice, closes his eyes in relief.

TWO SHOT—MISS CLARK AND MISS WALSH

Miss Clark picks one, looks at it, looks around. There are two left. Miss Walsh takes one, looks at it.

SHOT—HALLAM

Forced to take the last straw, looks at it with dismay.

CLOSE-UP—THE STRAW IN HIS HAND

A short one.

GROUP—INCLUDING SINCLAIR

They eye each other for telltale signs.

> SINCLAIR
> Hold up your straws.
> (they do; beat)
> Miss Clark and Mr. Hallam will not be
> going with us.

SHOT—HALLAM

Jumping to his feet, his face full of desperation.

> HALLAM
> It wasn't fair! I didn't have a choice!

> SINCLAIR'S VOICE
> Sit down, Mr. Hallam. Someone had to be last.

The CAMERA MOVES IN as Hallam sinks to his seat in despair.

FADE OUT

FADE IN:

INT. OPERATIONS BUILDING—HALLWAY—DAY

Hallam and Miss Clark sit on a bench beside the briefing room door. He chews his gum aggressively; she is resigned.

> HALLAM
> I don't see why you're so anxious to go
> home. One of them in there could have a
> heart attack or something.

> MISS CLARK
> And then what would we do—draw straws
> again to see which of us goes?

> HALLAM
> Sure. Why not?
> (beat)
> Listen, if they had let me do it my
> way, you think I'd be sitting
> out here?

CLOSER—HALLAM AND MISS CLARK

She looks at him as if he were a hideous biological specimen.

> MISS CLARK
> You mean you'd have—fixed the cards?

> HALLAM
> Honey, when your life depends on it, you
> *do* something.

>   MISS CLARK
> Even if it means pain or misfortune for others?
>   (beat)
> I would say, Mr. Hallam, that you have not
> advanced very far from your one-celled
> progenitors.

>   HALLAM
> Hey, what's that—some kind of wisecrack?

She gets up, eyes him disdainfully.

>   MISS CLARK
> I've seen your kind on slides under microscopes,
> that is what I mean.

She turns, starts away.

ANGLE TO WINDOW

She reaches it, looks out.

>   MISS CLARK
> Bacteria do not have consciences either.

Hallam joins her.

>   HALLAM
> But the way they did it—how do you know
> that Vickers didn't run it the way he wanted?

>   MISS CLARK
> It was fair, and we lost.
>   (beat)
> As for myself, I am ready to go home when
> they let me go.

                    HALLAM
                  (curled lip)
          Yeah, go ahead, give up. That's what you
          learned in your school. But let me tell you
          something: that's not what I learned in mine.

A door opens o.s. They turn to it. Instantly Hallam's manner changes to
one of optimistic expansiveness.

ANGLE ON DOOR

As Sinclair, Vickers, McKenna and the six colonists emerge, talking ad-lib.
Sinclair moves to the f.g. with Vickers. Hallam ENTERS FRAME. He smiles.

                    HALLAM
          General…

Sinclair turns to him.

                    HALLAM
                  (con't)
          General, I'm sorry I blew up before, but—
          well, it was a pretty hard thing to take, and
          it hit me pretty hard.

Sinclair puts a hand on his shoulder.

                    SINCLAIR
          Believe me, I understand, Mr. Hallam.

                    HALLAM
          I suppose everything's all set and ready
          to go?

                    SINCLAIR
                  (looks at watch)
          They've had their final instructions. The ship
          lifts off in about seventy-two minutes.

> HALLAM
> Gee, that's swell, I mean that everything's
> worked out, no hitches…Look, do you
> think it would be okay if I saw them to the
> ship? You know, wish everybody bon voyage
> and all that?

> SINCLAIR
> Of course you can.

Sinclair moves off with Vickers. Miss Blaze joins Hallam.

> MISS BLAZE
> That's not like you, Mr. Hallam, wishing
> anybody but yourself good luck. Why the
> change of heart?

> HALLAM
> You can't win 'em all. You ought to know
> that.

> MISS BLAZE
> That's not what you told me before.

> HALLAM
> That's what I'm telling you now.

> SINCLAIR'S VOICE
> Miss Blaze…

ANGLE PAST GROUP IN F.G.

and TOWARD Miss Blaze and Hallam.

> SINCLAIR
> We're going out to the ship.
> (turning)
> Follow me, everyone.

EXT. OPERATIONS BUILDING—CLOSE ON DOOR

An armed guard stands at the door, which opens. Sinclair comes out, followed by Vickers, McKenna, and the colonists, Hallam being the last. He would follow the others, who move off. The guard steps in his way. Hallam looks at him with irritation.

> HALLAM
> General Sinclair said I could say goodbye
> to them in the ship.

The guard turns to Sinclair o.s.

ANGLE TO GROUP—*VARUNA I* IN B.G.

They wait as two other guards move to join them. Sinclair looks toward the o.s. guard.

> SINCLAIR
> It's all right.

BACK TO GUARD AND HALLAM

The guard lets him go.

GROUP—STARTING OFF ACROSS CONCRETE APRON

One armed guard precedes Sinclair; everyone else follows in single file, the second guard bringing up the rear after Hallam.

ANGLE TO BASE OF SHIP—CLOSE ON LADDER

They move INTO FRAME, Sinclair moving to the ladder, but the others turn to look off, occupied with thoughts.

SHOT—MISS BLAZE

Her eyes begin to wet with tears.

                    MISS BLAZE
          You know, it was a rat race, but I think I'm
          going to miss it.

SHOT—WINTERROTH

Looking up at the sky.

                    WINTERROTH
          The sky's like this over Traverse City. There's
          a place there I used to fish...I'm gonna miss
          that.

TWO SHOT—JEWELL AND HALLAM

Hallam is tense, watches the others.

                    JEWELL
          It just doesn't seem possible...to think that
          all this is going to change...

                    SINCLAIR'S VOICE
          We'd better get aboard.

They turn toward the ladder.

INT. SPACESHIP—ANGLE DOWN CORRIDOR TO EXIT

They climb through into the corridor, Sinclair first, then a guard, followed by Vickers, McKenna and the others.

INT. CONTROL ROOM—FULL SHOT

Sinclair comes in with Vickers and McKenna, moves into the f.g. as the others enter the room. Sinclair looks at his watch.

                    SINCLAIR
          How much time do we have?

> VICKERS
> (glancing at watch)
> Eight minutes. We'll check the engines.

ANGLE TOWARD DOOR

The colonists move about, looking the room over curiously as Vickers and McKenna go through a door at the side of the control console.

SHOT—MISS BLAZE

Seeing the close quarters.

> MISS BLAZE
> I feel like a sardine already.

> SINCLAIR'S VOICE
> Let me have your attention...We have only
> a few minutes.

GROUP

It moves toward Sinclair, but Hallam takes a few steps to be near a guard, CAMERA FOLLOWING.

SHOT—SINCLAIR

He looks at them all gravely.

> SINCLAIR
> The President has asked me to extend his
> blessings and his hopes for a safe journey....

PAN SHOT—COLONISTS' FACES

Sober, reflecting the solemnity of the moment.

                    SINCLAIR'S VOICE
          ...Also he wanted me to remind you
          of the hardships that must be before you,
          and that in all the years to come you
          must not lose sight of your purpose, your
          goal...

TWO SHOT—HALLAM AND GUARD

Halam wets his lips, moves closer to the guard, who is absorbed in Sinclair's
remarks.

                    SINCLAIR'S VOICE
          ...for in each of you are the seeds of all the
          generations that will surely come...It will be
          your trust to nurture the first generation...

MED. SHOT—JEWELL

He listens attentively, a little separated from the others.

                    SINCLAIR'S VOICE
          ...for upon it man will be built anew after we
          are all forgot—

A SHOT rings out. Jewell falls. There are CRIES of alarm.

                                                    CUT TO:

TWO SHOT—SINCLAIR AND GUARD

They whirl, the guard reaching for his gun.

                    HALLAM'S VOICE
          Hold it!

ANGLE TO HALLAM

The guard from whom he took the pistol moves away as Hallam gestures with the gun. When the guard is far enough away, Hallam turns victoriously to Sinclair o.s.

> HALLAM
> Now, General, since Dr. Jewell won't be making
> the trip, as his reserve, I'm electing myself to take
> his place. He didn't want to go anyway, remember?

SHOT—SINCLAIR

Recovering from his shock.

> SINCLAIR
> Do you think these people would have you
> after what you've done?

MED. SHOT—HALLAM

He chews his gum joyously.

> HALLAM
> We're through with pretty speeches.
> (gestures with gun)
> General, you and your two guards get out
> of here, and take the doctor with you.

FULL SHOT

Hallam moves back to sit on the console by the other door. Nobody moves.

> HALLAM
> Did you hear what I said?

The guards took to Sinclair.

> SINCLAIR
> Do as he says.

MED. SHOT—HALLAM

He chuckles.

> HALLAM
> That's better.
> (looks o.s.)
> Well, Miss Blaze?

SHOT—MISS BLAZE

She looks at him hatefully.

> MISS BLAZE
> What do we do now, start calling you Little
> Caeser?

SHOT—CONRAD

Almost clinical.

> CONRAD
> Just what do you expect to gain by this—
> this murder?

MED. SHOT—HALLAM

Enjoying himself, sitting on the console, holding the gun easily, almost lazily.

> HALLAM
> Life, my friend…Oh, maybe you think you'll
> punish me, but you won't. You wouldn't
> hurt one of the eight surviving human beings.
> You're going to need me.
> (now to Miss Blaze)
> And as for you, Miss Blaze, a man gambles,
> he loses a hand here and there, but the game

isn't over until the last card's been played.
You remember that.

The door behind Hallam suddenly opens and Vickers and McKenna start through. Hallam wrenches around to face them, but Vickers, seeing in a flash what has happened, attacks him. McKenna would help, but the gun moves wildly. As it is pointed toward the control panel—

SHOT—INSTRUMENT PANEL

The gun FIRES, the bullet penetrating one of the dials. There is a brief, violent sputtering of electrical flashes; smoke eddies out into the room.

TWO SHOT—HALLAM AND VICKERS

Again McKenna tries to intervene, but Hallam suddenly wrenches free, quickly brings the gun to bear on Vickers. There is a SHOT. Hallam twists, falls to his knees, tries to raise the gun, falls heavily to the floor, the gun clattering away across the floor.

MED. TWO SHOT—GUARD AND JEWELL

The second guard stands with his gun still leveled. At his side Dr. Jewell is trying to get up, grimacing, holding his shoulder. O.s. there is pandemonium. Sinclair ENTERS FRAME.

> SINCLAIR
> (helping Jewell)
> Are you all right?

> JEWELL
> It's my shoulder.

> VICKERS' VOICE
> General!

The guard has put away his gun, takes Jewell from Sinclair.

ANGLE TO CONSOLE

Vickers points to the damaged dial from which some smoke still emerges, the colonists gathering around as Sinclair ENTERS FRAME.

> VICKERS
> We won't be leaving, General.

> SINCLAIR
> Can't that be repaired?

> VICKERS
> Not the telemetry system. There is no
> replacement available. It would take days
> to merely assess the damage.

Sinclair turns away to look gravely at the faces of the stunned colonists.

> SINCLAIR
> I wish I knew what to say to you…

They turn to look o.s.

ANGLE PAST HALLAM'S BODY IN F.G.

and SHOOTING UP to the colonists who look at it.

> CONRAD
> Just because he wasn't going…

> MISS BLAZE
> He was right…He said he was lucky. Now
> he won't have to face what's coming.

An o.s. siren is faintly HEARD.

EXT. APRON—HIGH ANGLE SHOT—SHOOTING DOWN

An army vehicle rushes toward the ship, its siren going. It skids to a stop. An OFFICER jumps out, looks up, shouts:

> OFFICER
> General Sinclair!

EXT. SHIP—ANGLE TO EXIT

Sinclair appears there, looking down. Others join him.

INT. SHIP—ANGLE TO EXIT

The officer reaches the exit, enters the ship. His demeanor is that of a man with glad tidings.

> OFFICER
> This just came in, sir.

He hands Sinclair a message, hardly able to conceal his exuberance.

SHOT—SINCLAIR

He reads eagerly, his face brightening. He looks up.

> SINCLAIR
> I am happy to be able to tell you the danger
> is past. The President informs me that the
> gravitational forces encountered by Wanderer
> in the solar system have torn it apart.

SHOT—WINTERROTH

Incredulous.

> WINTERROTH
> You mean it's not gonna hit the earth?

SHOT—SINCLAIR

> SINCLAIR
> (refers to message)
> It has been torn into five pieces. All of them
> will miss us by many thousands of miles.

SHOT DOWN CORRIDOR

There is instant jubilation. The would-be colonists slap each other on the back, shake hands—and Sinclair smiles for the first time.

TWO SHOT—MISS BLAZE AND VICKERS

In the melee they suddenly find themselves face to face. They pause for a moment, looking at each other, probing with their eyes, then he kisses her soundly, they part, he takes her hand as if to lead her off the ship.

> MISS BLAZE
> Wait a minute.

She pulls him the other way.

INT. CONTROL ROOM—ANGLE PAST HALLAM'S BODY IN F.G.

and SHOOTING UP toward the door. Miss Blaze appears there with Vickers behind her. She waves to the body.

> MISS BLAZE
> So long, sucker.

They go, CAMERA PANNING DOWN to HOLD on the body.

> SERLING'S VOICE
> Earth was doomed, everyone was marked
> for death…but when the danger was past,
> Jody Hallam, professional gambler, who

played a desperate last card in an effort to
stay alive, was, ironically, the only man among
the billions on earth who died as a direct result
of it.

FADE OUT

THE END

The Twilight Zone
Who Am I?

FADE IN:

EXT. APARTMENT HOUSE—FULL SHOT—DAY

A deluxe complex nicely landscaped, with flower beds and a fountain in the entrance gardens. Modernistic, expensive looking.

INT. APARTMENT BEDROOM—CLOSE ON CLOCK

It reads: 7:30. It RINGS. A hand ENTERS FRAME, fumbles with it, turns it off, CAMERA DRAWING BACK to show GLENN HOLBROOK in bed, his displeasure at the clock visible as he glares at it just this side of sleep. He is a good-looking young man, clean-cut and at the moment struggling with that part of himself that knows he must awaken. He sinks back to his pillow with a sigh, closes his eyes.

TWO SHOT—GLENN AND CLAIRE

Glenn smiles as he would sink back into blissful sleep. At his side, CLAIRE HOLBROOK, his pretty wife, lifts her arm, jabs at him with her elbow without opening her eyes or giving evidence or being awake. Glenn's eyes open languorously, then the lids come down slowly—until she jabs him again. He sighs awake.

GLENN
All right, all right.

He reaches for her elbow, lifts it, looks at it.

>   GLENN
>   (con't)
>   Your elbow gets sharper every morning.

He lets it drop, moves to sit up.

ANOTHER ANGLE—FAVORING GLENN

He lifts his legs over the side of the bed, yawns sleepily, slips into his slippers, reaches for his robe. He sits staring vacantly ahead until Claire's elbow jabs him again. He grimaces, turns to her.

>   GLENN
>   You keep doing that, you'll get a callus.

Claire does not move. Glenn gets to his feet, tightening his robe belt.

ANGLE TO WINDOW

Glenn moving to it, opening it, looking out. His face is full of good humor. He takes a deep breath, bends over, touches his toes several times, does a deep-knee bend, grunts, shakes his head, straightens, massaging his knee. He turns toward the bed, starts off.

FULL SHOT—BEDROOM

Glenn moving from the window to the bed, rocking the bed with his hand when he reaches it. Claire stirs.

>   CLAIRE
>   (sleepily)
>   Stop it!

>   GLENN
>   It's an earthquake. Flee for your life.

She lashes out at him, Glenn nimbly stepping aside with a laugh. He starts off.

INT. BATHROOM—FULL SHOT

Glenn coming in, turning on the light. The CAMERA is so situated we do not see his reflection in the mirror as, with one hand, he massages his scalp, opens a drawer, gets out his shaving equipment.

OVER-SHOULDER SHOT—GLENN

We see him preparing to shave. CAMERA is placed so we cannot see his reflection in the mirror; Glenn is so absorbed with his preparations and with the song he is HUMMING, that he does not look in the mirror. In this way, we become familiar with the back of his head. When he is ready to begin shaving, the CAMERA MOVES so that we see his reflection at the same time he does. We discover with him that the face does not belong to him. His reaction is one of extreme shock.

CLOSE SHOT—GLENN

Staring at his mirror image with disbelief and growing horror. His mouth drops open, his eyes widen. There is no similarity between this face and the face of Glenn Holbrook we saw in the opening scenes.

OVER-SHOULDER SHOT—GLENN

As he shakes his head in bewilderment as he continues to look at the mirror image. He raises a hand to feel the beard stubble. There is a small scar on his cheek. He runs a finger down this, watching himself in wonderment. He withdraws his hand, closes his eyes tightly, grimacing, then opens them wide, leans toward the mirror. The stranger looks back at him with the same expression.

ANOTHER ANGLE

Glenn frantically opening drawers until he finds a small portable shaving mirror. He holds this up to look into it.

ANGLE PAST REAR OF MIRROR IN F.G.

and TOWARD the new Glenn, staring at himself. Slowly he lowers the mirror, stares off into space, trying to make sense out of what he has seen. Then:

> GLENN
> (strained)
> Claire…

He turns away.

INT. BEDROOM—ANGLE TO BED

Glenn coming out, moving to the bed, shaking it violently.

> GLENN
> Claire!

> CLAIRE
> (stirring)
> I'll get up…promise.

Glenn turns from the bed, frantically moves off.

ANGLE TO DRESSER

Glenn moving to it, looking at his reflection in the mirror. The new Glenn stares back. He feels of his face again, then turns slowly, looks toward the bed.

> GLENN
> (in agony)
> Claire…

ANGLE TO BED

Claire moving to a sitting position, yawning, stretching, looking toward the brightness at the window, squinting.

                    CLAIRE
        It's going to be hot again today.

Glenn ENTERS FRAME to stare down at her agitatedly.

                    GLENN
        Claire, look at me!

CLOSE ON CLAIRE

Turning away from the window to look at him curiously.

                    CLAIRE
        Hmm?

CLOSE ON GLENN

Not knowing what to expect.

                    GLENN
        What do you see?

TWO SHOT—CLAIRE AND GLENN

She frowns in puzzlement.

                    CLAIRE
        Am I supposed to see something?

                    GLENN
        Me!—No, it's not me! I've changed! I'm
        different!

                    CLAIRE
        Now that you mention it, you *are* different.

CAMERA MOVES IN as he sits beside her on the bed.

                    GLENN
                (touching his face)
        This scar, for instance. See?

                    CLAIRE
                (looking at it)
        It looks the same to me.

                    GLENN
        No, it's my face—it's different.

                    CLAIRE
        Of course it is, darling. It's the face
        of an upset man, and that's not like
        you at all.

                    GLENN
                (backing away)
        But Claire—! This face—it's—
        not mine!

LONG SHOT TO BED

Glenn getting up, moving toward CAMERA, which TURNS to look
into the dresser mirror as Glenn approaches to look at himself again, feeling of his face, Claire getting out of bed to come to stand beside him,
staring at him in amazement.

                    SERLING'S VOICE
        Witness one Glenn Holbrook, a man long
        accustomed to his own face, now understandably
        confused by what he sees in the mirror.

SHOT—SERLING

                    SERLING
        Who is this stranger who stares back at
        him? Mr. Holbrook will never know, for

a basic rule of cause and effect has been
suddenly changed; it changed the moment
he entered The Twilight Zone.

FADE OUT

FADE IN:

INT. BEDROOM—FULL SHOT—DAY

Claire is sitting on the edge of the bed watching Glenn walk back and
forth before her agitatedly. Her eyes betray her concern.

> GLENN
> How could it happen? How can a man
> go to bed one person and wake up
> another person?

> CLAIRE
> But you're not a different person!

He stops to face her.

> GLENN
> How can you say that?
> (approaching her)
> Take a good look and then tell me I'm
> the same Glenn Holbrook.

TWO SHOT—CLAIRE AND GLENN

Glenn glowering down at her, Claire on the verge of tears.

> CLAIRE
> Darling, I *know* you.

> GLENN
> Not as well as *I* know me. I know the
> face I grew up with.

> CLAIRE
> You're the same man I married.

> GLENN
> Scar and all?

> CLAIRE
> Don't you remember? You were awfully
> touchy about that scar. You were—
> defensive. You always fancied people
> were looking at it.

The CAMERA MOVES IN as he sits beside her, takes her hand.

> GLENN
> Claire, I swear to you I never had a scar
> before this morning.

> CLAIRE
> That's impossible.

> GLENN
> Why?

> CLAIRE
> Because it simply isn't true. You've always
> been sensitive about it. It was years
> before you told me how it happened.

> GLENN
> And how did it?

> CLAIRE
> You don't remember?

> GLENN
> Would I be asking you if I remembered?

> CLAIRE
> (looking away)
> You were a child…You and some other
> boys were playing at war, throwing things
> …A sharp stone hit you, gashing your
> cheek. It required seven stitches. Your
> mother was hysterical about it.
> (beat; looks back)
> I've always thought she was responsible
> for your attitude toward it.

Glenn makes a sour face, gets to his feet, CAMERA MOVING IN on his face. Slowly:

> GLENN
> No…No. It never happened. I never
> played at war with anybody as a kid.

He looks o.s., starts off.

ANGLE TO DRESSER MIRROR

Glenn moving toward it, looking at himself. Claire is in the b.g. in the mirror watching him.

> GLENN
> These eyes are brown. My eyes are
> supposed to be blue. The planes of
> my face—the hair line—the lips…
> None of it is mine.

> CLAIRE
> Please, Glenn.

He turns.

ANGLE TO CLAIRE

Sitting uneasily on the bed.

> CLAIRE
> Don't talk like that. It—frightens me.

Glenn ENTERS FRAME.

> GLENN
> If it frightens you, then think of what
> it's doing to me. I had a face—I like
> to think it was a good-looking face—

He stops, arrested by a thought. Then:

> GLENN
> (con't)
> Where's the snapshot album?

He moves off.

ANGLE TO CLOSET

Glenn moving to it, opening the door, shoving things around on the shelf.

> GLENN
> Pictures don't lie.

He moves boxes and hats around, finds what he wants, a photo album, brings it down.

> GLENN
> (con't)
> Now we'll see.

He opens it, finds the picture he wants, looks to Claire o.s. triumphantly, starts for her.

GLENN
(con't)
Take a look at this.

ANGLE TO BED

Glenn reaching it with the album, handing it to her, pointing to a picture.

GLENN
Now tell me this isn't me.

OVER-SHOULDER SHOT—CLAIRE

We see the picture in the album with her. It is a photograph of the Glenn Holbrook we saw initially.

GLENN'S VOICE
Well?

TWO SHOT—CLAIRE AND GLENN

Claire deeply troubled as she looks up to him.

CLAIRE
It's you.

GLENN
(victoriously)
Of course it's me. That's what I've
been telling you.

CLAIRE
But it's the same, Glenn, the same as
you are now. You haven't changed.

Glenn stands dumbfounded for a long moment, then reaches down, takes the photo album in one hand, Claire's arm in the other, forcing her to rise and go with him.

ANGLE TO MIRROR

They reach it. Glenn holds up the photograph so that it and his face show in the mirror. Claire looks at the picture and at his face in the mirror.

> GLENN
> Now tell me they're the same. See?
> The eyes are different—wider apart.
> The lips are fuller. The jaw…

> CLAIRE
> (beside herself)
> They're the same. I swear it.

Glenn lets the photo album slowly sink to the dresser top, the CAMERA MOVING IN. There is agony in his eyes. Suddenly Claire is in his arms.

> CLAIRE
> Glenn, stop it! I don't want you to
> go on like this.

His eyes drift to the photo album on the dresser.

> GLENN
> I don't know what's happening to me,
> Claire.

Glenn reaches over, closes the photo album.

> CLAIRE
> Don't think about it.
> (smiling)
> Go to work as if nothing—

He breaks away.

GLENN
Go to work! How could I face old
McClosky looking like this? He'd throw
me out, an impostor.

CLAIRE
No, he wouldn't. You're *you.* *I* know
you. So will he—and Harry and everybody
else.

GLENN
(labored)
Underneath I'm me, but—
(turns to mirror)
—on the surface—who am I?

He brings up a hand to his face as Claire moves off.

CLAIRE
I'll get breakfast.

DISSOLVE

EXT. OFFICE BUILDING—FULL SHOT—DAY

A modern business edifice, tall, imposing.

DISSOLVE THROUGH TO:

INT. BUILDING—ANGLE ON DOOR

The door bears the wording: J.J. MCCLOSKY / ADVERTISING. Glenn,
clean-shaven and in a neat business suit, ENTERS FRAME, moves to the
door, reaches for the doorknob, draws back uneasily.

CLOSE SHOT—GLENN

Beset by doubts. He draws himself up, braces his shoulders, reaches for the doorknob again.

REVERSE ANGLE

Glenn opening the door, moving through it hesitatingly, glancing around uneasily as he stops.

POV SHOT—RECEPTIONIST

Seated at a desk. She looks up, smiles.

> RECEPTIONIST
> Good morning, Mr. Holbrook.

SHOT—GLENN—MOVING

Crossing the floor to the receptionist.

> GLENN
> You recognize me?

> RECEPTIONIST
> Of course, Mr. Holbrook.
> (beat)
> Is there something wrong?

Glenn sighs, turns away.

> GLENN
> No. Everything's just dandy.

INT. OUTER OFFICE—FULL SHOT

Glenn comes through the door, closes it behind him. MISS BENTLEY, a young secretary, looks up.

> MISS BENTLEY
> Good morning, Mr. Holbrook.

He moves to stand before her. She eyes him curiously.

> GLENN
> Isn't there something different about me
> today?

> MISS BENTLEY
> Different? In what way?

> GLENN
> Are you sure it's me?

> MISS BENTLEY
> (going along)
> Unless it's your twin brother.

She stands, picks up a memo pad, refers to it as Glenn snatches her compact from the desk, snaps it open and looks at himself in the mirror.

TWO SHOT—MISS BENTLEY AND GLENN

Glenn absorbed in his image, Miss Bentley checking off items on the pad.

> MISS BENTLEY
> Mr. Ashton's already called this morning and
> wants you to call him back the minute you
> get in. And production is ready for your
> opinion on the new Dorrance layout. And...

She looks up, sees his absorption with the compact, reacts, for a surprised moment says nothing. Then:

> MISS BENTLEY
> (con't)
> Mr. Holbrook...

Glenn tears himself away from the mirror, snaps it shut, with a little laugh puts it on the desk.

>   GLENN
> Just seeing what I look like this morning.

>   MISS BENTLEY
> One of those mornings?

>   GLENN
> Not really.
>   (beat; earnestly)
> You're sure I'm the same man you worked
> for yesterday.

>   MISS BENTLEY
>   (considering it)
> Well, yes…except—

>   GLENN
> Except?

>   MISS BENTLEY
> Maybe a few more crow's feet around the
> eyes.
>   (beat)
> Am I missing something?

>   GLENN
> Just everything, that's all.

>   MISS BENTLEY
> Then it *is* one of those mornings.

>   GLENN
> Listen: what would you do if you woke
> up one morning and found someone else
> looking out at you from the mirror?

> MISS BENTLEY
> If that ever happens, I hope it's an improvement.
> I do the best I can, but with my face—

> GLENN
> (starting off)
> You're lucky. You've got the face you
> were born with.

She looks after him puzzledly, then:

> MISS BENTLEY
> Mr. Holbrook—about Mr. Ashton and
> the production—which do you want first?

ANGLE TO DOOR TO INNER OFFICE

Glenn turning, his hand on the doorknob.

> GLENN
> Neither. Ask Harry to come in, will you?

He goes in.

INT. INNER OFFICE—FULL SHOT

Glenn comes in, hangs his hat and coat on a clothes tree, glances toward his desk as the intercom BUZZES. He moves to it, depresses a lever.

> GLENN
> Yes?

> MISS BENTLEY'S VOICE
> Mr. Ashton on line one, Mr. Holbrook.

> GLENN
> Tell him I'll call him back. And get Harry
> in here.

He slips up the toggle, starts off.

ANGLE TO WASHROOM

Glenn moving to the door, opening it. Inside there is a medicine cabinet with a mirror, and a sink. Glenn adjusts the door so that he will not be visible to anyone coming in, then examines himself in the mirror.

CLOSE ON GLENN

He examines himself critically, touches the edges of his eyes.

> GLENN
> Crow's feet, all right.

There is a KNOCK at the o.s. door. Glenn reacts with alarm, then composes himself.

> GLENN
> (con't)
> Come in.

ANGLE TO DOOR

It opens; HARRY comes in. Harry is a man younger than Glenn, attired in a conservative suit. He looks around, not seeing Glenn.

> HARRY
> Glenn?

> GLENN'S VOICE
> Be with you in a minute. Have a chair.

Harry moves to one of the chairs before the desk, the CAMERA FOLLOWING.

CLOSE ON GLENN

Thinking furiously.

> HARRY'S VOICE
> What's up, Glenn?

> GLENN
> Harry, I want you to do me a favor.

> HARRY'S VOICE
> You've got troubles?

> GLENN
> No. Just tell me what I look like.

SHOT—HARRY

Reacting.

> HARRY
> What you look like?

> GLENN'S VOICE
> Yes. Describe me.

> HARRY
> Is this some kind of gag, Glenn?

> GLENN'S VOICE
> It's no gag. Go ahead. Tell me. It's
> important.

CLOSE ON GLENN

Examining himself as Harry describes him.

> HARRY'S VOICE
> Well...you're five feet nine...or
> thereabouts...

>   GLENN
>   (impatiently)
>   Never mind that. What about my face?
>   What does it look like?

>   HARRY'S VOICE
>   Glenn, I don't see what—

>   GLENN
>   Go *on*, tell me.

>   HARRY'S VOICE
>   It's a florid face, dark hair, aquiline
>   nose, brown eyes...

Glenn reacts to the description of the eyes.

>   GLENN
>   You're sure about the eyes?

SHOT—HARRY

>   HARRY
>   Sure, I'm sure. After all, we've been
>   working together for old McClosky
>   for three years, haven't we?
>   (beat)
>   What's this all about, Glenn?

>   GLENN'S VOICE
>   Do I have any identifying marks?

>   HARRY
>   Not that I know of.

SHOT—GLENN

                    GLENN
                 (exultantly)
          No scars?

Glenn's face falls as he hears:

                    HARRY'S VOICE
                 (slight laugh)
          Oh, I forgot about that scar on your
          cheek.

ANGLE PAST HARRY IN F.G.

and TOWARD the washroom door, which Glenn opens and steps out
from, closing the door behind him.

                    HARRY
          How'd I do?

                    GLENN
                 (moving to desk)
          You get an A-plus, I'm sorry to say.

He sinks wearily into his chair.

                    HARRY
          What's wrong, Glenn?

                    GLENN
          If I told you, you wouldn't believe me.
          Thanks anyway, Harry.

                    HARRY
                 (getting up)
          I'll be getting back.

Glenn nods, the intercom BUZZES as Harry moves off. Glenn flips the
toggle.

> GLENN
> Yes?

> MISS BENTLEY'S VOICE
> Mr. Crawford's ready in production anytime
> you are, Mr. Holbrook.

> GLENN
> Tell him I'll talk to him later.

Glenn sinks back, puts his hands over his face, sighs, then brings the chair forward.

CLOSE ON GLENN

He opens a drawer, gets out a bottle of whiskey, sets it down on the desk, the CAMERA MOVING IN to HOLD on the bottle.

> LAP DISSOLVE

CLOSE ON BOTTLE

It is half gone. CAMERA DRAWS BACK to show Glenn still sitting in the chair, a glass in his hand. He swallows what is in it, shakes his head, gets up tipsily.

ANGLE TO WASHROOM

Glenn reaching the door, jerking it open, moving to the sink, running water into the glass, drinking it. As he lowers the glass, he looks at his reflection, glaring at himself hatefully. Suddenly he throws the glass at the cabinet mirror. It shatters.

ANGLE TO DOOR TO OUTER OFFICE

It bursts open, Miss Bentley coming in, leaving the door open.

> MISS BENTLEY
> Mr. Holbrook!

ANGLE TO WASHROOM

Glenn leaning against the door grinning rather drunkenly at Miss Bentley as she ENTERS FRAME.

> GLENN
> Lucky Miss Bentley, the lady with her
> own face.

ANGLE TO DOOR TO OUTER OFFICE

Through the door comes J.J. MCCLOSKY, an older man, the prototype of the big boss, followed by Harry. CAMERA FOLLOWS McClosky to the washroom to join Miss Bentley and Glenn.

> MCCLOSKY
> What's going on in here?

> MISS BENTLEY
> There was a crash—

> GLENN
> I broke the little old mirror, Mr. McClosky.

McClosky sizes up the situation, eyeing the bottle on the desk, frowning his displeasure.

> MCCLOSKY
> You've been drinking.

> GLENN
> I didn't like my reflection.

> MCCLOSKY
> (to the others)
> Leave us alone.

ANOTHER ANGLE

Miss Bentley and Harry move off, McClosky moving to the desk, nodding to the chair behind the desk.

> MCCLOSKY
> Sit down, Holbrook.

Glenn moves to his desk to take the chair, the CAMERA MOVING IN.

> GLENN
> I say down with all mirrors. What do
> you say?

> MCCLOSKY
> Never mind about the mirror.

> GLENN
> Drink?

McClosky takes the bottle.

> MCCLOSKY
> And you've had enough.
> (beat)
> You're a good man, Holbrook, but even a
> good man can push himself too hard and
> too far.

> GLENN
> So I'll buy a new mirror, but I'll have
> to paint it black.

> MCCLOSKY
> You've been acting strangely lately, and this
> morning you won't talk to Ashton, and you've
> got Crawford sitting on his hands in
> production. What's wrong with you?

> GLENN

In a nutshell, J.J., I don't like my new face.
Do you?

> MCCLOSKY

You've got to get hold of yourself before it's
too late.

> GLENN

The damage is already done.

> MCCLOSKY

If I thought so, I wouldn't be talking to you
like a father.
> (beat)

You're in no condition to discuss it. You're
not yourself.

> GLENN
> (laughing)

Not myself?
> (convulsed)

Thank you, Mr. McClosky, thank you
very much.

> MCCLOSKY

Holbrook—

> GLENN

Those are the two kindest words I've
heard all day.

Glenn continues to laugh; McClosky continues to glare.

> FADE OUT

FADE IN:

INT. PSYCHIATRIST'S OFFICE—ANGLE TO DESK—DAY

Soothing decor, the usual framed licenses, bookcases, art calculated to placate, the desk and chairs heavy and steady, as is DR. ERNST BLACKWOOD, who wears an air of infinite patience as he leans back in his swivel chair, a small gold pencil in his hands, a pad of paper on the desk before him, watching Glenn Holbrook as he walks nervously to and fro before him.

> BLACKWOOD
> Why don't you sit down, Mr, Holbrook?

> GLENN
> How can I sit down after all that's
> happened to me?

ANGLE TO BLACKWOOD

Easing up on his chair with a sigh, checking off items on the pad with his pencil.

> BLACKWOOD
> Let's examine the facts. You say you
> woke up with a face that isn't yours—

Glenn ENTERS FRAME to lean on the desk to address him.

> GLENN
> It's not just in my *mind*, doctor.

> BLACKWOOD
> Let me finish.

Glenn moves OUT OF FRAME as Blackwood continues:

> BLACKWOOD
> (con't)
> You went to your office expecting no
> one to recognize you, but they all did.

So you started drinking—

Glenn ENTERS FRAME to lean on the desk again.

> GLENN
> And I smashed a mirror. Don't forget
> about that. Old McClosky never will.

Blackwood looks up at him steadily.

> BLACKWOOD
> Mr. McClosky is responsible for your
> being here. He thinks a lot of you, Mr.
> Holbrook.

> GLENN
> Why shouldn't he? I've given him five
> years of my life already and he has an
> option on all the rest.

> BLACKWOOD
> He thinks you're worth salvaging.

> GLENN
> Salvaging!

ANOTHER ANGLE

as Glenn makes a why face, straightens and turns toward CAMERA to
walk a few steps.

> GLENN
> Let's look at the old wrecked car, see
> what it's worth.

> BLACKWOOD
> You are demeaning yourself again, Mr.
> Holbrook.

Glenn turns back to him, to lean on the desk again.

> GLENN
> How would you like it if you had to
> wear this face the rest of your natural
> life?

> BLACKWOOD
> The question is why. Sit down.
> (as Glenn sits)
> Doesn't it seem strange to you that you
> are the only one who thinks your face
> is not your own?

> GLENN
> That is stating it mildly.

> BLACKWOOD
> But it is the truth?

> GLENN
> (grudgingly)
> I suppose so.

CLOSER TWO SHOT—BLACKWOOD AND GLENN

Blackwood nodding.

> BLACKWOOD
> Then they are seeing you as you were.
> Right?

> GLENN
> That would explain it, but—

> BLACKWOOD
> Don't interrupt.
> (beat)

> Now, if everyone sees you as you were,
> then you are the only one who sees you
> as you are now. Isn't that right?

> GLENN
> (dubiously)
> I guess so.

> BLACKWOOD
> Then the trouble is not with them, but with
> you.

> GLENN
> I knew you'd get around to putting it that
> way. It's all in my mind.

> BLACKWOOD
> Precisely.

Blackwood gets up.

ANGLE TO BOOK SHELVES

Blackwood reaching them. He runs his hand along the books, thick volumes of case histories and psychiatric studies.

> BLACKWOOD
> These books are filled with cases, most of
> them far more bizarre than yours, Mr.
> Holbrook.

He starts back to the desk, CAMERA FOLLOWING. When he reaches it:

> BLACKWOOD
> (con't)
> When a man finds the world he lives in too
> hostile, too evil, too miserable, he sometimes

invents a new one—one that fits him better.
He then leaves this world, although he is
still in it.

> GLENN
> You mean that's happened to me?

> BLACKWOOD
> It fits the pattern.

ANGLE FAVORING GLENN

He considers it solemnly as Blackwood moves to his side.

> GLENN
> But why would I invent a face like this?

> BLACKWOOD
> Because your inner self is trying to tell you
> something. The thing to do is to live with
> it, accept it.

> GLENN
> That won't be easy.

> BLACKWOOD
> Nothing is easy, Mr. Holbrook.

Blackwood moves off.

ANGLE TO DESK

as Blackwood moves around it to take his chair.

> BLACKWOOD
> And I would suggest a series of treatments—
> at the start three times a week. Is that
> agreeable?

GLENN
If it will bring back the face I was born with—

Blackwood makes a tent of his hands.

BLACKWOOD
That will be up to you, but I would say the
prognosis is most favorable.

DISSOLVE

INT. GLENN'S OFFICE—ANGLE TO WASHROOM—DAY

Glenn finishes putting a new mirror in the cabinet. Harry stands by, watching.

HARRY
Old McClosky's going to be pleased,
your putting in a new mirror.

GLENN
The least I could do, Harry.

HARRY
You really had him going. Now if
I'd broken that mirror, I'd be out on
my ear.

CLOSE SHOT—GLENN

He breathes on the mirror, wipes it dry with a towel, grins at his reflected image, salutes it.

GLENN
Hi, ugly.

ANGLE TO DOOR

McClosky coming in, CAMERA FOLLOWING him to Glenn and Harry.

>   MCCLOSKY
>   You didn't have to do that, Holbrook.

>   GLENN
>   On the contrary, Mr. McClosky.

>   HARRY
>   (uneasily)
>   I'll be getting back.

Harry starts off.

ANGLE PAST DESK IN F.G.

and TOWARD Glenn and McClosky, Glenn hanging up the towel, giving himself a last look in the mirror, closing the door and moving toward
the desk.

>   GLENN
>   I have to make amends, and this is a
>   start.

>   MCCLOSKY
>   You're taking it well. Dr. Blackwood
>   thinks so, too.

>   GLENN
>   It's back to the status quo, as they say.

>   MCCLOSKY
>   A man has a right to let go once in a while.
>   (beat; fondly)
>   I've done some funny things in my time, too.

>   GLENN
>   Really, Mr. McClosky?

> MCCLOSKY
> (gruffly)
> Tell you about them someday.
> (beat)
> Right now I want to welcome you
> back. We'll go on as if nothing
> happened. Okay?

McClosky extends his hand, Glenn takes it with a smile.

> GLENN
> It's all over, Mr. McClosky. It's onward
> and upward with McClosky Advertising.

> MCCLOSKY
> That's the spirit, my boy.

DISSOLVE

INT. BEDROOM—FULL SHOT—NIGHT

Claire sits at the dressing table, brushing her hair. Glenn comes in. They are in night clothes.

> GLENN
> Everything's locked up and I'm about
> to wind the clock.

He crosses to the beside table, picks up the clock, winds it.

> GLENN
> (con't)
> If we had a cat, I'd put it out.

ANGLE TO DRESSER

Claire watching him in the mirror.

> CLAIRE
> My, aren't we chipper tonight.

Glenn moves to the window, opens it, looks out, breathes deeply.

> GLENN
> Smell that air. It's good to be alive
> again.

> CLAIRE
> I'm glad you feel that way. For a while
> there...

Glenn moves to her, kisses the back of her neck.

> GLENN
> That's over. McClosky, Dr. Blackwood
> and I all shook hands on it.

She looks up at him in the mirror with an edge of worry.

> CLAIRE
> But you still think—

> GLENN
> Yes, it's not my face, but I'll have to
> live with it.

> CLAIRE
> Is that what the psychiatrist said?

ANOTHER ANGLE

Glenn moving away, bending over to touch his toes in exercise.

> GLENN
> Looking at Dr. Blackwood across his
> desk, I thought: It could have been worse.

                    CLAIRE
What do you mean?

                    GLENN
I could have awakened with his face—
or old McClosky's. How would you like that?

                    CLAIRE
I like you the way you are.

Glenn stops his exercising, moves beside her at the mirror.

TWO SHOT—CLAIRE AND GLENN

Glenn peering into the mirror.

                    GLENN
You know, when I first looked at it, it
seemed distorted and—well, ugly. But
that's because it's so different.
          (beat)
Now I'm beginning to think it's not such
a bad old face.

                    CLAIRE
It's a good face. I've always thought it was.

                    GLENN
Firm chin, good cheekbones. I even think
now that the scar gives it a certain air of
distinction.

                    CLAIRE
Charm is the word.

                    GLENN
          (turning to her)
Since it's no stranger to you…

He cups his hands behind her head, leans down, kisses her.

>GLENN
>(con't)
>How's that?

>CLAIRE
>I'd say it was a good beginning.

He takes her arm; she gets up, moves to him. CAMERA PANS to the open window.

>LAP DISSOLVE

ANGLE TO WINDOW—DAY

A gentle breeze blows the curtains.

CLOSE ON CLOCK

It reads: 7:30. It RINGS. A hand ENTERS FRAME, fumbles with it, turns it off, CAMERA DRAWING BACK to show Glenn in bed, his face registering his usual displeasure with the clock. He sinks back to the pillow, closes his eyes with a sigh.

TWO SHOT—GLENN AND CLAIRE

Claire lifts her arm, jabs at him with her elbow without waking. Glenn's eyes open, the lids coming down slowly as he would sink into sleep again. Claire's elbow comes in hard, Glenn jerking awake.

>GLENN
>All right, all right.

With effort, Glenn slips his feet out of bed, sits up, shaking his head, scratching his scalp, yawning.

>   GLENN
>   (con't)
> I wish I knew which is going to give out
> first—your elbow or my ribs.

ANOTHER ANGLE

Glenn putting on his slippers, reaching for his robe. He sits with it, looks o.s. gloomily, hears the rustle of sheets as Claire would jab him in the ribs again, slips away from her.

>   GLENN
>   (victoriously)
>   Never touched me.

He tightens his robe, moves off.

ANGLE TO WINDOW

Glenn moving to it, looking out. His face is full of what good humor he can muster. He takes a deep breath, bends over, touches his toes, does a deep-knee bend, grunts, gets up, massages his knee, starts off.

ANGLE TO BED

Glenn reaching it, rocking the bed with his hand. Claire stirs.

>   CLAIRE
>   (sleepily)
>   Lemme alone.

>   GLENN
> There's a tiger loose in the apartment.
> On your feet.

>   CLAIRE
> Go away.

Glenn grins, starts off.

INT. BATHROOM—FULL SHOT

Glenn coming in, turning on the light. The CAMERA is again so situated that we do not see his reflection in the mirror as, with one hand, he continues to massage his scalp, opens a drawer, gets out his shaving equipment.

OVER-SHOULDER SHOT—GLENN

We see him preparing to shave. CAMERA is again placed so we cannot see his reflection in the mirror; Glenn is absorbed, does not look into it. When he is ready to shave, the CAMERA MOVES so that we see his reflection at the same time he does. It is an altogether different face.

CLOSE SHOT—GLENN

Stupefied at his new mirror image. Then, in agony:

> GLENN
> Oh, *no!*

He closes his eyes tightly, opens them.

ANGLE TO MIRROR

Still the radically new face. He raises a hand to feel it, runs a finger along where the scar used to be.

> GLENN
> (weakly)
> Claire…

ANGLE TO BATHROOM DOOR

Claire reaching it, looking in sleepily.

>   CLAIRE
>   Hmm?

Glenn joins her, pointing in consternation to his face.

>   GLENN
>   My face—it's changed again.

>   CLAIRE
>   Your face?

>   GLENN
>   The scar—it's gone, too.

>   CLAIRE
>   What scar? Glenn, you never had a scar.

>   GLENN
>   I had one yesterday!

>   CLAIRE
>   You've been dreaming.
>   (stifles a yawn)
>   I'll get breakfast. We'll both feel better
>   after a cup of coffee.

She goes, Glenn staring after her.

ANGLE TO MIRROR

Glenn moving to the mirror to touch his new face in maddening, compounding wonderment.

>   FADE OUT

                    THE END

Alfred Hitchcock Presents

Wife Errant

Ben Davenport, a neat, bespectacled, unimpressive-looking man in his forties, locks a door that bears these words on its glass panel: CITY TREASURER. He walks down a hallway and out to a parking lot behind the City Hall, nodding to friends on the way. He gets into his car and drives away.

We see him drive into his garage at home, get out and come to the front of the house, stepping up on the porch. The door is locked. He looks in the mailbox. Several letters. One of these he tears open. It is a letter from the bank notifying him that his account is overdrawn.

Ben frowns as he unlocks the door and walks in. He calls out for his wife, Sylvia. She does not appear. Moving to the kitchen, he sees what a mess it is, the breakfast dishes still in the sink, trash basket overflowing, orange rinds on the sink top. A bottle of bourbon, nearly empty, is on the kitchen table, and next to this are two glasses.

Ben stares at all this for a long moment. We can see his anger mounting. Suddenly he takes the two glasses, one in each hand, grips them hard and throws them in a frenzy to the floor where they shatter. Immediately his fury vanishes and we see that he has, in fact, been a little startled by his sudden show of violence. He gets out a pan and whisk broom and cleans up the shards. Next he dons an apron and starts to work on the dishes.

A squeal of brakes out in front. Ben moves quickly through the house to the front room to look out the window. Sylvia, a beautiful, shapely woman, steps out of a convertible driven by a man in his fifties. This man, who has the soft look of the easy life, playfully grabs her arm, pulls her back down to the seat and kisses her. We see Ben's reaction. Sylvia laughs, draws away and gets out. She is in her early thirties. If it weren't for the fact that everything about her is overdone—her mannerisms, bleached hair, eye shadow, mascara and lipstick—she would be a very attractive woman. She waves at the man, he waves in return, grins, and then starts the car. From their actions it is evident they have been drinking.

Sylvia, elegantly attired for this hour of the day, swings her fur piece over her shoulder and swings her hips as she clicks in high heels to the porch. When she comes in, she throws the fur piece to a chair, sees Ben's gloomy face, and makes a face at him, trying to duplicate his. Ben is not amused.

Sylvia does not give him a chance to talk, but starts right in telling him she doesn't want to hear a lecture, she's not going to tell him where she's been or who the man was. She walks into the kitchen where she picks up the bottle of bourbon, keeping up a running chatter all the while.

Ben has said nothing, but now he savagely grabs the bottle away from her, tells her she has gone too far. During the past six months she has run through the money they've had in the bank making ridiculous purchases, "like that fur piece." His savings have dwindled to the danger point, he says, and now she has added insult to injury by taking up with another man. He tells her it was disgraceful to bring him into the house and drink with him and then kiss him out in the street in broad daylight. He tells her he has had enough, it is going to have to end.

Ben is winded from this harangue. Now Sylvia steps in to coolly tell him she's convinced he's worried only because he's a public official, he's only concerned with what people will think of him, not with her feelings. He tells her this is not true.

"What's happened to us?" he asks. He says they used to be so happy together before she started to drink and cheapen herself with all these cosmetics, fantastic hair-dos, ridiculous clothes, exaggerated mannerisms, and now other men. He is sincere when he asks her if it's something he's done or hasn't done. "What is it that's bothering you, Sylvia?"

She is not moved. She accuses him of being niggardly, never taking her anyplace. Ben calmly states that his whole life seems to be spent in an effort to please her, that as a matter of fact they have a date with Dr. Lindsay Bromley and his wife, Grace, for that evening, as they have had before. Sylvia makes a face, calls them fuddy-duddies.

He angrily tells her it would be better for her to cultivate people like the Bromleys instead of the phonies she's been running with. She laughs at him, tells him he's the biggest phony in town, what with his record in Pennsylvania.

Ben is startled, dismayed. He says he regrets now that he ever told her about that. It was only because he wanted to be honest and above-board with her that he told her about his year in the penitentiary in Pennsylvania when he was twenty years old, a year spent atoning for a foolish mistake. It was here that he began to learn something about bookkeeping and vowed he'd never swerve from the straight and narrow. And he never has. "That was twenty-five years ago," he says. "It's better forgotten."

Sylvia says sweetly that she could bring it up at any time. What would the city council think of having an ex-convict for a city treasurer?

Furious, Ben says he could cheerfully kill her if she did a thing like that.

She tells him to get off her back, then. She's tired of his carping ways. She's only trying to get a little fun out of life.

Ben tells her he means what he says, that he'll throw her out the next time she takes up with another man.

Sylvia says she doesn't think he will, and leaves the room.

Ben is left in the kitchen with the bottle he's taken from her. He looks at it, opens it and pours what's left in it for a drink for himself. He makes a wry face as he swallows.

During the evening out with the Bromleys, Sylvia is very attentive to Dr. Bromley, a man in his fifties, distinguished, intelligent, and of good humor. This attentiveness embarrasses Grace and Ben, particularly when Sylvia dances very close to Bromley. She also drinks too much and is quite giddy.

At one point Sylvia attempts to light a cigarette, can't get her lighter flame lined up with her cigarette. Bromley moves her hand to light it, and Sylvia giggles.

When Grace and Sylvia go to the powder room, Ben apologizes to Bromley. The doctor laughs it off, saying he's sure Sylvia means nothing by it, but he does agree with Ben that she is drinking too much.

In the conversation that ensues, we learn that Bromley was the doctor for Ben's first wife, Margaret, and that their friendship grew out of his long care for her. Bromley is a close-enough friend to be able to say there certainly is a great deal of difference between Margaret and Sylvia.

Ben gloomily agrees. He says even though he devoted perhaps the best ten years of his life to Margaret, looked to her every comfort until the day she died, he never regretted it, but that he seems to have made a mistake in marrying Sylvia. He recalls ruefully that after Margaret's death he sought gaiety and something alive and bright and happy to make up for the sad days he wanted to forget. He met and married Sylvia. They were happy, too, and he can't understand what's happened to her. "Sylvia changed about six months ago. The honeymoon suddenly ended and now I feel more like a meal ticket than a husband."

Bromley suggests he come in for an examination, but Ben says it's nothing like that, he's been more than attentive to Sylvia. Bromley asks him if he thought Sylvia loved him when they wed. Ben says yes, he's sure she did. But she seems now to be growing farther and farther away from him, doesn't seem like the same woman.

Grace Bromley returns, says Sylvia stopped to talk to someone. They look up to see her talking to a man in the band who is shaking his head. Sylvia is agitated. She wants to play the drums. The band man hesitates, but Sylvia is so beguiling he finally smiles and lifts her to the bandstand. Sylvia tries to play the drums, but makes a botch of it. Her new friend, the drummer, shows her how to play. Sylvia sets herself in motion on the bandstand, doing a little suggestive dance to his beat. There is scattered applause, and Sylvia, encouraged by this, steps to the floor to do a larger version of the dance while members of the band return to the bandstand one by one to take up the rhythm.

When Sylvia starts a striptease, Ben rushes to her and takes her off the floor.

At home Ben tells her that she was a fool to drink so much, to make such a spectacle of herself. Sylvia is not high-spirited now. The effects of the night are in her face. She tells him she does not feel good, she has a headache. He tells her it's no wonder, the way she'd been drinking. She says she's sorry, that she'll try to behave, will he ever forgive her, etc. Ben, surprised and mollified by this change in attitude, takes her into his arms. She does not object.

In much the same scene as the opening one, Ben locks the door of his office, walks down the hallway and out to the parking lot behind the City Hall, nodding to his friends along the way. He is cheerful, and his step is jaunty. He gets in his car and drives away.

We see him drive into his garage, but as he does this he sees a car parked in front of his house—the same convertible he saw his wife get out of before. He walks quickly from his car around to the front of the house, his eyes angry. He comes up on the porch, walks into the house, stops.

There on the davenport, embracing, are his wife and the man who owns the car. Before them, on the coffee table, is a half-filled bottle of bourbon and two glasses. Ben, his face livid, advances on the man, who gets to his feet, frightened. He backs away, goes around the davenport and scoots out the door. We hear his feet clomp down the steps, hear him start his car and roar off.

Ben has turned to his wife. He tells her to get out, to start packing, he's had enough, he can't take any more. She tells him she has no intention of leaving the house. We feel Ben wants to strike her and he makes several moves in this direction, but Sylvia moves out of his reach, saying he can't make her leave. Finally he says all right, he'll leave then. She calmly tells him she has no intention of his doing that either. "What do you mean by that?" Ben asks. "You know what I mean," she says. "You're stuck with me, Ben. Stuck for good, for better or worse. It's either that or the little story about Pennsylvania in the papers tomorrow."

He stares at her. "You wouldn't do that," he says, refusing to believe it.

She says she certainly will, unless he reconsiders.

Ben looks at her with extreme hate. We have the feeling he would truly like to kill her now. He wilts, his shoulders droop, and he drops to the davenport, a beaten man, apparently. "All right," he says wearily, "you win." After a moment, he says, "I need a drink." He reaches for the bottle and Sylvia tells him there's mix in the refrigerator. "I know you don't like it straight."

Ben gets up, goes to the kitchen, gets the mix, opens a drawer to get a bottle opener, sees a long knife there. He stares at it fascinatedly, wraps his fingers tentatively around the handle. Then he drops it back, takes out the bottle opener, prepares two drinks. His manner becomes more cheerful. He hands her her drink as she comes in and says, "Since we can't go on the way we were, we'll have to start with a different understanding."

Sylvia is surprised by this change, gets out a cigarette as she studies him. He gallantly lights it for her, telling her he'd been wrong, there's no reason why they can't live together, she living her life and he living his.

Sylvia is not entirely convinced, but with each passing moment she is more so. Ben goes on telling her how they will reorganize their lives for the mutual good. She lets him talk.

Suddenly Ben cocks his head, frowns, asks her if she heard anything. A little frightened by his actions, she says she heard nothing. He says it seemed to come from the basement. He tiptoes to the basement door, jerks it open. He gasps, says with urgency, "Come here!" Sylvia does.

There is nothing to see, but as she pushes past him to look, he gives her a shove that sends her sprawling down the steps to the cold concrete below. He stands for a long time looking down at her. Then he calmly goes down the stairs, steps over her prostrate figure to step on the cigarette that had fallen from her hand during her descent. Sylvia is quite dead.

Ben comes upstairs, puts his drink on the kitchen table, goes to the telephone. He lifts the receiver, dials the operator, asks for the police. Before an answer the front door chimes sound. He hangs up, goes to the door.

It is Dr. Bromley. He comes in, says he stopped by the City Hall but Ben had already left. What he has to say he'd rather say in person. "It's about Sylvia."

Startled, Ben says, "What about Sylvia?" in a rather shrill voice. Dr. Bromley tells him Sylvia had come to see him a few days ago, she'd been suffering nausea in the morning, frequent headaches and didn't feel herself.

Ben says in a strangled voice, "You mean she's pregnant?"

Bromley asks him if he remembers three nights ago when they went out on the town, if he recalls the difficulty Sylvia had in lighting her cigarette. "I suspected it then, but I couldn't be sure it wasn't caused by alcohol. Then it was Grace who told me Sylvia confessed she'd taken up drinking to get rid of her terrific headaches, it was the only thing that seemed to do it."

The doctor says he would have told Sylvia herself if it were nothing serious. "But I have to tell you, instead. You must keep it from her. An analysis of the X-rays shows she has an inoperable brain tumor. It is pressing on her optic nerve and alters her vision. That's why she couldn't find the end of her cigarette, why she lacked visual judgment, why she seemed to change character."

Ben, whose face shows increased anguish, says, "That's why, for the past six months…"

The doctor nods.

Ben sinks his face into his hands.

■

Growing Up With Daddy

by Jennifer Sohl

When I was a child in bed at night, the only sound I heard was the curtains brushing against the wall below the window in a breeze that brought with it the far-off sound of a cricket's lullaby, only to be drowned out by the cicada's ear-piercing hum.

When the tap-tap-tapping rhythm of the typewriter began, it was a welcome relief. Soon the cicada's tune would vanish. Down the hall, just a few doors away, my father skillfully wove a thread using just his two index fingers, middle fingers and thumbs. He typed paintings—pictures with words. Into another world, his mind entered an imaginary dimension where the characters came to life on a single sheet of yellow paper inserted in his Remington typewriter. He was very fast, sounding something like rata tata tata tata tata tat *ring*, rata tata tata tat tat tata *ring*. Eighty words a minute, if not faster. It was a comforting rhythm, and it lulled me to sleep.

We moved out to California in 1958 so my father could write for television. I was old enough then to realize life growing up with a writer father wasn't commonplace. I felt I was bragging when I would have to go into a lengthy explanation, which was okay some of the time.

I remember us all gathering around in front of the television set to watch one of my father's stories airing that night. What a thrill to see my dad's name in print right there on that screen for all the world to see.

We used to play double solitaire while sitting on the living room floor, waiting until lunch was ready. He'd have his deck of cards spread out in front of him and I would have mine. It was very exciting. I tried my best to catch up, but he always won.

We used to watch movies together…Well, sometimes I would start first by myself, and just as the end neared my father would appear and sit down next to me. This happened with *Imitation of Life*. The final scene gets you, when the character does her "That's my momma!" piece. When the film ended my father went into the bathroom and blew his nose. I asked Mom what was wrong with Daddy. She said, "Your father was very moved." And then I felt silly for having hid my own tears.

My father was my best friend. I could call him anytime; he would always stop what he was doing, and we would just talk about stuff. I always felt better no matter what it was that was bothering me. I could ask him about anything.

In later years we used to listen to opera artists' demo CDs, both weeping silently to ourselves. I remember looking over at him and seeing the tears streaming down his cheeks. I knew we had shared a moment, and that moment I shall always have with me every time I listen to *Madame Butterfly*, which was his favorite.

In his failing years, his hearing and his sense of self faded away, and the father I knew departed. I remember listening to the radio on my way to work one morning when the Adagio of Massenet's *Meditation* (Thais) came on. It was so beautiful—I had never heard this piece before, and I was very moved, as he would have been. I knew then I was listening to it with him.

■

Later Tales

Notes on Jerry Sohl

by George Clayton Johnson

Let me tell you something about Jerry Sohl.

You know that if you want to make instant coffee you put the coffee powder into the cup and add hot water.

If you want to hear something remarkable the next time you do it, try making a series of ringing taps with your spoon on the rim of the cup and listen to the ascending note that is made as the powder goes into the solution with the water as the water temperature lowers. Keep tapping and you can tell when the process has been completed and the coffee is ready to drink.

I noticed that Jerry would always do this with the expression on his face of a scientist who found satisfaction in thus seeing the linkage between harmonics and temperature and in knowing that the laws of physics were absolute and unvarying.

This deliberative, contemplative quality was characteristic of Jerry, always low key and unexcited, able to work steadily for hours with the pace of a journeyman Linotype operator which is what he had been for many years.

Jerry was one of that small group of wise men that I chose to be my teachers and held warmly in my heart through all those years who included among their number Ray Bradbury, Theodore Sturgeon, A.E. Van Vogt, Forrest J. Ackerman, Rod Serling, Robert Bloch, Richard Matheson, Charles Beaumont, William F. Nolan, John Tomerlin, Frank M. Robinson and Ray Russell.

They were an intense group of creative people who, when gathered together in numbers, threw off such sparks that I often, when among them, believed myself to be somewhere near the chewy center. Where else could I find truth, beauty, honesty, knowledge, wonder, amazement, fun—

and a curious kind of holiness—come together in one place?

But being alone with any one of these gifted men was often an even more dazzling experience. Finding myself the total focus of that much questioning awareness proved to be consciousness-expanding.

The relationship between me and Jerry Sohl was established within a few days back in 1958.

The place we met was the Alexandria Hotel in downtown Los Angeles, then a decaying pile of somber elegance, dark and imposing throughout its vaulted chambers.

The occasion was the World Science Fiction Convention where Richard Matheson was the Guest of Honor and Robert Bloch, even then a Grand Master of Fantasy and Science Fiction, was Master of Ceremonies.

My wife Lola and I had come as guests of Charles Beaumont. Charles was on several panels and was scheduled to be auctioned off to the highest bidder as a dinner companion to some lucky fan.

This was our first convention and when Charles was whisked away to meet some people we were left alone for a few minutes. Lola and I clung to each other, a little intimidated, not knowing anyone and feeling excluded by small knots of people who hurried about on mysterious errands, greeting each other with easy familiarity while seeming to look through us.

I looked around for a friendly face.

Someone was coming down the big staircase with a "Don't I know you?" look on his face. He was about my age, and alone.

I took advantage of the opportunity. "Hello," I said. "I'm George."

"Why, hello, chum," he said, warmly. "I'm Jerry."

I relaxed and introduced him to Lola.

I've always gotten along well with people named Jerry.

We all know that Jerry Sohl wrote for *Star Trek, The Twilight Zone* and *The Outer Limits.*

Some of us are aware that he also wrote for *G.E. Theatre, Alfred Hitchcock Presents* and *Route 66.*

Few of us remember that he also wrote for other, less-celebrated shows when he was breaking into writing for television like *Naked City, The Invaders,* and *M Squad.*

M Squad was Jerry Sohl's first television credit. It just happens he was staying at my house when he got this assignment which launched his career in Hollywood writing episodic television.

I had a small hand in getting him the assignment.

Taking advantage of being a guest at the Science Fiction Worldcon that year he decided that this would be a good time to try to break into TV.

He had established himself as a novelist (*The Haploids, Point Ultimate*) and short-story writer and hoped to use these as qualifications to help break down the door.

I could understand something like this. Wasn't I also someone who yearned to break into writing for television? We were instant soul brothers on the quest.

Both of us wanted to break into TV because that was where the money was.

His New York literary agent had arranged for a West Coast agent to represent Jerry in TV and movies.

His new Hollywood agent was trying to set up a few interviews for him but Jerry needed a place to stay for a few days while he waited to see what might come of it.

Such was our growing friendship that Lola and I invited him to stay with us in our little G.I. Bill house in Pacoima along with our son Paul and newborn Judy.

When he contacted his agent from my house the day after he arrived he learned that his agent had arranged an appointment the following morning to meet with the producer of *M Squad*. It was a series about a police detective in seamy Chicago that starred Lee Marvin as a no-nonsense cop.

I remember after he got the news that morning, sitting with him in a small booth in a coffee shop near my home, pitching each other story ideas we thought suitable for Lee Marvin's cop show, learning the art of the story conference.

One of those original ideas got Jerry the writing assignment that allowed him to return to his wife and children in Boulder Creek, California where he would do the work to lead on to other assignments.

While he was still here I introduced him to the Beaumont crowd, which quickly accepted him as one of their own.

Having mutual friends like Beaumont and Matheson kept us in the same orbit so that over the years we became friends encountering each other at conventions, book signings and at the studios where we often found ourselves writing for the same shows.

Jerry had ambitions that reached beyond television and movies. He was hard at work on a serious novel, *The Lemon Eaters*. He had also cobbled together a group of reprint stories resurrected from the pages of old magazines that he hoped he might sell as a book and help him remain in idyllic Boulder Creek to finish *The Lemon Eaters.* He called the collection *Filet of Sohl.*

By the mid-70s, such had our friendship grown that we joined together with Matheson and Theodore Sturgeon to form a company to create a series of our own.

We called our company "The Green Hand" in honor of Beaumont who had coined the name to designate the remarkable group of writers who were his friends. We called our proposed series *A Touch of Strange,* a Sturgeon title, and hoped to carry on the *Twilight Zone* tradition in a different format on network television.

We got both MGM and Bing Crosby Productions to hire us to develop several different proposals but at network meetings with these studios behind us we were consistently shot down.

I now believe things would have been different if Jerry had been the president and spokesman of our little group but unfortunately they selected me.

I am sure that his mildness and willingness to cooperate would have served us better than my verbal dexterity when it came to talking to network executives....

I will close with a quote from Jerry's *The Lemon Eaters.*

"He was still closer to those who had so recently shaken his hand and said their goodbyes, faces to begin with but people to end with, and they were precious to him for what they had shared with him. He would never forget Olive, or Gene, or Allison or Clio, or any of the others, and they would be added to the sum of all the lives he had known, all very dear to him, veterans of the battle for hope and resolution against torment and uncertainty and fear."

Jerry Sohl was a dear figure in the sum of all the lives I have known. I will never forget him.

■

Mr. Moyachki

They were astonished when he was wheeled in, because they weren't prepared for the bright-blue eyes and the extreme whiteness of his skin. But most of all, they were surprised to find him so alive, so seemingly *aware*, for they had been told Mr. Moyachki lived in his own private world and never said anything to anyone anymore; yet there he was, number 28098, looking anything but inward, eyes darting about, blinking. And listening. Mr. Moyachki looked as if he would answer if any of them put a question to him, for new doctors were allowed to do that and in other years some had even tried to, but Mr. Moyachki never answered when they did. When they addressed him by name, all he did was sweat a little more. Sometimes he trembled. Or passed air. One year one of the new residents said he looked like a man waiting for the blindfold before his execution, and Dr. Humboldt wrote that in the record and even mentioned it as his own observation in ensuing presentations.

"What you're going to see," Dr. Humboldt had said, referring to a neatly typed case history in a folder, "is a man in his sixties, a man who was found wandering the streets in the Garment District after midnight about twenty years ago. He ran away when approached by police officers. He might not have been caught if he hadn't collided with a light standard as he was running around a corner." He paused.

"He was taken to Bellevue, where his condition was diagnosed as an acute and agitated anxiety state. A week later, he was transferred to Central Islip State Hospital on Long Island. Eighteen years ago, he was brought here. He's been in the Davidson Building, Ward D, ever since. For your information, that's a back ward. For therapy he sees a doctor now maybe once a year. His state is one of classic manic-depressive psychosis that seems to have begun as a manic episode, deteriorated to malignant depression, and then to depressive stupor, where it has been arrested." He leafed through pages, found the one he wanted. "The official diagnosis is catatonic schizophrenia."

The new residents stirred. Humboldt paused while a late arrival came in and said, "Excuse me, doctor." Humboldt eyed him coldly. Other doctors turned, not so much to see the new arrival as to ogle once again Coralee Swithers, a busty, blonde-haired resident appointee who defied tradition and wore a miniskirt. Coralee smiled appreciatively. Everybody settled down.

"Was he hurt when he hit the light pole?" a redheaded resident at the rear of the room asked.

"Nothing to indicate he was," Humboldt said tiredly, "except for a bump on the head."

"Organic brain syndrome," a thin young man in the front row ventured.

"It would be hard to say, since no one knew the patient's natural or usual behavior."

"Subdural hematoma?" Coralee volunteered brightly.

"No. You should know he started to run when he saw the police officers, and when he was caught he talked a blue streak."

"What did he say?"

"Nothing that made any sense. Someone on the service reported he thought he was speaking in tongues."

"Any identification?"

"None."

"General adaptation syndrome."

"Who said that?"

"I did," said one of the residents in the middle of the group. "He was in alarm reaction when he saw the police, the stage of resistance when they caught him, and he quickly progressed to a stage of exhaustion, where he's been ever since."

"What's your name?" Humboldt asked.

"Savery. Matthew Savery."

"Doctor, would you like to work with this man?"

"I don't know," Savery said. "I haven't even seen him yet."

"Is that a prerequisite?"

"Is it, doctor?"

There was a vacuum. In it some of the residents laughed a little self-consciously. Then Humboldt smiled and the tension evaporated.

The man they had taken to calling Mr. Moyachki was wheeled in, and Moyachki thought, Well, at least it's something different, not the dreary ward but a brighter place and the usual number of blurred faces and the big man with the walrus mustache and the folder in his hand. They would look at him, the big doctor would gesture to him and they'd talk. He wished he understood what they were saying, but he'd been wishing that for years and it hadn't done any good.

Once, he had understood everybody, had understood everybody for years. Then one day he woke up and it was as if everybody were speaking a foreign language. Something had gone wrong in his brain, just like with all the people he saw around him. They had deliberately made him that way because of what he'd done with the sausages. He was crazy. He'd been crazy for…it bothered him that he did not know for how long he'd been crazy. He squirmed in the wheelchair. He hated the damn thing. Why did they insist he sit in it when he came into this lecture room? What good did it do them to look at him, poke him, prod him, talk to him, make fun of him? He was tired of it. But of course there was no way out.

Why had they taken his glasses so long ago? What was it they didn't want him to see? Why wouldn't they let him have them for even a little while? What did they really want of him?

If only I could see clearly, he thought. Then I could better bear up under all this, even though I am bearing up under it.

"Aphasia," one resident said.

"Agraphia," said another.

"Of course he can't talk," Humboldt said with a degree of disgust. "Or won't talk." He glared at the eager faces. "As for agraphia…" He turned to Moyachki and smiled a bit ruefully. "Mr. Moyachki's an artist, aren't you, Mr. Moyachki?"

Moyachki blinked at the walrus mustache. He could barely make out the white teeth behind the patronizing smile.

"Why, sir?" a resident asked. "Why do you say that?"

"He finger-paints on walls in solitary with fecal matter," Dr. Humboldt said as if he were proud of it.

"What did he paint?" Coralee wanted to know.

"Shit," said the redheaded resident.

Everybody laughed, including Dr. Humboldt, who then fixed the young man with a stare.

"Maybe you'd like to try your luck with this patient, doctor."

The resident said uncomfortably, "What can you do with a catatonic?"

"You can keep your mouth as shut as he keeps his," Humboldt said.

There was, of course, more laughter.

The man they called Moyachki closed his eyes and remembered, immersing himself in the quiet loveliness of the river in the smoke-colored autumn. Did it still freeze over most of the winter? His mind drifted to the breathless beauty of ballet and Chopin crisp and clear, breath-holding, and everybody an aristocrat in the big concert hall. And then there were other days, holidays in the park, dust motes dancing in the afternoon sun, bearded old men playing chess, young lovers spellbound on the grass, old ladies in long coats feeding the pigeons with seeds they withdrew from brown paper bags and threw to the winds. There were the squat little fishing boats, the long barges, sea gulls soaring and dipping and forever hungry, dashing waves and rain and thick clouds. Yes, there was all of that, and it still lives, it must still be. Beyond these walls.

Then there was the prison. Warmth leached from Moyachki as the recollection of locker-white walls and lone light bulbs in ceilings crept along his veins like refrigerated embalming fluid and made him shiver. But at least those in the prison had understood him, and he had understood them. The guards, he could talk to them. The doctors, he could tell them how he felt; they always wanted to know how he felt. Now he knew why.

"How do you feel this morning?" they'd ask when they came to his room in the infirmary.

He'd been arrested because he'd been hungry, he'd had too much to drink and he thought no one would miss the sausages he stuffed into his overcoat pockets. He was only going to take them home to Irina; maybe they had some wine left and would celebrate because he was feeling so good, he couldn't remember.

But they had taken him away, the uniformed men had. The store manager had made him stay until the police came. They took him to that awful place, the prison with its twelve-foot-thick walls, and they wouldn't let him get a word to Irina. When he asked why, they shrugged, said they were sorry, but somebody was going to have to serve as an example, there had been too many thefts from stores, mostly food, and this was setting a bad precedent, people would begin thinking they didn't have to work anymore, just go into stores and pick up what they needed without paying. It had to be stopped. Then they had taken his picture and put it in the paper. They showed it to him. He was a common criminal. No wonder his wife never came to see him!

Endless days, hours strung out in quiet agony until the real pain, the day he'd had his first headache. Then the days ran quickly together and the pain became worse. Excruciating. That is when he was taken to the infirmary: when he could no longer stand up but just lie on his bunk, rolling and moaning and not caring what they did with him because he was so sick and wanted to die.

The doctors seemed glad to see him, kept nodding their heads and rubbing their hands together.

"What's wrong with me?" he gasped.

A doctor, one young enough to be his son, said, "A neoplasm," but an older doctor said gently, "A tumor. A brain tumor."

And when he said, "Am I going to die?" the old doctor said, "We're going to try an experiment," and they injected him with something. Gradually, the pain went away.

It was then that he knew they were lying. No one recovers from a brain tumor. They were experimenting on him. First, something in his food, then the pain, then the injections. He'd heard such things happened in prisons.

He should have known. He began to feel good. Better than good. And everybody was so cheerful and happy and considerate. Was that because of what they were planning for him? Or was it because they were feeling sorry for him because he was going to have to go back to those narrow, dank halls, the dingy cells, the place of fetid smells, the place where the rats were? They were smiling and telling him what a lucky man he was, and they kept taking his blood pressure and samples of his urine and blood.

He could not stand to wait and see. He would escape, that is what he would do. He'd do it before he went back to the main prison, for there was no way out of there, but in the infirmary it was different; there were fewer guards and he had a lot of freedom. He could walk to the solarium, to the day room, stroll the bright, sun-lighted corridors and nod at people and stop to look out the windows at the beautiful city. It would be easy.

It was.

"He closes his eyes," red hair said. "Why does he do that?"

"Why don't you ask him?"

"Mr. Moyachki"—whereupon Moyachki opened his eyes—"why do you close your eyes?"

Savery said, "He closes his eyes because he can't stand the sight of you."

Dr. Humboldt broke into the laughter to say, "A primitive psychosomatic language. We all do it: shutting out the world, it's called. You'll see a lot of that here."

"By the staff?" someone said, but nobody acknowledged it, though Humboldt ran his eyes over all the faces.

"Irrelevant language," Savery said, leaning forward and staring straight into Moyachki's eyes.

"Follow that," Humboldt said, interested.

Savery considered it. "You said he talked once, but the words, phrases and utterances had no meaning. Perhaps they had meaning to Mr. Moyachki. Has anyone thought of that?"

"How many schizophrenics have you listened to?" Humboldt asked.

"I've listened to a lot of autistic children and hebephrenic teenagers in a children's hospital."

"Then you know it's all their creation. They invent their world and they live in it, close you out. Each is safe in his own delusional system. Their talk, if any, is armor plate."

"More like a portcullis." Savery said.

"Exactly."

But Savery wasn't satisfied. "It puzzles me that Mr. Moyachki spoke once but doesn't speak anymore."

Coralee Swithers said, "Dr. Humboldt, you stated his first words were jerky, explosive and irregular. Couldn't that be asynergic or ataxic speech?"

"Of course," Dr. Humboldt said with a wry smile and a glance at her pretty legs. "You've been studying."

"I won't deny it."

"Well, we thought of a disease of the cerebellum, Dr. Swithers, yes, we did that. But it was negative."

Savery said, "How did he react to the examination?"

"He didn't like it."

"Would you say he overreacted?"

"Yes."

"Any idea why?"

"No. Do you have a guess?"

"No." Savery sank back, as baffled as the rest.

"For a moment," Dr. Humboldt said dryly, "I was expecting a miracle. Do any of you believe in miracles?"

Moyachki closed his eyes again and went back twenty years to the infirmary, to the solarium where, during one of his days, he unlocked a window. He was surprised to find it unlocked the next day. And the next.

Finally, he exited through it at night, dropping to the ground twenty feet below, being thankful he'd had sense enough to bend his knees. As it was, he hit his chin on his knees when he landed, nearly breaking his neck. He rolled, then lay silent for a long time, letting noises of the night come into him: the murmur of traffic, faraway voices, bells and insect sounds. He looked up at the stars, expected a head to come poking out of the window he'd just dropped from. At last he got up, was surprised to find that he could stand, walked through wet grass to the sidewalk. No trouble at all getting his bearings from the sky and the first bridge he came to. No question where the piers and the ships lay: on the island. And so he moved through mist, crossed the canal and moved along the river when he came to it and crossed to the island. There would be a ship there, a big one, a ship that would carry him from here to a place that would sparkle in the sun and be warm, where the maidens would be dusky, as he'd once read they were, and danced naked on the sand, and followed you to wherever you wanted to take them, their long, black hair shifting lazily in the tropical breeze. The fall and the sudden freedom had made him giddy.

It was a midnight walk along the embankment, his breath visible, cold seeping into him. It was a walk such as lovers might take, and he took warmth in it. Wasn't he with a lover? The figment of his favorite dancing girl? Not the pristine prettiness of the ballerinas but the sultry wanting-to-please brown-eyed beauties who could not take their eyes off him, girls who waited for him at the end of the world.

He was so lost in thoughts of faraway places that he was on the island before he knew it, and there in her berth was the ship for him, a forbidding, dark shape as tall as a building.

He approached from the stern past the name JALOKIVI illuminated by a lone light high on a post near a dockside crane and not thinking about it, only about the fact that it was a ship, that it was there and he would be aboard her soon. Moving cautiously, he came amidships to the gangway steps. He stood for a moment to listen, heard nothing unusual, started up toward the light at the top. There would be someone there, of course.

His eyes came level with the deck. He could see two sailors standing nearby, talking in low tones. He stayed where he was until one yawned and the other slapped him jovially on the back and pushed him toward a companionway. The watch sailor darted a glance toward the gangway before quickly moving down the steps to follow the other sailor.

Moyachki waited a moment, then darted up to the deck, explored and found an open hatch. In less than a minute he had hidden himself among crates in the freight hold. After his racing heart slowed to normal, he fell asleep to dream about endless stretches of white sand, blue lagoons and grass huts wherein he dwelt and was visited whenever he wished by any number of soft, brown-skinned girls with flowers in their hair.

When the man who would later be called Moyachki came to his senses, he thought he was back in the infirmary and that they had done something terrible to him, because he couldn't see. Then he knew he was somewhere else, because the smells were different, the room was different, the doctors were different. When he had the strength, he put his hand up to his eyes. His glasses were gone.

"My glasses," he said with alarm. "I need my glasses."

Nils Ladoga, medical officer of the *Jalokivi*, a freighter of Finnish registry, heard him, came to look down at him. "So you can speak, can you? Well, save your strength. You are still pretty dehydrated." He took out the I.V.s that had been keeping Moyachki alive.

Moyachki had been frightened at the hospital. Now, being somewhere else and seeing nothing but a series of depressing blurs and the vague face of Nils Ladoga saying something he did not understand, he became more frightened than ever. What had they done to his brain? Where was this? He squinted and tried to sit up in the sick bay.

"Easy, now," Ladoga said, pushing Moyachki down. "You rest."

Moyachki was nauseated and weak. This was worse than the prison infirmary. There he could at least see and there he could understand what was being said. What they had done to him was to take his glasses away and render his brain twisted and incapable of understanding words.

His heart commenced jackhammering and only with great effort of will was he able to force himself to relax. He was so successful he even closed his eyes and slept. When he opened them, he did so only to narrow slits. He saw nothing moving among the blurs. He blinked and sat up. Nothing. He swung his legs off the table. He was weak and felt near collapse, but he made himself sit up until he felt halfway normal, then he got off and stood, swaying, dizzy. He had to get out of there.

He moved slowly up the companionways until he reached the deck, found it was still night out and wondered how that could be; surely more hours had passed than that. He stopped, listened. Not a sound. The ship was not rocking or rolling, its engines were not running, so it had not yet moved out. He started across the deck to the bulwarks and, with his hand on the rail, stepped toward where he thought the gangway would be, stumbling sometimes, moving around equipment he saw only as blurred, dark hulks, always coming back to the railing, until he finally came to the break and the dockside steps.

"Hey—you!" The cry came from some distance away and he heard the sound of feet pounding on the deck. He did not understand the words, but there could be no doubt of what the words meant.

Moyachki started down the gangway as fast as his feet would go, and when he reached the solidity of the wood of the pier, he ran toward the lights.

Later, he wandered about streets looking for the canal. He was sure he would be able to find it even though he was without his glasses, but before he was able to, he ran into the police. There was no mistake about these men who suddenly loomed before him. They reeked of authority, of menace, of danger.

"What are you doing here?"

He did not like the sound of the voice, veered away from them. They reached for him. He began to run fast down the street, hearing their shouts, the soles of their shoes slapping the pavement. Moyachki did not see the light standard in time, because, as he rounded the corner, he turned to look behind him and was pleased to see nothing, though he could still hear them coming. When he turned back, there was the pole and he collided with it. It sent daggers of light to piercing his brain, shattering into myriad fragments as he fell unconscious to the sidewalk.

Moyachki, after having been treated for the bump on his forehead, was taken to a small cubicle and left with a man in a white smock who sat at a table and motioned for him to sit down. Moyachki was better able to see the motion than he was the man's arm.

"Hello," the man said cheerfully.

Moyachki stared at him. This man spoke like the rest, he was probably a doctor and very learned, and Moyachki knew now with crushing despair that whatever words he would hear in the world, he would never understand them.

"What day is this?" the man said.

Moyachki shook his head. Maybe they would understand him if he spoke. "I want my eyeglasses, please."

"Do you know where you are?"

"Please, my eyeglasses. I can't do anything without my eyeglasses. I can only see that you are a face, nothing more. I will behave, if only you will return my eyeglasses. I'm sorry for all I've done and I'll obey all the rules. You see, something's happened to my brain, they've done something to it and I don't understand what people say anymore."

"Is it raining outside?" And when Moyachki started in again about how much he needed his eyeglasses, the doctor said, "Let me put it another way. Was it raining when you were brought in?"

"My eyeglasses, please. I beg you."

"What is your name?"

"My eyeglasses," Moyachki said without hope as the doctor began to write something down.

The first day he ran about, shouting, "My eyeglasses, I need my eyeglasses! Can't anybody understand? My eyeglasses, please, I beg you! My eyeglasses, please!" But he knew it was useless.

They put him in restraint and filled him with chlorpromazine and abruptly his eyeglasses weren't important anymore.

Because he could not see clocks, he had to rely on his inner time sense to tell him when to join lines of silent people who shuffled up to nursing carts to receive paper cups of liquid. He did not care anymore what it was. He drank the Thorazine.

He ambled about in loose-fitting garb, the blue pajama pants and top and white cloth slippers, all with BELLEVUE stenciled on them.

Then he was transferred to another place with a lot of other prisoners. And after an indeterminate period there—since he could not read calendars, he did not know how long it was—he was transferred to still another place. This one.

It was here that he decided to end his miserable life.

The reason was, though he could not see anything in any detail, he did see attendants choke an old man who never stopped singing at the top of his voice. They choked him into silence and, finally, in their anger, into death.

Then there was the bald-headed man who kept standing up in bed, shouting, lecturing. He wouldn't stop even when Moyachki went up to him and said, "Stop it or they'll choke you if you don't, don't you realize that? They'll choke you to death."

The man paid him no attention. The attendants came in, tied the man down, and when the man gnawed through the ropes and stood up and started his harangue again, they put him in a strait jacket; he couldn't speak, because he kept spitting at the flies that kept gathering around his mouth.

They wanted to use Moyachki, so they sent him to the kitchen to work, but he kept bumping into things, knocking them over. "Listen, pinhead," the cook said, "you break one more thing, I'll see it's the hole for you."

When he inadvertently dumped over a whole tray of dishes after he stumbled into a cart, he was taken away, stripped of his clothes and put in a small, chilly solitary-isolation cell that contained only a ceiling bulb and a mattress on the floor. At first he ran around the mattress, shouting for his glasses. Then he thought how much like the man in the bed he was being, so he quieted and wrote on the wall in big letters instead.

Two weeks later he was taken out, put in a shower, given a new set of pajamas and slippers and taken before another man in a white smock, a man with a walrus mustache.

"I'm Dr. Humboldt."

"My eyeglasses. Please."

"Do you know where you are?"

"My eyeglasses!"

"Do you know what day it is? What year? Do you know who the President of the United States is?"

Moyachki cried inside. What was the use of living if he couldn't see anything? Even if they set him free, what good would it do to walk through sunny streets, through the park, and not see the people, the clouds, the trees, the lovers, the freshly-mowed grass, the old ladies and men, and the flowers swaying in the breeze in their beds along the parkway?

He broke open a medicine cabinet at a nurse's station and was in the middle of gulping down all the medicine in the bottles when attendants rushed him and pulled him away, the nurses screaming in fright.

They pumped his stomach.

He did not ask for his glasses.

He was put in solitary for a month.

He did not ask for his glasses.

He went on a fast. He would fast until the end.

They came in, took him to another room, tied him down on a table, forced a tube into his stomach, put a funnel at the other end and let gruel flow down.

"You can't starve here, Mr. Moyachki," Humboldt said. "We won't let you. Every other day it will be food down the tube. The choice is yours." This doctor with the mustache came around to look down at him. "I imagine you don't care much for this, do you, Mr. Moyachki?"

He gave up the fast.

He also gave up talking. He would speak no more.

Humboldt told them, "Mr. Moyachki was not always as weak and submissive as you see him today. He just seemed to cave in one day. If you had him, Dr. Savery, what would you do with him?"

Savery, whose sun-tanned face was a study, said, "I don't know. It's a puzzle. There's something strange here." The other residents laughed and Coralee tittered. Some of the residents used the occasion to dart admiring glances to her. Savery went on, "He can't understand."

"Sensory aphasia," said a resident who wanted to make points. "Plus anarthria."

Savery, who had stood first in his class in medical school and had made waves as a medical intern, said with heavy sarcasm, "OK, let's drag it all out, all the jargon. Sure, he can't talk. But maybe he doesn't want to talk. He's given up. So let's be technical and call it lalophobia and say he's afraid of talking. Does that make everybody happy?"

"Dr. Savery," Humboldt said severely, "I must ask—"

"Is there any paralysis?" Savery interrupted.

"You mean of the speech muscles?"

Savery nodded wearily. "Yes, of the speech muscles. Laloplegia, if you want me to say it. I've studied, too, you know."

"What's your point, doctor?"

"I think it must be simpler than it appears, that's all."

"Is that a fact?" Humboldt said dryly. "Then how would you explain eighteen years of his being a patient without any bright young doctor like you discovering this 'simplicity' you seem so sure about?"

"You say he doesn't communicate."

"You can see that for yourself."

"Yet you said he wrote on a wall."

"In broad, smelly strokes, if you want to be factual."

"What did he write on the wall?"

"Are you trying to make a fool out of me, doctor?"

"I'm asking you a serious question."

"The hospital should immortalize words written in excrement by a crazy man?" Humboldt fairly bristled. "Is that what you're implying?"

"It's a form of communication, doctor."

"The attendant who looked through the peephole and saw him doing this was rewarded with some of it in his eye."

"Mr. Moyachki did that?"

"He certainly did."

"Then you know what he thinks of the attendant and probably the hospital itself."

"Dr. Savery, why don't you give us the benefit of your infinite wisdom and tell us what you're driving at."

"I say this man is sane."

Humboldt looked at him for a long moment. "I would like you to prove that, doctor."

Savery said, "I can't. At least not right now."

"How long do you think it would take?"

"I don't know. I just have a feeling. Call it intuitive validity, if you want. There's just something about him, that's all."

Addressing the residents, Dr. Humboldt said, "The genius residing in Dr. Savery is going to unravel for us in the next few months—or will it be days, doctor?—what we have been trying to unravel for years."

At that moment there was a commotion at the door and Dr. Harold Lindgren, head of the service, who had opened the door without ceremony, ushered in three people. Humboldt, who would have been outraged had it not been Lindgren, was nonetheless put out at this disruption and seemed on the verge of saying so, having more than tenure, but Lindgren was acting strangely. He brought the three persons—a woman and two men, who were dressed rather severely—to the lectern and introduced them to Humboldt and the residents as if they were royalty:

"Dr. Maria Bassinov, a director of the Serbsky Institute for Forensic Psychiatry in Moscow; Dr. Nikolai Paskar, head of the special hospital at Chernyakhovsk; and Dr. Axel Chelny, chief of research at the Institute of Psychology of the Georgian Academy of Sciences."

Dr. Humboldt was impressed and shook their hands as Lindgren explained to the visitors his position in the hospital and, in answer to Humboldt's questioning gaze, explained in turn that the Russians were touring mental-health facilities in the United States as guests of the Government.

The residents sat in quiet expectation. Moyachki blinked his eyes and showed interest as the three Russians turned their attention to him.

Humboldt said, "We were in the middle of a case presentation here." He pointed to Moyachki. "Eighteen-year schizophrenic. Moyachki."

Maria laughed easily. "Your pronunciation, doctor. And you have them on. Have you been studying Russian long?"

"I beg your pardon?"

Dr. Paskar eyed her severely and said to her, "*Ne smeites' nad amerikantsami kotorie izuchaiut nash iazik.*" ("You should not make fun of Americans if they are trying to learn our language.")

Dr. Chelny, with a glance at Humboldt, said, "*Mne kazhetsia shto vy ego obideli.*" ("I think you hurt his feelings.")

Moyachki jumped from the wheelchair, faced them excitedly. "*Ia vas ponimaiu! Ia vas ponimaiu!*" ("I can understand you! I can understand you!")

Maria said, "*On govorit po russki!*" ("He speaks Russian!")

"*Konechno ia govoriu po russki. Ia russki. Ia rodilsia i vyros v Leningrade kogda on escho byl Petrograd.*" ("Of course I speak Russian. I am a Russian. I was born and raised in Leningrad when it was Petrograd.")

The residents stared as Moyachki began to sob his relief, taking in great gulps of air, putting his hands to his face. Humboldt and Lindgren didn't know what to do. The Russian visitors were visibly moved. Moyachiki said, "I kept asking for my glasses. I kept saying '*Moi ochki*' over and over and that's why they call me Moiochki."

Dr. Chelny said crisply, "What is your name?"

"My name is Michael Pimen."

Maria said to Humboldt, "This man has been here eighteen years?"

Humboldt, numbed by the revelations, nodded dumbly.

"He must be released at once," Dr. Paskar said with some authority.

"He is a Russian subject."

Maria said she wanted to know how Pimen came to be their charge and Humboldt haltingly explained it, trying to make everyone involved look good.

"Get me out of here," Pimen said. "And please, my eyeglasses!"

"But don't you see," Maria Bassinov said excitedly, waving the sheaf of papers in her hand, "you're an important man. You're important to every man wherever he lives—in Russia, the United States—it doesn't matter where."

Michael Pimen sat luxuriating in the softness of a lounging chair in the main room of the hotel suite, not excited at all. It was enough to be away from the hospital, to be away from the plastic cups that contained the liquid that dulled his mind, his senses. His brain, after years of numbing drugs, had come alive again. He was not the same man; those years were behind him. They said they were taking him back, and he was frankly worried about that, but for now, in the cool room with the whispering air conditioning....

"Tell me about the Krasnaia Strela," he said. "Is it still running?"

"Yes, yes," Maria said impatiently, "the *Red Arrow* still eases into the Moskovskii Voksal the way it always did. The train is as luxurious as ever. But—"

"Do they still play the hymn in the station?"

"Yes."

It was Glière's *Hymn to the City* and Michael loved it. When he heard it on the public-address system, he couldn't get it out of his head for days.

"They certainly play it loud enough," Maria said absently. Then she moved to him. "You had a brain tumor. Do you remember that?"

"I could not have had a brain tumor."

"But we checked and you did. You volunteered to be a guinea pig— you and twenty-seven others with cancers of one kind or another."

Michael wondered what she looked like, really. She had a very nice voice. Very soft, very warm. Unlike those at the hospital. Soon he would have his glasses. They had taken him to a New York optometrist who understood Russian. Yes, soon Nikolai and Axel would be back with his eyeglasses. "*Moi ochki*," he would say as he took them. He had to smile at the thought. After all these years...

"And," Maria was saying, "you were administered the Plasskoy serum. That was Dr. Plasskov who was working on you when you decided to run off. Didn't you know that?"

"Serum?"

"For a horse, actually. It works on the reticulo-endothelial systems. It annihilated your brain tumor, comrade. Yours and yours alone. Doesn't that mean anything to you?"

Michael sighed. "When will they return with my eyeglasses?"

"Any minute now." Maria walked to the windows, put the papers on the table between them. "Why did you do what you did? Didn't you trust Dr. Plasskov?"

"I would have been sent back to prison when I was cured. What did it matter?"

"That is not true. You would have become a celebrity—what you are now in the eyes of the Central Committee. They have heard about you, you know." She came to him, put a hand on his shoulder. "What happened inside your body to kill the cancer is important to all of mankind. You will be given a medal."

"What happened to the others?"

"I don't understand."

"The other...twenty-seven."

"The other volunteers? It didn't work on them. They died. That's why what happened to you is—"

"So important. Yes, I know. That's what you say." They had been feeding him well and he felt strong again. He was lucky. He had been lucky all along.

Maria fiddled with the papers on the table. "The report says you jumped out of the hospital window and fled into the night. They expected to find you dead when the others began to drop off, except that when the *Jewel* reached New York—"

"The *Jewel?*"

"The Finnish ship—the *Jalokivi*—the ship you were on. You were in the freight hold for nearly two weeks, unconscious, overcome by fumes from cargo chemicals. It's lucky that you didn't die."

Yes, he'd been lucky. And that is why he hadn't understood...

"Then, when they fed you intravenously and you got your senses back, you ran out and off the boat and wandered about the city of New York."

Michael smiled wryly. "I thought this was Leningrad. I thought I'd been on the ship only that night. No wonder I wasn't able to find the Obvodny Canal."

"Or the Fontanka River."

"I survived."

"Yes, you did that. You have done that."

"I thought the police…"

"That is understandable," Maria said quietly. Then, coldly, "What is not understandable, however, is the idiocy of the people here. Isn't there anyone here who understands Russian?"

"Oh, yes. There was a man—two men. One was a Muscovite and he sang songs at the top of his voice and…"

"Didn't you talk to him?"

"I tried to, but he wouldn't stop singing."

"What happened to him?"

"They choked him to death."

"And the other man?"

"He would stand up in his bed, lecturing. He was one of the volunteers for the *Opolchenie*—the People's Army who defended Leningrad—"

Maria said stiffly, "I am aware of the heroes of Leningrad, comrade. My uncle—but never mind. Couldn't you talk to him?"

"I tried to. I told him what they did to the other Russian, but he never stopped his shouting about how they all died before the westward advance toward Berlin, how horrible it was, the famine, how they all had allotted to them seven bullets a day."

"A rifleman, no doubt. What happened to him?"

"They tied him down, he bit through the ropes, they put him in restraints and he finally died."

Maria snorted. "Because they did not want him reciting the glories of the People's Army, no doubt."

There was a silence. Michael said, "Have you any word of my wife, Irina?"

"Dead."

"They questioned her, I suppose."

"Of course they questioned her. Would you not do the same?"

Irina was a shadowy figure now buried deep in the crevices of his brain. He could not even remember the color of her eyes. He wondered how she had died.

Nikolai Paskar and Axel Chelny came back to the hotel and entered the suite, Paskar carrying the new glasses in their case. They made Michael sit near the window while they put them on and adjusted them for him.

Instantly for Michael the air that had hung outside the windows like a mist became clear and he could see everything, including the building across the street, the dark smoked glass of the windows, very strange for windows.

They made him stand up and look down, and he beheld, far below, variously colored insects crawling in orderly rows down pathways, stopping at other intersecting pathways momentarily, then starting up again. He realized they were automobiles, and he was overcome by the sight, by the clarity with which he could see them, by the fact that man had created all this, that he was part of it, that he should be so high above them and still be safe and cool.

He sank back to his lounge chair, his chin quivering, his eyes wet. A tear rolled out and down his cheek and for a moment, before he blinked his eyes, he was seeing the world through a mist again.

Then there was Maria and she was standing before him. He was hypnotized by the young sweetness of her face, the blue black of her eyes, the pores he could now see, her full lips.

"What do you think?" Nikolai Paskar asked jovially. "What do you think, eh, Michael?"

When he looked at the men and saw how severely they were looking at him, he thought: NKVD. When they saw his face darken, Paskar asked, "What is it, Michael Pimen? What is wrong?"

"NKVD," Michael said miserably. "You're NKVD."

There was a hush. And then Maria moved even closer, turned his face to hers, smiled wanly. "There is no more NKVD, Michael."

"I don't believe you." He had to say it.

"It's been changed to the MVD." Then she blinked at him, said sharply, "But it has nothing to do with you. We are not MVD. We are scientists. Doctors. We will take you back, yes, but not to prison. You will return a hero, as I've told you. You must believe, Michael."

"Michael Pimen," Axel Chelny said gently, moving to stand beside Maria Bassinov, "what has happened to you has happened to no other man. We must find out why. We must find out how so we can make it happen to others. Do you understand?"

He didn't believe them or care much about what they were talking about. They didn't talk like NKVD. Maybe they were right. His eyes strayed to the window and he got up to look out. "I want to go down there," he said.

"No," Nikolai said. "We can't take a chance like that."

"You must stay here in this suite," Maria said. "We are all flying back in the morning."

So he *was* a prisoner.

Or maybe he wasn't. Maybe they were right, nothing would happen to him when they got back. But he had to get down there. He had to see this world before he left it, this world he had never seen. But he knew better than to ask permission. He'd wait. Maybe in the night, when they were asleep, he'd go out, see it all, if it was possible.

It was after midnight and it was cold and The Turtle was about ready to tell Honest John it was a waste of time, nobody would be dumb enough to enter Central Park at this hour, there were other places. He knew what Honest John would say. He would tell him there were a lot of dumb people in the world. And he'd be right. The Turtle rubbed his hands together, did a couple of deep-knee bends before Honest John, who could hear what others could not, banged him on the shoulder and made him quit.

The Turtle stopped and looked to where Honest John was pointing. They saw an old man, a man in his sixties maybe, coming up the path, looking around as if it were the first day of spring. What could he be thinking of? How dumb could you get?

They waited until he came up to where they were, then Honest John simply stepped out from the bushes to take his stand behind the man, putting the knife to his throat. "Not one word, baby," Honest John said. "Not one word."

The Turtle saw the man's eyes behind the glasses. They were wide and bulging with fear. His mouth kept opening and closing as he breathed hard. The Turtle made his search quick and neat but found absolutely nothing on the man, in his coat, in his pockets, no jewelry, not anything. He was surprised.

The man twisted away unexpectedly, something they never did. Honest John took a couple of steps and grabbed him again, pushing the blade hard against the throat. "That wasn't very nice, old man. Not nice at all." Honest John was mad.

"He's got nothing," The Turtle said. "Nothing at all. Nothing anywhere."

"Nothing? What do you mean, nothing?" Honest John was fit to be tied, The Turtle could see that.

The man started squirming. Honest John was so annoyed he batted the stranger on the head, sent him flying, glasses sailing into the grass. They watched the old man get to his hands and knees.

"*Moi ochki*," the man said, patting the area around him, searching, then looking toward them. Next, he screamed it: "*Moi ochki!*"

That was when Honest John had to finish him off.

■

The Service

- Mr. Cade?

What?

- Mr. Dexter Cade?

Yes. Who the devil are you?

- I'm sorry if I've startled you, sir.

How long have you been standing there like that?

- Not long.

How did you get in?

- With this key.

Oh!…Then—you must be the one…

- Yes, Mr. Cade, I am.

Oh, my God!

- There's no need to be upset, sir. There's no rule that says I have to stay.

It's not that. It's—it's—I didn't think he meant it. I didn't think he meant it even after he asked me for the key and I gave it to him.

- If it pains you, sir…

I thought he was just trying to placate me, make me feel good, get me to cling to something.

- They're good at that, Mr. Cade. But then that's their job.

It was so unbearable, so hopeless…I tried to make him see that.

- You don't have to worry about it now, sir.

I still can't believe it!

- And, as I said, I don't have to stay, but I must warn you that if you ask me to leave no one else from the Service will be coming back. You must understand that. Do you, Mr. Cade?

Yes, yes.

- We want you to be happy with us.

Oh, I am! I am!

- And you must want to go through with it.

I do…but since it's going to be—well, there are certain things I'd like to know more about first.

- There's nothing more to know, sir. It's what it is and that's all. I've been told it's been explained to you, and the Service is never wrong. Is it that you want me to leave?

Have you done this sort of thing before?

- Certainly, Mr. Cade. It's my job.

Many times?

- Oh, many times.

When will it—happen?

- Whenever you're ready, sir.

You know, you're not what I expected.

- They all say that. Most of them do, anyway. They expect a sadist or a maniac or something vile. Actually, we are very ordinary persons…with a specialty.

You're certainly different from the people who've been taking care of me, if you can call it that.

- In what way, sir?

With them I could always see what was coming in their eyes, in their faces, in the way they said things to me and to each other. Sometimes they thought I couldn't hear them, but I did. And then there was the way I felt. I know why they've let me come home.

- An increase in hearing acuity is not at all unusual in people in your situation. And I believe home is best, if I may say so, Mr. Cade.

You know, I like you. I can't say I see anything at all deceptive or ulterior about you.

- Thank you. We in the Service like to think of ourselves as truth— the final truth, if you will—the truth that the others won't admit, even to themselves. The reason is obvious, of course. It contravenes what they stand for. And it shakes them, shakes them to their very foundations. That's why there is such a need for the Service.

Yes, I can see that. I suppose one could even feel sorry for them, for the stance they have to take.

- The human animal is a complex thing, Mr. Cade. In vain effort he sometimes pushes and pulls at the same time.

May I ask you something?

- Of course.

Doesn't this bother you at all?

- No. We're trained for it. I'm sure you were told that.

I was, but I should think it would bother you anyway.

- Not when you consider that pain no longer lays upon those we visit, if I may paraphrase Aeschylus. The Service has its dedication, too, you see; and with it comes its own blessings, its own rewards.

I wish I were able to get up.

- It's all right, sir, if by that you were thinking of the amenities. It is considerate of you, but I can manage. It should not be any trouble for you. Can I get you some coffee? Some tea?

Tea would be fine. You will find everything in the kitchen.

- Here is your tea, Mr. Cade.

Thank you.

- Can I prop you up?

If you would, please.

- There.

Thank you. Good tea. Why didn't they ever offer me tea?

- They never do.

Very good tea, indeed.

- Thank you.

You know, I don't even know your name. What should I call you?

- Friend.

Just "friend"?

- It fits better than any given name, Mr. Cade. Are you comfortable?

Oh, yes.

- What did you do, what was your profession, if you don't mind my asking?

I was a photographer. I'd have thought you'd heard of me. I was a photographer of women.

- Yes, come to think of it, I have heard of you. One of the world's foremost, if memory serves.

I like to think so. Or let's say I wanted to be the very best at the beginning. In the end it didn't matter.

- I don't quite understand, Mr. Cade.

Well, I was in later years not driven so much by power and money as I was by beauty. I loved every woman I photographed.

- It shows in the photographs.

I don't mean that in a carnal sense. I—transcended that.

- Could you explain that?

Let's say that I drew my subjects to me through the lens and in that way I coveted them, for what walked out through the studio door after the session was in no way as perfect and beautiful as what I had captured on film.

- Would you say you gave them life?

I would say that through the magic of the camera's eye I evoked rather than described. I added a dimension or two, made them more than what they were. Even the ordinary models I gave a presence to, an immortality, so to speak. Yes, I guess you could say I breathed into them and gave them life.

- You possessed a kind of divine power. Would you say that?

I suppose one could say that. Strobes popping constantly, banks of electric flash units going off all the time, all of it mechanical, artificial. Yet what came out of it was anything but inanimate or sterile. People said I had a unique gift for creating essence, and I did. I guess it was because I talked to the girls while shooting, said things to them I'd never say even over cocktails. I was able to create a kind of mysterious balance, an enchanting mood that was impossible to achieve any other way. Claudia Frankes was nothing before she came to me. Neither was Penelope Wykoff, Susan Harrison or Calla Parrish.

- They are beautiful women still, but I realize when I visualize them that I am only seeing them as you photographed them.

I was able to do what I did by virtue of contrast. Put a beautiful woman in the harsh, angular reality of a rocky creek bed at high noon, and she becomes more beautiful than she would be reclining on a soft chaise lounge. Of course the lighting, dress and pose must be exactly right.

- Mr. Cade, of all your models, who was your favorite?

Why do you ask me that?

- You seem to hesitate now and then, choose your words so. It's as if you're seeing someone you're not talking about.

They train you well in the Service, friend.

- We try not to miss anything, Mr. Cade. Who was she?

Elena Cassell.

- She was your first model, wasn't she?

She was. Her real name was Helen Chassell. Abigail Lasson sent her to me when I said I wanted to photograph people rather than ash trays and table settings and draped cloth. She was inexperienced; rather, she was born to that half of the world in front of the camera's eye. She should not have been named Helen. I knew that the moment I saw her, that instant she stepped into my studio and brightened it with her presence the way no one else had before or since. So I made her Elena. The fair Elena. She was a woman, friend. There has never been another like her.

- You have photographs of beautiful women hanging on the walls of this room, but I see none of Elena Cassell.

Just as one could not live with Puccini twenty-four hours a day one could not live with the face of Elena peering out at you. Or at least I could not.

- But you do have photographs of her, do you not?

Yes. I used to get them out and look at them, but it always made me sad when I did.

- Where do you keep them?

In that closet over there. I have them in a pack on the top shelf. But I don't think—

- You loved her.

Yes…Where are you going?

- There they are, Mr. Cade, the six you say you like the best, each on an easel.

Oh, God, what memories those bring back!

- Follow them.

Elena had that rare quality of influencing her surroundings. For example, it was as if the room darkened when she let her head drop forward. Do you see it there in that first one? Look at the way she sits on that old stool, so pensive, yet so alive. I set this one up in an abandoned barn on some rolling farmland near Frederick, Maryland. As you can see, the barn is bright with sun; yet there is darkness there because Elena has made it so with her bent back, her arched neck, and her lowered eyes staring so moodily at the straw strands on the old wood floor. The pose makes you want to cry out to her, doesn't it? It makes you want her to look at you…and she did, you know, right after the sitting. It was like an electric shock. Or should I say electrocution, for I was struck dumb by what her eyes could do to me. I was in awe of her.

- She is truly beautiful, sir.

You see her rushing across that meadow in the second one, running toward you? That was taken at Haypress Meadows, high in the desolation wilderness near Lake Tahoe. There is a fresh, wild gaiety in the way she moves, something she always had. She was like an uncaged animal sometimes, the way she moved, and she could always draw you into moods with her. See her yellow hair splashing, her blue skirt billowing?

- She is like a young doe.

And the third there, at the edge of the forest. The photo's like something out of Eadweard Muybridge or Carleton Emmons Watkins because it was like many they had taken so many years ago near Fort Bragg. The way she stands so quiet, listening to voices we can't hear, her beautiful eyes closed. So like the old photographs worn and browned with time. Seeing Elena this way was like sipping gamay beaujolais; it was just as uplifting. I was so taken with her this day that I ran out of film here. When I told her I had, she grinned impishly and darted into the redwood forest behind her. So enchanted was I that I followed her, leaving my expensive equipment behind. I just didn't care. I had to have her, be where she was, for when she left where she'd been, all that was life would go with her. She was light and fast on her feet, and her laughter drifted back to me as I ran, and soon she emerged into a meadow, a beautiful place full of daisies. She laughed when she saw me so near.

- You caught her.

Yes, I caught her and held her. It was the first time I'd done that. She trembled, whether with excitement or fear or desire, I didn't know then. But when she drew away I saw in her eyes the dream I know she must have seen in mine...and then she took my hand and we—we said not a word but lay down together in the meadow in midday. It was—it was—

- If you can't go on, sir...

No, no. I'll be all right. Let me get to the fourth picture. It's in the same general area—we loved Sonoma and Mendocino—only it is some weeks later. She is stepping out of a willow thicket. What would you say is the look on her face?

- Rapture.

Yes.

- It is the look of a woman well-loved, Mr. Cade.

And she was. Sometimes I could not believe she was real and found myself looking to see if she cast a shadow. Elena had no awkward moments. Her arms flowed with her body, and she always looked at things as if seeing them for the first time. She was marvelous. Everything was always new and beautiful and wonderful with Elena.

- She projects an ethereal air.

Yes. It's as if at any moment she might evaporate, she was that rare. Now look at the fifth one. Do you see how, though the shutter has caught her and frozen her in motion as she runs up that hill, she looks as if she is flowing on anyway, like some animal made of amber?

- Yes. And the last one. Is that grief?

In her most ordinary gesture there was grandeur, and so it was with her weeping. It was as if she were crying for the world, for all humanity.

- How did you get her to do it?

I told her I loved her. She always cried when I told her that. When I asked her why that should make her weep, she said it was because she loved me so much and all she needed to do was imagine life without me and the tears came.

- She is grieving for you, then.

It was strange. Just as she could read into ordinary events, see things that weren't there, so she somehow knew. I had decided that a vibrant, high-strung young gazelle like Elena must have had access to the higher reaches, don't ask me how. Her eyes were tragic those last few days. I had no idea why. It was a prescience, an intimation of her mortality, I suppose. A week later she was dead, drowned with fifty-three others when her plane went down in the Mediterranean near Crete, where I was to follow in a few days on assignment. It was—horrible.

- Don't dwell on it, Mr. Cade.

The last photographs I'd taken of her I could never develop. I destroyed them.

- But you did go on.

Yes. I didn't know then I would never find another Elena. So I set out to find her. In my lifetime I must have photographed five thousand other women. I saw parts of Elena in the twist of this wrist, the flicking of that eye, a turn of an ankle, and I loved them all, as I've said, but no one ever came close to Elena. Even now I'm not sure she ever existed, except that I know she must have because of these stills.

- I know what you must feel, Mr. Cade.

I have never told anyone how it was…now suddenly I'm very tired, my friend.

- Of course.

And I know now I'm ready. Or was it already in the tea?

- A little in the tea, sir. If you are really sure you're ready now...

Yes, I am sure. How long will it take?

- It will be intravenous and I will control it. You will feel nothing, as you have already felt nothing.

Dr. Hedron was right about all this. He said—

- Just relax now, sir. Tell me what you see, what you think...There.

Ah...I hadn't...I didn't expect...

- What is it, Mr. Cade?

I could swear I saw Elena move! Yes, she *is* moving—there at the edge of the woods! But how is it possible?

- All things are possible now, sir.

Elena! Wait for me!

- Easy, sir.

I love you, Elena! Let me hold you! Oh, God, how I've missed you! Come, take my hand...

- Take her into the meadow.

Elena...

- Now, sir, *la mort douce*...

Ah...

- ...the sweet death.

Thank you...thank you...very...much....

∎

Karma, Kruse and the Rollerboard Man

At first he thought if he hadn't started to walk to keep his lunch date with Angela he wouldn't have encountered the rollerboard man, but in the end he knew this wasn't true.

As it was, Randall Kruse saw the man vigorously propelling himself toward him on the sidewalk, his misshapen lower half concealed by an array of discolored rags, a pied patchwork of old blankets. In either fist he held his means of locomotion: cloth-covered handles attached to blocks of wood, the bottoms of which were fitted with cut tire treads.

It wasn't that Kruse had never seen the roller man; he was usually parked near crowds, his tin cup held out, nodding, mumbling thanks to those who dropped in a coin or two. It was that this day he was in motion, rhythmically bobbing, arms swinging, roller wheels humming. Kruse thought he would pass him by, so great was his speed, but with a sudden braking action of the treads the rollerboard man came to a stop in front of him.

The maneuver was so unexpected, the man so agile, Kruse stopped in surprise, the perfect target in his pinstripes, shiny shoes and power tie. He stared down into bloodshot brown eyes, stubbly like-leather face and a crooked smile that said, go ahead, look at my palsied head, my gnarled and yellowed teeth, see a real object of pity, and see if I care. Kruse caught a whiff of bad breath, old sweat and rancid oily rags.

Kruse would have moved around him but the man dropped one of the propelling blocks to his lap, held up his hand, moved his shoulders in a spasmed clonic reflex, and said, "See this?" Spittle appeared on his chin. At the same time he flipped his hand and a half-dollar size coin appeared in his palm.

When Kruse, repulsed, moved to go on, the man quickly wrenched himself around to intercept, holding the coin higher and nearer. Kruse was astonished to see such a clean silver piece agleam in the afternoon sun in the dirty hand of this revolting mass of flesh, bone and rags. A word on the coin was written in strange letters: ᚪ ᚦ ᚦ ᛒ ✿ ᐤ

An idiotic grin. "It's yours, Mr. Kruse." The man snapped his hand closed and pulled back to hold the coin against his chest. "But you have to ask for it."

Recovering, Kruse snorted in disgust, pushed past and started walking away. He heard the rollerboard behind him, ignored it as it glided by on humming wheels. In another amazing flash the man deftly whipped it around to a quick stop so they were facing each other again.

"Don't you want it, Sport?" He flashed the coin at him.

Controlling flaring anger, Kruse turned to the curb, walked into the street, hailed an empty cab and got in. The cabbie grinned. "How's it goin', Mr. Kruse?" This was Freddie Harmon, as his license proclaimed, and Kruse had ridden with him before. Most people knew Kruse, his face on his *Love Kruse* show every weekday night at eleven-thirty. Freddie gave him a look in the rear-view mirror. "Roller Balls get to you?"

"Is that what they're calling him now?"

With a laugh Freddie said, "That's not all they're calling him. People don't take kindly to being pestered for spare change. Where you headed?"

"Carrington's. You know what his real name is?"

"I've seen write-ups in the papers, but I forget. Been around awhile. Probably makes more than me."

Kruse had seen beggars in Cairo. You couldn't escape them. From the moment he got off the plane into the searing heat of the day until he was safe in his hotel it was a strident cry of *baksheesh* from every blind, deformed or emaciated person, hand outstretched, fingers clutching, clawing, children and old people as well. It started the moment he stepped out anywhere until he closed a door behind him somewhere else. He set no precedent by giving any of them anything. He'd never gotten used to the cries, often heard them in his sleep.

"Here we are," Freddie announced as they rolled to a stop in front of Carrington's.

He found Angela reading a script at a table for two in the Red Room, a glass of white wine beside her. She looked wonderfully beautiful. Angela was one of those persons who had no bad side; no light was unflattering to her no matter what she was doing. Her pert face always brightened the air around her. Her eyes spoke to you: we love you. Angela Parsons was one of the leads in Levin Gower's *Choice Parts*, his sophisticated television comedy series. She was also Mrs. Kruse. As he approached, her head turned, her eyes warmed at the sight of him, her face blossoming in a happy smile. She said, "And I thought *I* was early."

He gently brushed her lips with his and took his chair, explaining that he'd taken a cab.

"You said you were going to walk." She put her hand over his. "You *need* to walk, Randy. It's only six blocks. I'd have walked from the lot if it were nearer."

"No you wouldn't. Not with all the paparazzi out there, unless you had somebody running interference."

"How about you? Six blocks and you take a taxi."

He told her about the man on the rollerboard, and as he talked he saw her stiffen, face whiten, eyes widen, until he stopped and said, "What's the matter?"

Before she could answer, their waiter appeared. After they ordered, Angela said, "I've seen that crippled man on the board. I know I should feel pity, but he frightens me. He's been watching me. Every time I turn around, there he is on his rollerboard, staring at me."

"Not on the set, I hope."

"No. Never inside the studio gates."

"What does he say? Does he try to hurt you, touch you or anything?"

"No. It's his eyes. They're not just leering. There's a craftiness about them, maybe a meanness would better describe it. I've heard about him. He's a beggar, has places he hangs out, holds out a tin cup, so they say. But for me, he does nothing. He never speaks. Sometimes I want to give him a hard kick, but I could never do that." She wet her lips. "I didn't mean to go on so. What's wrong with him, anyway?"

Kruse said he didn't know but he was going to find out. "Did he *offer* you anything? Show you a coin the way he did me?"

"No. He just *looks* at me. In a strange, intense way." She gave a little shudder, shook her head. "Let's talk about something else." After she'd sipped her wine, she said, "We finished early. Eleven o'clock, can you imagine? We've got a good director, Mort Selvin. Fewer takes. Lets you work out the scene yourself, the tone, mood and inflection. It's going to be a good segment." She leaned closer, eyes smoldering. "Can't figure out what to do with the rest of the day. You have any ideas? Or aren't you the boss where you are?"

Kruse grinned. "Tonight's show will take care of itself. I'll call Hal Endersby right now, tell him I won't be back until just before air time."

"You *are* in charge, aren't you."

He made a growling sound in his throat and said, "You betcha."

Her laugh was softly suggestive and warmly encouraging.

The rollerboard man was waiting for them outside Carrington's, whizzing out of the shadows to come to an abrupt stop directly in front of them. His eyes were on Angela, and Kruse saw what she meant by his piercing gaze. "Mr. Kruse." He held the coin toward him in an outstretched hand, his eyes devouring Angela. Angela took Kruse's arm, clutched it tightly.

"Bug off," Kruse snarled at the man as Angela pulled him. Kruse reached out with his foot, gave the rollerboard man a hard shove backward so they could pass to where a taxicab had been summoned by the restaurant's doorman.

"That wasn't very nice, Sport," the rollerboard man said from where he'd braked the board.

"You're not very nice," Kruse said in an imitative voice as he entered the cab after Angela. He slammed the door. The taxi started up. Kruse gave directions.

"Hideous little man," Angela said. "Reminds me of one of those gargoyles you see on the cathedral of Notre Dame."

That night, before the *Love Kruse* show, Kruse told his research staff to amass all the information they could about the rollerboard man, and for the next several days Kruse avoided contact with him by keeping to his car to and from home. That did not stop him from seeing the roller. Twice the man gave him the finger. Kruse reciprocated.

When the material was assembled, he went over it with his people. There were feature stories, most of them with pictures, and interviews, including one TV sound bite, but not produced by Kruse's station. His staff said they'd seen most of it before but felt the man was not worth bringing to Kruse's attention, did he want to book him? He thanked them, took the gathered items to his office and immersed himself in them.

He saw that the rollerboard man was clever, articulate and engaging. His outlook was optimistic despite his handicap and he was brash and more than well-educated. From all of the interviews curious inconsistencies and discrepancies emerged. In Totec City he said he was Krevin Seidman and he'd lost his legs in the Vietnam War but he'd educated himself by spending all his spare time in libraries. Checking, the staff had found there was a Krevin Seidman in Totec City but that he was not handicapped; he was vice president of the Kendall County Bank and on the job. Caught up in Carverville, the rollerboard man said his name was Grantland Emery and he'd lost his legs to a fast freight train during a stormy night; he'd been educated at Harvard and had been a law professor at UCLA, but he was enjoying a sabbatical in the Midwest, and enjoying it he was, he told Kruse's people. In the short video he said he was from Allentown and his name was Halstead Johnstone; he'd been with the U.S. Geological Survey before losing his legs in an automobile accident near his digs at the Ripley formation in Mississippi. A check showed there was a Halstead Johnstone with the Survey, but he was at his office in Washington, and contacted there, said he never gave interviews. None of these persons ever heard of the rollerboard man and were snappish about it and cut the staffers short.

Kruse was intrigued. The man in all the pictures and the video was Roller Balls, no doubt of it. To keep himself alive and well, he begged. Perhaps he did make more money than Freddie Harmon, the taxi driver. But why did he say he was someone he was not? There was no mention of his offering a coin to anyone, and he did not seem to be obnoxious, or a leering lecher. Kruse came to the conclusion he might be worth a spot on his show, but he would have to learn more about him before risking booking him. Did he have an agent? Probably not. He'd have to sign more than the usual waivers.

In pursuit of the truth Randall Kruse left his office, took the staff elevator to the ground floor and exited the building by the rear entrance to go to his car in the parking lot. He drove out and was not at all surprised to see the rollerboard man waiting for him up the street. This time Kruse pulled over, got out of the car and moved to the man who had positioned himself in the shade of a stately California pepper tree. Roller Balls' demeanor was one of quiet patience. He seemed to know what Kruse wanted. Disheveled as ever, he did not smile or offer the coin. Kruse thought he looked, at best, tired, at worst, like death warmed over.

When he reached him Kruse said, "What's your name?"

The man brightened. "You've changed your mind about the coin."

"No. Look, all I want to do is talk to you, but I can't do that without knowing your name. Your *real* name."

"Why? That's not important."

"It is to me."

The roller man took a deep, resigned breath. "Mr. Kruse, it really doesn't matter. Let's get this over with." He opened his hand. There lay the coin. "All I want you to do is accept my gift to you. Then it will be over. Doesn't that make more sense than us standing here jawboning?"

"Are you Krevin Seidman and did you lose your legs in the Vietnam War?"

The roller man was startled. "No. What makes you ask that?"

Kruse decided the man was either a gifted liar or he was telling the truth.

"Are you Professor Grantland Emery?"

"No. Never heard of him."

"Halstead Johnstone?"

"No. What is all this?"

They gazed at each other for a long moment before the rollerboard man said, "My name is Glover Taggart, if it really matters all that much to you."

"How did you lose your legs?"

"I can't tell you." He held up the coin. "Just ask me for this coin and I'll be on my way and you'll never see me again."

"Why should I do that?"

"Because it will change your life, Mr. Kruse. Let's say you will find it a rich learning experience."

Kruse examined the coin but didn't move to take it. "What do those letters on the coin mean?"

"You will be able to read them when you ask for and accept the coin. All will be answered then."

"Why do you offer me a coin but ask everyone else for donations?"

"A man has to live, Mr. Kruse, so I solicit donations. As for the coin, that I offer you because you are deserving of it. As I say, when you have it, truth will be revealed to you."

Kruse was getting tired of it. He said severely, "Why do you harass my wife?"

Taggart wasn't shocked. He was merely amused. "Angela Parsons is one of the most beautiful women I have ever seen. I'm in love with her too, you see? But I do not harass her, as you say. Neither would I harm her in any way. I watch her in person. Others watch her on television. Is there much difference? You are a lucky man, Mr. Kruse. If you ask for and accept this coin I promise I will never look at your wife again."

"I think not," Kruse said coldly, deciding to have done with it. "I'm warning you, if you persist in watching my wife or continue to bother either of us I'll have to do something about it and you'll be sorry."

For the first time Taggart smiled. "Those are threatening words," Taggart said, "but that's all they are, Sport. You can do nothing to me."

"What makes you so sure of that?"

"Because I'm a lawyer."

"I don't believe you. I think you're a pathological liar and ought to be put away."

Taggart seemed to enjoy it. "I'm not harming myself and I'm not a danger to anyone else. I would be out in seventy-two hours or less."

"You're a danger to my wife."

"You would have no legal case, Mr. Kruse. I didn't peep through a window. I only appreciated what scenery there was, which was free, and it was beautiful. To see Angela under such circumstances is any man's right."

The man's imperturbability angered Kruse. He said harshly, "I'm telling you, don't come near me or my wife again. If you do…" He didn't finish, just let it hang there. Then he turned on his heel, strode to his car and got in. He felt better for having told him off, but something told him this was not the end of it. But what to do? The man might really be a lawyer, so threats were of no use.

There was force. He considered it. No, he decided, he would never resort to violence. Taggart was quite right, the man had violated no law. There had to be some other way. Perhaps he should have taken the damned coin and have done with it, see if he'd stop bothering them. One thing was sure, Glover Taggart was never going to be seen on the *Love Kruse* show.

Saturday night Kruse and his wife attended a party of the cast of *Choice Parts* at Levin Gower's and with others were driven home in a stretch limo during a blinding rainstorm, being let out at their house with a borrowed umbrella.

As the limo pulled away and they started up the walk to go between the light standards at the end of a privet hedge on either side they saw him.

Glover Taggart, the roller man, was waiting for them on his board. He was completely soaked, rain running down his hair and face, then in rivulets down his rag-tag blankets.

"Out of the way," Kruse ordered, ready to kick the board.

"No," Taggart said, holding out the coin. "You must ask for and take this."

"Randy," Angela said in annoyance, pulling at him.

He gave her the umbrella as he said, "All right, Taggart. Let me have the coin. Quickly, now." As he took it he said, "Remember your promise not to bother us."

He looked down at the coin to see the single word there: K A R M A. He realized then he was rain-soaked.

Looking up, he saw Kruse following Angela to the house. Suddenly understanding, he shouted, "Hey!"

Angela used her key, opened the door and went in as Kruse turned to regard him with a nasty smile.

Furious, he threw the coin at Kruse.

Kruse caught it, deftly tossed it back to him from the safety of the portico, saying, "You're going to need this, Sport."

The coin fell, turning over and over in the rain, landing on the sloping sidewalk, not on its side but on its milled edge.

It started to roll toward him, but he could not get the hang of how to reach down for it from the rollerboard.

To his dismay he saw it roll underneath the board.

He turned his head, saw it roll down the walk to the curb. He heard it plop down and hit something metallic.

When he managed to roll to the curb he saw the piece of silver teetering on the steel grillwork to one side, water rushing over it down the drain.

Even in his wetness as he strained to reach for it, with horror he watched it fall through the grating.

■

Afterword:
A Science Fiction Life
by Allan Sohl

Let us imagine an ordinary soul (no pun intended) such as myself, who has gotten tired of living exciting lives and dying horrible deaths, and decides to take some time off from the excitement to find a nice working-class family in the "mid western US of A." This life will be simple and undemanding. He won't have to think very much or take a stand on anything. Dad is in the "Army Air Corps" and life is fairly mundane. Things go much as expected until the kid gets old enough to understand human speech in enough detail to learn that Dad doesn't work in a factory, build houses or sell automobiles. Dad works for a newspaper. He doesn't hang out with other dads who pat each other on the back and tell each who the greatest cat in the world is. He reads *books*, plays the piano and tells interesting stories. At times, one might even think of him as "visionary."

It was clear that this was not going as I expected. It would not be as easy as I thought. *What will my friends think? There must be some kind of mistake....*

Viewing life as a series of dramas would come naturally to the son of a writer of fiction. Viewing one's life as one in an infinite series of lives from which there is no escape would come more naturally to the son of Jerry Sohl, a writer of Science Fiction.

We didn't do sports. Sometimes we sat on the floor in front of the record player with a piano reduction of a symphonic work of Tchaikovsky or Rimsky-Korsakov attempting to follow the sound of the recording in the printed score. I was inspired by the fact that the shapes printed on the page corresponded with the sounds which we were hearing.

259

My sisters and I all benefited from our dad's approach to teaching us to think. Today we would say that he wanted us to think "outside of the box." I was age six or seven when he explained how a refrigerator works: how it uses a compressor and a special gas along with coils of tubing to absorb the heat inside and move it to the radiator on the back. There was a reason for explaining this. He had a puzzle for me to solve:

"Suppose you put a refrigerator in an insulated room (no heat can get in or out). You plug this refrigerator into an electrical outlet in the wall, open its door, turn it on, then leave the room, closing the door to the room behind you. When you come back a week later, is the room warmer or cooler?"

My answer was *cooler*, of course. It seemed obvious. That is not the correct answer.

The purpose of the puzzle was not just to see if I remembered how a refrigerator works. It was to introduce me to the *idea* that it takes energy or power to do things like pump the heat out of the inside of a refrigerator. The actual explanation was necessary, yet incidental, almost a red herring.

My introduction to politics (and trust) was just as unique:

One day my dad brought home some firecrackers. I was excited about them and wanted to light some right away.

"No," he said. "It is illegal to have firecrackers. We could be arrested."

"If they are illegal, how did *you* get them?" I asked.

He said, "A friend brought them back from Missouri, where they *are* legal."

"Why are they illegal?" I said, playing right along.

"Sometimes people do not seem to be very smart," he said. "They have hurt themselves or others by not understanding how dangerous they can be. Politicians have made firecrackers illegal to show that they have done something about it. As you can see, that hasn't stopped people from getting them. It has only made it more difficult." Then he said, "When we go to Grandma and Grandpa's farm this weekend, we can light some."

He had given the packages to me and then explained what they were. He trusted that I would be careful with them once he explained how. Years later I realized how unusual this was for the time and place.

I did have this question, though: "Have you known anyone who has been injured by firecrackers?"

"No," he said. "Not during the time that I have been working for the newspaper."

It was clear that my dad did not have a high regard for people who made useless laws for the purpose of getting votes. Today, he would probably say that this political "sleight-of-hand" is actually a public form of "Munchausen by Proxy," where a problem is created to match symptoms that don't really exist.

No, this was not what I was expecting. It was much more interesting than a working-class family in Middle America.

As with any family or relationship, there were difficult times. I have long since forgiven my dad (and mom) for those times and I can see that even the act of forgiving is something that I learned about from him.

When other kids were picking on me for being different, he had an explanation: "The reason those kids are picking on you is because you are not afraid to be yourself. They envy you for this. They would rather be your friends but they are too afraid."

At that age, it was hard to see how that could be. It was beyond my understanding. What I did understand was that when I was asked: "What does your father do?," I would have an easier time of it if I said my dad worked for a newspaper than I did if I said he wrote books.

Was Jerry Sohl always this inspiring teacher? He was quite often when I was very young. Of course as we got older and our lives became more complicated, I saw less of this side of him. Still, these (and many other) times are as powerful now as they ever were. I find that I honor him daily by viewing things in depth, looking for the issues behind the issues, always keeping in mind that the process of discovery is as important as that which is discovered. As my father was quite often in his stories, I try to be visionary too.

> – Allan Sohl
> Carlsbad, California
> December, 2002

A CLASSIC RETURNS!

Jerry Sohl's *Costigan's Needle*—
Available Again in Trade Paperback
from Xlibris!

First published in 1953, *Costigan's Needle* is Jerry Sohl's most famous science fiction novel—the story of a scientist who discovers a needle-shaped doorway into another world, and the first human beings who pass through it. Fast-paced and compulsively readable, *Costigan's Needle* was Jerry Sohl's own favorite among his SF novels, and represents the author at the height of his storytelling powers. Discover this 1950s classic for yourself!

Available from Xlibris Corporation

ISBN 0-7388-3659-1

Also available in e-Book format

To order:

1-888-7-XLIBRIS

Orders@Xlibris.com

http://www.xlibris.com

Have You Seen The Wind?
Selected Stories and Poems
by William F. Nolan

ISBN: 0-9714570-5-0   *$14.95*

With 75 books and over 300 anthology appearances to his credit, William F. Nolan (author of *Logan's Run*) is twice winner of the Edgar Allan Poe Special Award. Most recently, he accepted the International Guild's Living Legend Award for 2002.

This is the first collection of Nolan's horror fiction and verse to share a single volume. Six chilling tales of murder and madness, guns and obsession steam the pages of this haunting book, including "In Real Life," cited in *The Year's Best Fantasy and Horror*, and a brand new story written just for this collection: "Behind the Curtain."

Delve into Nolan's darkest worlds as he assembles tales of an ex-wife claiming revenge from beyond the grave… of an insane mind justifying the murder of his mate through the tall glass of a cold one… of a husband who refuses to stay dead… And top it all off with a celebration of this master's widely-praised poems, on topics ranging from Bradbury to Vienna, from Hammett to Hemingway.

COMMENTARY ON NOLAN'S PROSE

"William F. Nolan is a hell of a writer! I have real admiration for his stories."   —Peter Straub

"He makes a permanent dent in our memories. Nolan is able to create an atmosphere of ultimate terror, causing readers to live out his nightmares."   —Ray Bradbury

"He's incredibly talented … Each of his stories is like a psychiatric session from which the reader comes away knowing more about the human condition, due to Nolan's fascination with the topography of emotional torment and his infallible rendering of the troubled psyche."
—Richard Christian Matheson

AND ON HIS VERSE

"Nolan is a prime communicator … and although he writes only 'two or three' poems a year, he manages to communicate emotions better than most full-time poets."
—Small Press Review

___ YES, please send me ___ copies of *Have You Seen The Wind?* for just $14.95 each.

___ YES, I would like more information about your other publications.

Add $4 postage for up to 5 books. For non-US orders, please add $4 per book for airmail, in US funds. Payment must accompany all orders. Or buy online with Paypal at bearmanormedia.com.

My check or money order for $_____ is enclosed. Thank you.

NAME _____

ADDRESS_____

CITY/STATE/ZIP_____

EMAIL _____

Checks payable to: BearManor Media * P O Box 750 * Boalsburg, PA 16827
ben@musicdish.com